I0682018

A Challenging Duet

A Novel in Four Parts
First Movement

Kyah Merritt

ISBN: 978-1-7355459-6-7
Cover art created using postermywall.com

Published by Northern Horizon Books

Table of Contents

In this age devoted to completing the French Revolution and to beginning the Human Revolution, equality between the sexes being part of equality between men, a great woman was needed. Woman had to prove that she could have all our manly qualities without losing her angelic ones: that she could be strong without ceasing to be gentle: George Sand is that proof... she bequeathes to us the right of woman which draws its proof from woman's genius... Thus the Revolution is fulfilled.
—Victor Hugo

Overture

I was first properly introduced to the Polish composer Fryderyk Chopin in high school, when I checked out a book from the library called *Lives of the Musicians: Good Times, Bad Times (And What the Neighbors Thought)*, by Kathleen Krull and Kathryn Hewitt. I was so intrigued by the disastrous metaphorical honeymoon in Mallorca that he had shared with feminist author George Sand (formally Aurore Dudevant) that I had to know more about this man, who, I soon discovered, was the composer of the famous Funeral March (a connection I thought was very appropriate).

So began a glorious hyperfocus, leading to intensive research and eventually this novel, which is a combination of fact and fiction.

As I wrote, I considered my purpose. *What if*, I wondered, *what if things had gone differently? What if things had gone better? And what key factors would have needed to have been different for their relationship to have lasted?*

Armed with this purpose, I set about adjusting the narrative, tweaking history to guide the narrative away from the deadliest relational cliffs; the most heartbreaking deal-breakers. Most importantly, I chose to omit George Sand's previous marriage and her two children. Historically, her son Maurice and daughter Solange had a profound impact on her relationship with Fryderyk, coming between them in complex ways. As George never married Fryderyk, making him an official stepfather to her children, their relationship was always poorly-defined. George's bitterness toward the youthful puppy-love Solange came to show Fryderyk (which he returned with supportive, caring friendship), George's anger at Fryderyk's later unwillingness to side with her in a major family conflict, and Maurice's seething resentment at the continual presence of his mother's boyfriend, who was preventing him, as the only related male, from stepping into the role of man of the house, boiled up into a crescendo that would not be out-of-place on *Dr. Phil*.

After a physical family fight in 1847 in which someone was almost struck with a hammer, Fryderyk continued to refuse to take sides, George thanked him for nine years of friendship, and their long-standing relationship... was over. They saw one another only once more before Fryderyk's death in 1849.

But what if it hadn't gone that way? What if the greatest impediments to the success of their relationship had never gotten in their way? What if they had worked through their struggles and come through on the other side?

Come with me as we explore the mirror-world of what could have been, wandering untread paths of wisdom, grace, maturity, and communication to find our way to the joyful possibilities of what they might have shared if only things had been different. Join me in a wistful look at what might have been.

1   The Introduction

"Madame Sand, may I introduce Fryderyk Chopin."

George looked up at Franz Liszt's voice, her eyes bouncing from her friend to the man he was introducing. The elegant young gentleman walked gracefully through the crowd of guests, Parisian glitterati who had gathered for Marie d'Agoult's party, his green velvet jacket cut flatteringly on his small, slim frame, his fluffy white cravat tied right up to his pointed chin, his silky brown hair falling in a carefully-arranged swoop over his white forehead. His slender, white-gloved hand clutched his gold-topped walking stick, and the diamond pin on his breast caught the lamplight. So this was Fryderyk Chopin.

George put out her cigar, hopped up from the soft armchair in which she'd been sitting, and held out her hand, noticing with an internal smile that although Chopin was taller than she was, it wasn't to the extreme interval by which men usually towered over her. Although he didn't appear exactly ill, there was something about his stance, about the way he moved, about the intense pallor of his angular face and the extreme thinness of his body, that gave George a sense that he might blow away in a strong wind.

Chopin gave a small smile and shook her hand. How amazing to grasp a hand that was not much larger than hers. It was just as delicate as it looked— she felt like she could hurt him if she weren't careful— and it was cold even with the glove. And yet, at the same time, as she met his calm gaze, she caught an impression of a strength she had not encountered in even the most strapping former beau. Silently, she wondered what it was that caused such a strong spirit inside to be housed inside such a frail, almost sickly body.

"Madame Sand, Monsieur Chopin is a fellow composer of mine, and Monsieur Chopin, Madame Sand is an author. Perhaps you have read some of her books?"

Chopin's brown eyes traveled over George's top hat, her masculine suit jacket, her pressed trousers. His expression changed slightly, becoming pleasantly neutral; carefully polite. And her mind prickled as she wondered what he was thinking.

"I don't think so," he said almost haltingly, and this time, she could see on his face the question of what type of books a woman in trousers would write. "I'll have to choose one the next time I'm at the bookstore."

Trying to maintain eye contact as Chopin awkwardly looked away, George offered a gracious smile. "I'd be honored."

Chopin shook her hand once more, then let it go with a courteous nod. "It was nice to meet you, Madame Sand," he said, his simple words graced in a beautiful Polish accent. Offering a brief bow, he turned to greet someone else.

She let him go, watching him melt into the crowd of frockcoats and pleated skirts; the sea of artists that flickered in the warm lamplight that lit the evening scene.

"He was about to play," a voice said from over her shoulder. George looked up, and up again, to see Liszt towering over her again, the tall, rawboned Hungarian dressed in his usual all black. Franz nodded at a doorway leading to another part of the grand house in which they had gathered.

George felt her heart quicken with excitement, even as she wondered what had struck her so about the Polish composer. "Really?"

Franz smiled. "Better get a seat before they close the doors."

George hurried into the smaller *salon*, where a grand piano of shining, silky chestnut stood at the head of the cozy, green-wallpapered room, sitting down quietly among the smaller group of guests who had gathered for the performance. And with them, she waited.

"Presenting Fryderyk Chopin, who will perform his Ballade in G Minor," announced a servant, standing stiff and formal in his pressed black jacket and white gloves. George swallowed, twisting her hands in her lap almost nervously, fleetingly wondering where these feelings were coming from— from whence hailed this sudden ache of breathless anticipation? Why was her heart fluttering, her breath catching in her throat? What was this delicious feeling… that felt almost like fear? George swallowed, telling her quickening heart to be still. And every second of silence that passed seemed to drag.

Until the wave broke. A heartbeat later, the audience shifted in their chairs as a slender, graceful figure entered the room, offering a brief bow to the assembled guests before settling himself at the gleaming chestnut piano. He arranged his sheet music. He paused. The audience went silent, the air shimmering in anticipation.

And he began.

Ringing octaves marched up the keyboard, a gentle melody winding its way around the treble as the left hand kept a calm rhythm. George shuddered at the softness; at the delicacy with which those sweet, graceful notes elegantly whispered, murmuring sweet nothings that were somehow everything. Powerful chords now arose, the piece rising in speed and intensity as Chopin's delicate, long-fingered hands flew over the keys, the melody racing up and down the keyboard as the left hand continued measuring the steady rhythm. And George forgot to breathe as a storm of sound and emotion rose, whirling around the room as Chopin's fingers danced over the black and white keys of the piano. She forgot to breathe, forgot to think, forgot whose party she had come to as the music filled her soul, a wave of glorious sound washing away anything outside of itself in an overwhelming flood. She did not want anything outside of this. Nothing at all. Nothing in the world but this man's music.

Softening again, the piece introduced a new melody, delicately expounding upon it at some length. And again George shivered at the softness, the sensitivity with which the composer's long, delicate fingers brushed lovingly, intently, over the keys. Again intensity rose, and the hair on the back of George's neck rose as she closed her eyes, letting the music wash over her like water, like the wind, like the sun, like all the forces of nature blended into one glorious whole. Overwhelmed by art, she let it fill her up, drowning her in sound and emotion, an overflowing flood of everything she could ever want.

Up and down the music went, softening, intensifying, hammering out powerful chords and trilling delicate melodic lines, finally rising to an exhilarating crescendo that slowly, once again, softened. Suddenly, surprisingly, launching into a completely new melody, the ballade once again gained speed and volume, notes racing up and down the keyboard as the left and right hands seemed to chase one another. And with one final, powerful chord, it was over.

There was silence. And then the applause began, the assembled guests clapping politely as Chopin slowly rose, offering another brief bow and immediately exiting the room, raising his handkerchief to his mouth as he went as if to stifle a cough.

George sat there in her chair in overwhelmed silence, lost in the eye of a cyclone of exhilaration, floating adrift in the middle of a sea of bliss, alone in a universe of sheer beauty, speechless mind and body still reverberating with the overwhelming magnificence of what she had just heard. Already it was playing over in her mind, her breath catching once more at the mere memory of what she had just experienced. And again, she closed her eyes, sitting in stillness in the middle of the crowd of departing guests, experiencing its perfect beauty again in her imagination.

And she wondered if she was in love.

George went home to her Paris apartment with the ballade still echoing inside her mind, fell asleep with it tiptoeing around the edges of her mind, heard it winding through her dreams, found herself humming it as she wrote, walked the dog, made dinner. It followed her everywhere. And she was hungry, no, starving, for more.

George spent the summer in her country estate at Nohant, the grand house and acreage in the Berry region of central France. She had inherited the estate from her grandmother, and that was where she spent most of her summers. Over the summer, she wondered about Chopin. And as she returned to Paris, watching as the autumn of 1836 wore into winter, she brooded about him. And the author poured out her heart in words as she had so many times before, crafting a new story, a story of marriage and murder that swirled around the character of Bernard Mauprat, all the while questioning the role women were "supposed" to take in courtship and marriage; the singular path of domesticity down which the education they received shunted them.

She wrote, as she always did. And in her writing, amid all the tension of balancing what she knew was right for her with what the world wanted, the painful tension that felt like trying to stand up in a rowboat caught in a terrible storm, she sought happiness.

George got up every morning and put on her white shirt, her black trousers, her waistcoat of green or blue or brown, her cravat, her top hat, buttoning herself up, wrapping masculine clothing around the body of a woman. She put it on like armor, remembering with every button she did, every cravat she tied, every breakup, every failed romance, every emotional disaster she had undertaken with a man.

Every one of them had proven to her that she was bad. Too wild. Out of control. Too independent. Not a real, feminine woman. And so, over time, she had settled into the role into which they had cast her; stopped trying to be feminine. And she hid them away, her heart, her body, the name that her mother had given her in honor of the dawn, all her femininity; hid them away like precious jewels surrounded by a constricting fist of masculine strength, the masculine strength that was all that would get Amantine Lucile Aurore Dupin through this world alive.

George was out to lunch in Paris a few days into the new year of 1837, enjoying a large steak in a glamorous restaurant on a busy Saturday afternoon, when a voice she recognized, French words dignified with a refined, sophisticated Polish accent, sounded from the table behind her.

"And I'm hard at work on the etudes; I may be nearly done..."

George swallowed firmly and took a sip of red wine as her heart began to pound. She would talk to Monsieur Chopin when he was done eating.

George finished her steak almost without tasting it, so intently was she listening for the end of his conversation. When would he and his dining companion be done eating… George shoveled her meal down, staring at an empty plate long before the words of the composer and his fellow diner fell silent.

Finally, the clinking of forks and plates at the other table ceased. Slowly, George put down her fork and placed her money on the table. She adjusted her top hat. And she stood up, slowly, politely approaching Chopin's table.

He was dining with an older man, slightly heavyset, with the most impressive gray sideburns George had ever seen. Over empty plates, they remained deep in conversation.

Softly, George cleared her throat. Chopin stopped mid-word and looked up. And George watched his expression change as he recognized her.

"Madame Sand, how nice to see you," he said pleasantly, standing up to offer a bow, as did Elsner. As before, Chopin took in her jacket and trousers, but said nothing.

She smiled at him; his fair, angular face, his slender frame, his slim, delicate hands, his expensive-looking jacket of black velvet and the white cravat tied all the way up to his pointed chin. He looked as thin as he had when they had first met, and nearly as pale, but, thankfully, not any worse.

"Would you like to join us?"

George bobbed her head in a manly bow, then sat down in an empty chair, which Chopin carefully pulled out and pushed in for her before returning to his. "How have you been?"

He shrugged his thin shoulders. "Fairly well." He paused, straightening up. "Oh, may I introduce my former piano teacher,

Professor Józef Elsner. He's visiting Paris from Poland." Elsner offered a second bow before returning to his own chair.

"So, how are you enjoying Paris, *Pan* Elsner?" George asked, silently congratulating herself on remembering the Polish equivalent of *Monsieur*.

"Beautiful, very beautiful," he said with a smile and a nod. He, too, was either polite enough, forward-thinking enough, or embarrassed enough to say nothing of her attire. "A fine city such as this deserves an artist like Fryderyk. Or, should I say, a fine artist like Fryderyk deserves a city such as Paris. He was a blessing to Poland, and we hope we can return someday, after peace returns." The professor sighed. "As dear as Poland is to my heart, it is not a safe time to be in my homeland. Since Fryderyk's childhood, our nation has been divided between the possession of the Russians, the Prussians, and the Hapsburgs. And with every year that passes, the heart of our country, and Warsaw itself, are brought under more and more Russian oppression. Censorship, secret police spying on and persecuting the underground societies through which we cling to freedom, the Tsar crowning himself the King of Poland…"

There was a clatter. George looked at Chopin to see him slowly and deliberately picking up the fork that had skidded halfway across the table, having slipped out of the white-knuckled grip in which he'd been clutching it, his jaw visibly clenched.

Taking a deep breath, he picked it up again, looking down at it as he began to speak in a harsh, dead monotone. "Grand Duke Constantine has eliminated most of our traditional social associations and patriotic organizations and replaced Poles with Russians within our own government. In November of '30, the Russians tried to force the Polish army to stop the revolution in

Belgium and the one here in France. But we wouldn't do it. The soldiers took the Grand Duke's palace in Warsaw, and he fled. Then the rebels took the arsenal of Warsaw, and as their numbers grew, they forced the Russians out of the city. The rebellion, the Cadet Revolution, grew into a war, and we fought hard for nearly a year. And we poured out our blood on the battlefield. Until… until there was no more left to spill. I was out of the country, I was touring, when I learned that we'd been brought down… that I couldn't go home again. That assuming I had a home left to go back to, it would be in Russian-occupied territory, not an independent, sovereign Kingdom of Poland. And all I could hope… was that my father hadn't been hanged; that my mother and sisters hadn't been assaulted."

George caught her breath at the pain she saw in his eyes; the fear and anger she heard shivering through his words.

"Is your family safe?" she whispered once she hoped a respectful interval had elapsed.

He nodded, a small smile leavening the heavy sigh he released. "Yes. My family is all right— my parents, my sisters. We keep in touch… and they keep me abreast of how things are around Warsaw. But for now, at least… they are safe. Although I don't know… I truly don't know… when I'll be able to go home again. I settled into Paris on a temporary basis back in '31… and I've been here ever since."

Chopin sighed, biting his lip again. George couldn't help it; she reached out her hand, taking his gently in hers. As she had noticed before, it was very cold, despite the gloves he wore. He didn't pull his hand back; just looked down at it where it rested on the table, entwined with hers. Blushing, she cleared her throat, gave his hand a quick, friendly squeeze, and let go.

"They'll be in my prayers," she said through the lump in her throat. At least she hadn't completely given up her decorum by throwing her arms around him out of sheer sympathy and bursting into tears.

He sighed. "Thank you, Madame Sand. Mademoiselle Dupin. What would you like me to call you, Madame Sand?"

"*George*," she said. Silently, Chopin's eyebrows rose.

Breathlessly, George chuckled. "No, really, it's *George*. Or *Aurore*. I answer to that, too. But don't bother with *Madame Sand*. I'm really a Dupin, and I was almost a Dudevant." She looked down, then back at him, heart filling with breathless excitement again as the heaviness of what Chopin had just said slowly ebbed like clouds pushed along by a breeze. And she felt a smile touch her face as an almost painful ache propelled her forward, her sleepless hunger for Chopin's music pushing aside the careful manners with which she had sought to present herself. Her starstruck passion roared up again, begging for more beauty from the angel of music who sat across from her.

"I've been thinking about your music ever since Countess d'Agoult's party," she said abruptly, words tumbling out in a sudden gush. "I've never heard anything so beautiful… Are you playing anywhere else anytime soon? I'd love to hear it again… or anything of yours. Anything… at all."

Chopin gave a small smile. "I don't do many live performances… but the next time I have one, you'll be the first person I invite."

"Have you been composing anything new lately?" George went on in a rush. "I'm an author, and I've been writing day and night— I hope you're happy with how it's going, in any case—"

Softly, Chopin smiled. "It's been going very well."

Breathlessly, George smiled. "I… I'm glad. Mine is— mine is, too."

Chopin inclined his head. "I'm very glad to hear that."

An icy raindrop seemed to roll down George's spine as she felt another pair of eyes on her. Slowly and deliberately, she directed her gaze towards Professor Elsner, who was watching the composer and the author placidly, a soft, slightly amused smile on his gentle face. Closing her eyes for an instant, George gritted her teeth in silent shame. How had she completely forgotten he was there?

"I— I'm sorry—" she stammered, feeling her face growing hot as she looked down at her knees, convulsively adjusting her top hat and cravat as her hands began to sweat inside her white gloves. "I didn't mean to go on and on— thank you for being here, Professor, and I hope you enjoy the rest of your visit."

The professor just smiled as he rose from his seat. "I'm sure I shall, dear lady. It was a delight to meet you."

Releasing a deep breath, George looked at Chopin, who was gathering up his own hat and coat and preparing to pay for the meal he and the professor had shared. It was time for them to be going. And it was time for her to politely let them go.

George stood up. Again, she bobbed her head in a gentlemanly bow, then shook hands with both of them.

"It was good to see you, Monsieur Chopin. And to meet you, Professor Elsner."

The composer smiled again. "It was good to see you. And *Fryderyk*, please. Maybe…" What might have almost been a blush touched his pale cheek. "Maybe I'll see you around sometime. I live at Number Thirty-Eight rue de la Chaussée-d'Antin. You're welcome to call sometime, if you like."

George grinned, a wave of delight sweeping over her as her heart pounded. And all she could say was, "I will."

2   Curiosity

George wrote. And she brooded. And she wondered when she should take the composer up on his offer for her to call on him.

Today was as good a day as any, she decided. She put on her black frockcoat against the January day and set off from the Paris apartment to which she returned when she was not spending the summer in Nohant, making her way on foot to the rue de la Chaussée-d'Antin. A few minutes later, she was thumping on the door of Chopin's apartment. What felt like ages later there was a quiet pattering, and the door finally opened.

"Hello, Madame Sand," Chopin said, fair face lighting up in a smile. "Good to see you. Come in; come in." He stepped aside, welcoming her inside.

George peered into the apartment as she stepped over the threshold. The first thing she noticed was how little she could actually see— how dark it was. The heavy curtains were drawn, throwing the sitting room, crowded with large bookshelves and overstuffed furniture, into shadow. Somehow it reminded her of the house of the grandparents of one of her childhood friends; closed-off and stuffy; musty and too warm and dimly lit. It specifically reminded her of their home in the five years before they had died.

"Let me take your coat." George smiled gratefully as Chopin helped her remove her gentleman's-style coat, hanging it up for her beside his own on the coatrack. Carefully she stomped the snow from her boots, drying them as well as she could before entering his home. "Would you like to sit down?" Silently observing her shirt and trousers while yet again choosing not to

21

betray his thoughts on them, Chopin motioned to a chair that might have been upholstered in deep red velvet— it was too dark to tell. George smiled and sat down, loosening her cravat. She was sweating.

There was a *meow* at her feet. George looked down just as a lithe, striped tabby cat hopped into her lap.

"I hope you don't mind cats," Chopin said quickly as George blinked and adjusted. The cat happily walked two circles in her lap and lay down with its head resting on her knee, softly purring.

She shook her head, smiling at the cat on her lap. "Not a bit."

Chopin smiled, leaning back into the chair he'd taken across from George's. "This is Valdeck," he said. "I'm so glad I have him. He's such a comfort. He curls up in my lap and purrs when I'm sad or lonely, and he always sleeps next to me..."

George ran her hand over the cat, even as her heart twinged at her new friend's perhaps-unthinking emphasis on the frequency at which he seemed to find himself feeling sad or lonely. Valdeck purred again and closed his eyes, settling in as if he planned to stay there for a long time.

"Sounds like he's a blessing," she said. "I have a dog— a little white fuzzball named Marquis. There's just nothing in the world like our little furry companions, is there?"

Chopin just smiled.

George paused, peering through the darkness of the room, looking again at Chopin's pale face, which, although thankfully he appeared no worse than in their previous meetings, had grown no rosier.

"Have you been well?" she asked softly.

Chopin looked away with a small sigh, folding his thin, bony hands in his lap. "Well... to be honest, my health is not as good as

I would like. I have a cough that I just can't get rid of." He paused, then offered an attempt at a reassuring smile and a slight shake of his head. "But I'm all right. It's just… how things are for me. Winter isn't easy for me. Never has been. And my lungs… they've never been strong. It's just the way they do things… the hard way."

George sighed, looking away into the reflective silence that had settled like a gentle snowfall. Her eyes traveled over the comfortable furniture; over the shelves that loomed over the stately grand piano…

Her heart skipped a beat. "Monsieur Chopin," she begged almost before she could think of what she was saying, "would you play something for me? Please, please, please? I heard you play at Countess d'Agoult's party and it was the most beautiful thing I've ever heard in my entire life."

Chopin blushed. "Well, I don't usually do private performances for individuals… but I can see how much you care."

George nodded enthusiastically. "Oh, I do, I do; it was all I could think about for months…"

Chopin shook his head with a chuckle. "Say no more. I suppose you'd like to hear the ballade?"

"Yessss!" she almost moaned. He chuckled again, slowly standing up.

"Just let me get my sheet music, then."

George sat there trying not to wriggle with delight as Chopin looked through his library of sheet music. "Here we are," he said a moment later, bringing the folder of music to the piano and placing the sheets into the rack. Slowly, he sat down. He raised his hands. And he began to play.

Breathlessly, George closed her eyes, letting the music wash over her as it had the first time she had heard it. And once again, her soul was overwhelmed with longing; a hungry, aching need to fall into the arms of the music itself, to be swallowed up in it. Demandingly, her heart propelled her forward, every note drawing her like a magnet. She had to get closer. Closer.

As she listened, entranced, enthralled, hypnotized, enraptured, intoxicated by art, she found herself gently ushering the cat off her lap so she could stand up, creeping closer and closer to the enormous grand piano. Her very soul longed to climb inside the piano itself, drowning herself in the embrace of the music— that was not possible, but how close could she get?

Yes, she was enthralled— anyone would be. But what was it that made her long to get as close to the overwhelming power of the music as possible; to throw aside any vestige of normal manners, little though she cared for propriety in any case, and do something that made no sense? Because as the music soared, insistently demanding that she come closer and closer yet, she knew that she was about to do something crazy.

Slowly, she sat down on the floor, pressing her hands into the soft rug, inching her body closer and closer to the piano without even noticing that she was doing so, so enraptured was she, overwhelmed with a wild longing to become the music herself, for the composer to play *her*. Silently she crept closer, moving easily in her shirt and trousers, sneaking along barely daring to breathe, desperate to avoid distracting the angel who was creating such melodies. She never wanted the music to stop. Never.

She reached out, grasping the carved wooden piano leg, feeling the music echoing through its length, then pressed herself against it. Lost in the hypnotic trance of the music, she lay down on the floor beneath the powerful instrument itself, stretching out on her back within the embrace of the world that existed between the piano and the floor.

George closed her eyes, immersing herself within the flowing notes and powerful chords of the ballade. She could feel it reverberating through the floor, through her body, into her very soul, just as it had during Marie d'Agoult's party. She lay there on the floor, lost in the melody that was all around her, no longer aware of the day, the time, whether or not she was breathing; where she was or why she was there. She was lost, immersed, surrounded, enveloped in Chopin's music. This was heaven.

Suddenly the music stopped, the still air ringing with the abrupt silence; the icy vacuum of the stark, desolate void that threatened to devour her in a bleak, barren realm without music. George opened her eyes. Blinked. Took a breath. Looked around. And paused as the spell broke, as the dream ended, as she came to. Slowly, unwillingly, she emerged from the delicious rapture in which she had been immersed. Where was she? And how had she ended up underneath the piano?

Chopin bent down to look at her. "Uh, Madame Sand, what are you doing under there?"

"Immersing myself in the music," she sighed, the pure ecstasy from which she had just emerged overtaking the logical question of how she had made her way under the piano; ecstasy that soured into pain as her suddenly-deprived mind, heart, and soul demanded more.

He shook his head. "All right." Recapturing his intent focus, he started playing again. She shut her eyes and let it fill her up; let herself drown in it.

But had he truly recaptured that focus? Even in the celestial depths of George's transports of exquisite rapture, she noticed that the tempo of the piece kept changing, even in moments where it was not supposed to. Then Chopin gave a fumble. And the next line was definitely wrong. He played it again, but then he made another mistake. Clearly, the *maestro* was distracted. He stopped again, and in that ringing silence, she heard him lean over so he could see her. She opened her eyes again.

"Can you hear all right down there?"

"Oh, yes," she purred. "Amazingly."

He paused. "Are you comfortable? Do you want a pillow or a blanket or something?"

"Oh, no," she reassured him through the vexing eternity of grating silence that had interrupted his heavenly music, mind aching again in painful anticipation; in the breathless, insistent need for more. "I'm wonderful. Keep playing; keep playing!"

He returned to the ballade. When he began using the piano pedals, which made the echoing reverberation ring through the floor even more amazingly, he moved his legs in very small, stiff, careful motions, trying to keep his legs as close as he could to his body.

"It's all right," she reassured him. "You have plenty of room. You're not going to kick me."

"Are you sure?" he asked.

"If you do, it won't bother me," she said.

That quite obviously made him feel even more awkward.

She was still clearly on his mind, but Chopin made his way beautifully through the rest of the piece. And there was silence. Shining, shimmering, speechless silence. Slowly, breathlessly, George clambered out from under the piano, overcome by awe, glowing from the overwhelming experience. She grabbed the arm of the nearest chair and hauled herself to her feet, out of breath with rapture.

"That was beautiful, Monsieur Chopin," she beamed.

He smiled. "Thank you. And *Fryderyk*, please." Then he shrugged. "I wasn't particularly pleased with my playing; my... focus was poor."

"I wouldn't have any idea why," she said, teasing him. "Thank you for letting me lie under there."

"Why do you like being under there?" he asked, quirking a curious eyebrow.

"Well, I can fit pretty well, can't I; I'm not that tall," she said, sitting back down in her chair. Immediately the cat hopped into her lap again. Chuckling, she began petting him, then continued. "And it just lets me be closer to the music... inside it, almost. And anyway, that way I'm inconspicuous. You can just forget I'm there and play like you're alone."

"Actually, dear lady, you're a lot easier to forget about if you're sitting on the couch or someplace I can see you," Fryderyk admitted, still looking slightly embarrassed. "You can lie under there if you like, but it's actually very distracting."

George giggled. "Well, thank you for the experience."

Fryderyk paused, then coughed into his elbow. "Well, I... Thank you for coming to visit."

He was gracefully asking her to leave. George sighed, silently nodding to herself as she prepared herself to honor the parameters of her host's gracious hospitality. "All right, Valdeck; it was nice meeting you, but you need to get down now," she said to the cat, who was now snoozing in her lap.

"Come, Valdeck," Fryderyk said. Reluctantly, the cat stood up, stretched, and hopped off George's lap with a snort. "It was lovely to see you again, Madame Sand."

George stood up and put out her hand, feeling herself continuing to sweat in the overheated apartment. "George, please." From the piano bench where he still sat, Fryderyk smiled and shook her hand. His was freezing, and felt as fragile as ever. How could he possibly be cold in such a warm house?

"George. Here, let me get your coat…" Slowly rising and crossing to the entryway, he brought her coat and helped her on with it. "Well, I hope you have a lovely evening. I'd entertain you longer, but I… have work upstairs that I have to get back to." Hiding his face in his elbow once more, he coughed again.

George nodded slowly. Work? Had he been writing… or resting? "Well, thank you again for the music," she said fervently. Ever the gentleman, she bowed. "Until next time."

He gave a small bow. "Until next time."

George went home. And she shook her head, biting her lip in tender, compassionate concern, as she thought of Fryderyk. His pale face, his wispy frame, his skeletal hands, his slow, intentional movements that betrayed his awareness of the limitations of his physical strength; of the condition within whose unchangeable parameters he had pledged to live with strength and courage. *Had she ever seen any man so thin; so fragile?* she asked herself. And, by the same token, what was it that made him so attractive to her, this thin, frail, patient sufferer who seemed not unlikely to blow away in a gust of wind?

Something rose inside her, a rush of loving energy that longed to wrap Chopin in her strong arms and softly cradle him to her heart like a tender angel of domesticity. Like the angel in the back of her mind whom she could never be quite sure from one day to the next whether she wanted to emulate or not, unsure of whether domestic tenderness was an expression of weakness or of strength, at a loss as to how to balance the two extremes of independence and domesticity that she could never seem to bring together. The warm, loving energy that now filled her urged her to offer the almost motherly care she had also offered to the others who had come before Fryderyk; the others with whom George had lived, laughed, and loved— Jules, Musset, Didier, Mallefille, Casimir. Because this time... maybe it would work. After all, Chopin... he was weak. Vulnerable. And he needed help. Care. Support. Love. Could she... be the one to offer it?

He needs you, the voice of her grandmother; of a memory that was never very far away, seemed to whisper.

George smiled. *I think he does.*

"I just don't know, Claudette... He's so different from anyone I've ever courted before. Félicien Mallefille... that baron's son Casimir Dudevant... Jules Sandeau... Charles Didier... Alfred de Musset..."

Claudette sipped her wine, leaning back in the kitchen chair at which she was seated. Larger than George's Paris apartment, Claudette's was quite exotic; the lamps were swathed in rosy silk scarves, the rooms softened with cozy ottomans and luxurious chaise lounges, the floors graced with imported rugs.

"Tell me more."

George sighed, adjusting her cravat. Unlike Fryderyk's hot, stuffy apartment, Claudette's was cold, as she always liked to have the windows open, even in the depths of midwinter.

"At first, I thought it might just be a crush on his music itself, but…" She chuckled. "This time feels different. This time… something might happen."

The actress nodded knowingly, a lock of her long, brunette hair falling into her brown eyes. "*This time*. I see." She raised an eyebrow. "Well, what's different about him?"

George shook her head, smiling as she pictured Fryderyk; remembered the feeling of his hand in hers. "With the others, it was how manly they were— that was what I liked about them. And he…" She bit back another chuckle. "Well, you've seen him, haven't you?" Claudette just rolled her eyes. George tapped her chin. "He's different. Very different. But he…" Again, she smiled at the memories. "He's not a big lug who towers over me. His music… takes my breath away. And he's a suave, dashing young gentleman… so sweet and polite. He hasn't said a thing about my trousers. And…" Again, Claudette rolled her eyes, giving a sarcastic snort as George glowed. "I think he needs someone."

Claudette took another sip of wine. "So, what are you going to do about it?"

George gave half a smile. "So… now what? I care about him— I really do. But how can I show it?" She heaved a thoughtful sigh. "This is certainly not my first romance, but it just feels so different, somehow. Very different. And I… it's going to sound funny, but I would honestly appreciate any thoughts you had on how I might actually be able to make this work." With a wry chuckle, George shook her head. "Although I don't even know him properly yet— we've only just met— so what am I saying, *romance*? All I can say, I suppose, is that I think I know what my heart wants."

Claudette shook her head, looking down into her half-empty glass of wine. "All I have at this point in my life are friends. So, think of it this way. Every relationship, romantic or otherwise, begins with friendship. So, you're going to have to decide... do you care about him enough to start with being friends... and to stick with it even if it never goes anywhere else?"

George looked up and smiled. "So, that's it, then, I suppose," she said. "Just try to be his friend. I don't know where it'll go, but like you said, it certainly can't go anywhere if we're not friends first. And I can try... to be the friend he needs me to be."

Claudette smiled back. "Sounds like a plan, you lovestruck dreamer."

Help me figure this out, George prayed as she got ready for bed. *I like him. I really do. Please... help me do this right. And let things work out this time.*

3   Excitement

George put on her shirt the next morning, buttoning it up to protect the heart that had been battered by too many breakups. She put on her top hat, tucking away her long hair beneath the disguise that allowed her to slip undetected through town, going where she pleased and doing as she chose. She put on her boots, ready to stride independently through life; ready to step on those who got in her way or defend herself from any dangers she might encounter. And she put on her cravat, hiding her ivory neck, veiling her loveliness from those who could not appreciate it.

Now she was protected. She was protected against the eyes of ruffians who might see a petite woman walking alone as easy prey, protected against the prejudices of publishers and editors who might not see the female of the species as capable of being a career person, protected against stares and odd questions as she took herself shopping, out to dinner, or out to a bar. Protected from anyone and everyone who might insist upon telling her what she could or could not do, whether they meant well, wishing to protect her from the nastiness of the world, or whether they wanted to herd her back into the little box in which she might cook, sew, parent, and console as women had been doing for hundreds and hundreds of limiting years.

Not that she didn't enjoy cooking or sewing, she reflected with a shrug. She just wanted to do them on her own terms. And not because some random stranger thought they were all she could or should do.

She could earn her own money; live her own life. And she could make her home a beautiful, safe place through the cooking and sewing at which she also excelled; which also brought her joy. But not... all at the same time. Because between those two goals, two dreams, the dream of independence and the dream of domesticity, the world out there and the world within, the life of the fist and the life of the heart, there was an impassable chasm. A chasm over which George could leap, and leapt as often as she had to. But the jump... the jump itself was dangerous. And even though she could and did make it, day in and day out, there was no way to bring her incompatible dreams together. And so she jumped from one to the other and back again, wishing that there was some way to bring them together. Some way... to find balance. But there wasn't. And so, every day that she stepped out into the world of the independent career person, she began by putting on her armor.

George spent the next week in a writing frenzy, practically eating and sleeping at her desk. Pouring her heart and soul into her writing, wandering through a parallel world of dreams and mirrors, a thousand reflections of real life echoing out into infinity, she immersed herself in it so completely that she almost stopped thinking about Fryderyk.

But not quite.

George staggered to her editor's office, bleary-eyed from writing all night for a week and proudly carrying a folder containing the manuscript of her latest book. Tenderly leaving it in the care of her editor, she left the office with her advance. It always felt good to walk home with her advance after dropping off a manuscript that was ready for a new set of eyes to help prepare it for the world.

A carriage passed by— a carriage whose passenger, a slight, slender figure in a snappy top hat, made it a point to wave a white-gloved hand out his window. With a smile, George looked up and waved back.

She kept walking with a silent smile. Nothing needed to be said.

There was a hole in the knee of George's favorite trousers. So she went to the men's clothing store, the bell at the top of the doorframe tinkling merrily as she strode in. Purse jingling, she was ready to spend some of her advance; some of her hard-earned money that she could allocate as she chose.

As she entered the shop, she waved at Gisèle. The young woman had run the shop while Armand, the owner of the clothing store, had gone to fight in the insurrections of April of 1834, but now she was back to restocking empty shelves.

"We have a customer," Armand muttered, nodding toward the back of the shop. Rolling her eyes good-naturedly at George over Armand's shoulder, Gisèle excused herself, retreating to the back of the shop, where society insisted she remain. Even if she rather enjoyed counting money and was faster at calculating sale prices than Armand was.

Armand bent to examine a ledger, only half-looking up as his customer approached the counter. "What can I find for you today, Monsieur?" He set aside his ledger, straightening his spectacles as he took in his customer. And he blanched. "Oh— Madame Sand!" He took off his spectacles, wiping them on his sleeve as he stammered, eating his words. "Excuse me, Madame Sand," he faltered, bowing deeply.

She just grinned. That reaction... the blanch, the blinking, the stammering, the way they shrank back in shock… was always a rush. And she lived for it.

"I need a new pair of trousers, please— the same size as last time," she said, giving a roguish wink. "Red, please."

She carried on writing, healing her own soul through the act of releasing her thoughts, emotions, desires onto the waiting pages of her many notebooks; the searing pain she carried every day of the wounds that life had dealt her. Scars… that would never disappear. But maybe, if she thought hard enough, worked long enough, she would be able to heal the wounds her heart had taken over the long years of her hard life. Maybe, someday, she would complete the work that would finally truly heal her.

Through the complex relationship between George's heroine Edmée and her eventual beau Bernard she wrote, offering a critique wrapped in prose; a critique of the world around her and the way it prepared young women for nothing but marriage, training them to stand as passively as Rapunzel in her tower, waiting for men to approach them in courtship; to ask them (or their fathers) for their hands in marriage.

Inspired by her colleague Pierre Leroux, she built upon his philosophies to form her own, envisioning a future of humanitarian concern for the welfare of all, in which family, country, and property could be maintained, honored, and celebrated in a perfect union; the complete equality of a true democracy. And into the story of Edmée and Bernard she wove the American Revolution, with all of its dreams of the perfect union demonstrated by justice, domestic tranquility, the common defense, general welfare, and liberty for all. A story of liberty, justice, and equality that was still being written in the world around her.

"I bought red ones this time," George said, showing off her new trousers to her friend.

Claudette raised her hands as in wild applause. "Oh, you wonderful rebel, you."

George met Claudette for coffee or tea; invited her over for lunch or popped over to her apartment for dinner. Together they pored over the works of philosophers contemporary and historical, piecing together their own history of the systemic limitation of women by the societies in which they lived. Together they debated the past, in all its positives and negatives, the present in which they now dwelt, and the potential futures they might create. And together they discussed fashion, Claudette complimenting George's newest top hat or the cut of her trousers as they cheerfully filled the air with tobacco smoke from their matching cigars. Maybe Claudette didn't usually wear trousers— she loved her elegant gowns too much— but George's friend loved seeing her running free. Years ago, at the beginning of George's journey through life, Claudette had helped her set herself free.

They discussed life. And they discussed the political systems and structures that impacted their daily lives. The king and his cabinet worked together in an uncomfortable sort of dance— because only those who paid above a certain rate of taxes could vote, everyone but the richest men in France were excluded.

That was so. But George and Claudette, the trouser-wearing author and the forward-thinking actress, dreamed of a future in which they had an equal voice in matters of state.

George put away the clean laundry that had been delivered by the laundress, placing armloads of clean clothing back into her armoire. She hung up her starched jackets and gleaming white cravats, neat waistcoats, and snappy dress shirts alongside the many dresses, some simple and casual, some elegant, and others absurdly frilly and fluffy, that she also sometimes wore. A lifetime had brought many items to her wardrobe, accumulated over the years, shirts and skirts finding themselves side-by-side; top hats and tiny shoes, cravats and hair ribbons, ready to complete one look or another. She was an artist. And as such, she needed an entire palette of colors with which to paint on the canvas of her life.

She shrugged. Every day was different. Every occasion was unique. Dresses were pretty and feminine. But shirts and trousers were comfortable and freeing. She wore a dress when she wanted to be pretty. But when she wanted to be free… she wore her shirt and trousers.

Slowly, the spring of 1837 arrived, the gentle sun thawing the winter chill. And again, George felt her heart skipping a beat when one day, taking herself out for lunch at a local restaurant— this time on a quiet Monday— she heard a voice she recognized acknowledging the bill for luncheon.

She finished her langoustine bisque in breathless silence, then slowly, almost demurely, walked over to Chopin's table. Demure, maybe… but also grateful, as she had chosen to wear a shirt and trousers today, that he, of all people, didn't seem to mind her wardrobe choices.

Fryderyk was just finishing a plate of chicken and potatoes;

taking the last sip of the tea he had ordered. He heard someone approach. He looked up. And he smiled.

"Hello, Madame Sand," he said, standing up to shake her hand. George took his hand gently, giving it a light, polite shake that didn't threaten to injure his shoulder joint. He looked better than he had; although he was still fair, he didn't seem quite so pale. Today, a gray jacket and a white shirt were set off by a black cravat and matching top hat. If he was surprised at how similar George's outfit was to his, he gave no outward sign.

"Hello, Monsieur Chopin."

He smiled. "Fryderyk, please," he said at the same moment as she said,

"George, please."

They paused. "George," he said, tasting the single syllable.

"Fryderyk," she murmured, the name rolling gently off her tongue.

They paused again, the silence bubbling up into embarrassed chuckles.

"How have you been?" they both asked, again tripping over one another with their words. George laughed out loud.

"I've been well enough," she said before he could try to answer. "Been writing day and night."

Fryderyk smiled. "So have I," he replied. "Quite literally."

"That's good to hear," she said.

"Oh, how wonderful," he echoed. And again, they laughed.

Suddenly Fryderyk blinked, snapping to attention as he gestured at the seat across from him.

"Would you like to sit down?" he asked quickly, hurrying around to the other side of the table to pull out the empty chair. Gratefully George sat down, letting him push her in. "May I, ah, order you anything?" he asked. "Or did you eat, or—"

George nodded toward her table and the empty soup bowl. "I just had some soup for lunch," she said.

Fryderyk smiled. "I was actually just thinking of what I might order for dessert."

George smiled, even as she pushed away the whisper in the back of her mind of what her grandmother would say— that as her father's lad, she needed to be a gentleman toward others; not accept gentlemanly gestures that might be offered to her. Silently, she asked that voice to stop talking. And carefully, she found herself opening her well-protected heart... just a crack.

"Well... I wouldn't say no to a piece of apple tart."

Fryderyk chuckled. "Neither would I."

Fryderyk ordered for both of them, and they sat together at the table, occasionally commenting on the weather, until their dessert arrived. George ate her apple tart slowly, appreciating the flavor and the texture; trying not to get crumbs in her cravat. And thinking. Of how good it had felt to let Fryderyk be the gentleman. Of how... honored though she would have been to buy his dessert for him, and satisfying and thoroughly ordinary as it would have felt to split the bill down the middle... that had not been so bad. Not so bad at all. And how grateful she was that he had gone to the trouble of offering that gesture to her. Slowly they finished their dessert, finally setting down their forks and sitting back in their chairs in satisfaction.

Fryderyk looked at George. "I'd like to see you again sometime," he said softly.

She bubbled up inside. "Really?" she asked, her near-whisper holding back the excited squeal that was building inside her heart. "That sounds wonderful."

He smiled. "Could we go for a drive?"

"Whatever you like," she said, fighting to sound casual, so she would at least sound like a sane person. "I have a horse I hire."

"So have I," he said. "And a carriage."

"So, we could either go horseback riding together or ride in the carriage," she said. "Do you like horseback riding?"

"I think I prefer the carriage," he said.

"Sounds wonderful," she said again. "When are you free?"

He thought. "What is today— Monday? How about tomorrow?"

She smiled, blushing. "Tomorrow works for me. What time?"

Fryderyk bit his lip. "Well, I have to be back by eight in the evening; I have… things I need to accomplish, so… how about before dinner? Would four o'clock work for you?"

"Four o'clock is fine. Do you want to pick me up, or should I come to your house?"

He blushed, even as a question seemed to pass over his face. "I could come get you if you like. Of course, if you'd rather come over, or if you'd rather meet somewhere…"

"You can pick me up," she said. "That'll be just fine." Retrieving a slip of paper from her pocketbook, she scribbled down her address, then offered him the paper. "My apartment shouldn't be too hard to find."

He smiled nervously. "Four o'clock it is, then."

George nodded. "Four o'clock."

Fryderyk looked away shyly. George reached over and took his hand. It was cold. He smiled and let her hold it.

Fryderyk looked down at his empty plate. George's bowl, at her table, was empty, too, as were their smaller dessert plates. Lunchtime was over.

Fryderyk stood up, and so did George. She stuck out her hand to shake, and he took it gently. To her delicious surprise, he lifted it and kissed it.

A thousand feelings exploding inside her heart, she struggled to remain coherent. With an effort, she turned her extremely sappy smile into one that was hopefully intelligent and inclined her head.

"Until tomorrow, then, Fryderyk."

He smiled, inclining his head in turn. "Until tomorrow, George."

George somehow took her leave and floated home. Her feet scarcely touched the road… she hardly saw anything but the beautiful blue sky and the trees that were getting greener every day. She skipped home, laughing all the way. Because she was going to see Fryderyk tomorrow.

George rolled over and woke up. Immediately it hit her— today she was going driving with Fryderyk. Heart beginning to pound, she jumped out of her four-poster bed, fighting free from the red hangings that surrounded it, and ran past her desk, piled high with stacks of paper representing her works-in-progress, quick notes to herself regarding scenes yet unwritten, grocery lists, pens, and empty teacups, to her large armoire. She had to figure out what she was going to wear…

George stood at the open wardrobe, staring at her collection of options. If she were going horseback riding, she'd gravitate toward trousers, but since they were going to be driving in Fryderyk's carriage, her freedom of movement wasn't quite as important. And although he hadn't seemed to be scandalized by her masculine attire; hadn't divulged any opinion of it one way or the other, there was no harm in dressing ladylike for once. Like the woman her mother had been; the woman who lived in the back of her mind, henpecking her, telling her that if she had been a perfect, traditional, domesticated, angelic, feminine woman, things would have worked out with Casimir, with Jules, with Didier, with Musset, with Mallefille…

She went to the window and pulled back the curtain. It was sunny out, one of the first truly warm spring days of the year singing with birds and flowers. Good. She wouldn't have to worry about getting her clothes muddy. And a chilly, rainy day wasn't going to come and make Fryderyk sick.

George picked a dark blue and a dark green dress and agonized over her choice. Both were perfectly becoming, and neither would drag and get in her way. In the end, she picked the blue one.

George practically jumped into her corset and dress, lacing herself into the foundation of the structured undergarment more tightly than was strictly comfortable, and then attacked her head with her wooden hairbrush while trying to put on her high-heeled lady shoes one-handed. Then she realized— she was getting ready as if their date was for nine o'clock this morning. It wasn't until four this afternoon. She could slow down. She had plenty of time.

Plenty of time to wait. Not until four… Suddenly George felt like she was climbing through blancmange. Now she had the entirety of the long day to get through. What was she going to do until around three-thirty?

George groaned and put the brush down. She might as well get some breakfast, and fight with her hair later. After *lunch*, maybe. Ugh. How was she going to wait?

George dragged herself into the kitchen and slowly, slowly made muffins. Waiting for them to bake would kill time. She stood waiting by the kitchen window, feeling the spring sunshine on her face, humming and tapping on the windowsill. What was she humming? George smiled. It was the ballade Fryderyk had played at Marie d'Agoult's party. Why was she not surprised?

4   A Carriage Ride

Long past breakfast-time, George was finally eating a plate of hot muffins. But she didn't even enjoy them. They were only a way to waste time. After she finally got two muffins down, giving another to her little dog Marquis and putting the rest away for later, she sat at the kitchen table and added another chapter to her current manuscript, then wrote eight letters. That really *did* help to pass the time. She walked the dog around the block. And then she returned to the kitchen to make gingerbread cookies— she could send some home with Fryderyk. Once they were all set out to cool, she looked up at the clock— two fifty-three. Only an hour or so and he'd be here. She smiled, feeling excitement bubbling up inside her heart again. Time to really start getting ready.

George found the hairbrush again and began the fairly painful process of getting her hair presentably wrangled into a reasonably neat bun. Once that was finally accomplished and she had stopped crying from the pain, she straightened her dress and finished putting on her makeup; powdering her face, then dabbing on a tiny bit of rouge and a lip balm tinted the same shade of pink. She stuffed her feet into her high-heels, tottering about like a little pony and struggling not to lose her balance and turn her ankle. Finally, she hauled herself to the mirror to examine herself. How did she look?

Oh, if she had another hour, she could list all the tiny little things that were wrong with her appearance, or she could just let them go and smile that she was, indeed, presentable.

You look perfect, a voice seemed to coo inside her mind. George looked up at the words of the feminine ideal that lived inside her mind; the annoying personification of angelic perfection, domestic goddess and happy housewife extraordinaire. All pink cheeks and curled hair and starched aprons, the angel puttered about inside the cozy kitchen of George's heart, all but literally tied to the stove with the strings of that apron. *You look like a lady. A beautiful, sweet, demure, feminine lady. Just like you should be.*

George just shrugged. The idea that she "should" be demure and feminine at all times, she disagreed with. And yet, it was all so contextual. And it wasn't wrong to be a lady when the occasion called for it, was it? A lady who could fill her kitchen with homemade cookies… cookies that she carefully placed in a cute little basket, wrapping them in a white cloth.

She looked at the time again. Three forty-eight. Time to go outside and wait. Almost squealing with excitement, George took hold of her skirt to keep it out of her way and tripped outside to stand in front of her apartment building. She held the basket of cookies and tried to look ladylike.

She watched intently for Fryderyk's carriage. Every time a carriage went by, she brightened up, heart pounding as she wondered if it was him. No. Not yet. She sighed every time.

Finally, just as the clock in her sitting room chimed four o'clock, she grinned. This carriage she recognized. He was here.

George took a deep breath and tried to look calm. Slowly, she made her way toward the carriage.

She managed to turn her glorious feelings into a polite smile as she stood there on the steps, waving vaguely. The driver pulled the carriage up to a stop, the door slowly opening so the passenger inside could emerge. Slowly, a gold-topped walking stick held by a white-gloved hand poked itself out of the open door. Slowly, the rest of Fryderyk followed.

He'd really dressed up, George realized, trying not to give a sappy sigh. He shone in a dark green tailcoat she'd never seen before and a black top hat, a few tiny violets at his buttonhole. Gracefully, he leaned on the same gold-topped walking-stick he'd carried at Marie d'Agoult's party. Delicate white gloves and an ornately tied cravat, the whitest she'd ever seen, completed the picture.

George smiled at him, and shyly, he returned her smile. For a moment, neither spoke.

"You look very nice," they said at exactly the same time. George bit her lip with an embarrassed giggle as he gave a self-conscious chuckle of his own.

Doffing his top hat, Fryderyk stepped forward with a bow, and George had to fight to keep her knees from collapsing in sheer romantic delight as he softly kissed her hand. Blinking back her glorious amazement, she remembered the cookies she'd made, and presented the covered basket.

"I made you cookies," she said breathlessly, holding out the basket.

He smiled, taking the basket in his gloved hand. "Ooh, what kind?"

"Ginger," she said. "Spicy gingerbread cookies."

"Oh, these are my favorite!" he said with a grin. George smiled as she noticed that he had an adorable dimple in his cheek. "When I was fifteen, I visited my godfather in Toruń during school vacation, and that's where I had the best gingerbread I've ever eaten— *pierniki toruńskie*, we call it. I loved it so much I wrote to my friend Jasia about it, and sent some home to my family near

46

Warsaw. This is just like a little bit of home—thank you so much for making them." Carefully, he set the basket in the carriage, a delighted smile still playing about his mouth. "We can eat them on the way." Inclining his head, he offered his hand to her.

George looked at his hand. What a gentleman, offering to help her into the carriage. And yet... subtle as it was in his noble effort to conceal it, he had planted his feet to brace himself, preparing himself to support her. *Don't you dare let him help you*, her grandmother seemed to say, putting her hands on her hips. *Because he can't.* But George's mother Sophie shook her head, countering, *Be a lady. Let him be the man.*

Silently, George nodded, and she made her plan. Smiling politely, she took his hand as lightly as she could, grabbed firmly onto the frame of the carriage, supported her weight against it rather than his arm, and hopped in. *Well done*, her grandmother seemed to accede, nodding in satisfaction just as George's mother contradicted, *Why didn't you let him help you?*

Turning back toward Fryderyk, she extended her own hand. With a grateful nod, he accepted the boost. Internally, George smiled. That had felt good. She'd accepted his chivalry... and then turned around and helped him.

They settled into the carriage, sitting side-by-side. George put the basket of gingerbread on her lap; then reached around Fryderyk, shutting the door. The driver whistled to the horses, and a moment later, the carriage began moving.

George looked at Fryderyk. "So where are we going?" she asked.

"I thought just over to the pond, you know, next to the church," he said. "Maybe we could get out and sit for awhile."

She nodded. "Sounds wonderful." She opened the basket.

"Here, have a cookie."

Fryderyk took one, nibbling it so delicately that it made George feel like she ate like a horse. He brushed the crumbs from his mouth; then set about picking the remaining crumbs off his glove.

"They're very good," he said as soon as his mouth was empty. She smiled. What a delight to watch him enjoy eating something she'd made for him. "I haven't had these for the longest time."

George took one as well, making a real effort to eat politely. She succeeded, but couldn't pull it off as well as he could. Hopelessly, she tried to brush the cookie crumbs off her lap.

"Well, I'm a messy eater, aren't I?" she said. *Just like your father*, her grandmother's voice snapped at her from inside her head, snapping just like her fierce steel-blue eyes had snapped when Aurore had misbehaved. *Just like...* Now it took on a pleading tone. *Just like your dear, brave, wonderful papa... Just sit down, my lad. Just sit down.*

Just like a little farm boy, her mother's voice hissed. George could just see Sophie's brown eyes narrowing; her rouged lip curling as her daughter disappointed her. *Sit up straight. Hands in your lap. Take off your riding boots and get that grass out of your hair. Why did you choose that outfit? It doesn't show off how pretty you are.*

George shook her head, kicking at the memories, trying to shut them up. They scolded her like the little girl she had once been— the little girl they still made her feel like; the little girl she was not. But there was no use getting distracted by what they would have said to her. So, she looked at Fryderyk. And waited for his answer.

He gave her a teasing little smile, but didn't reply. "Yes, I am,"

48

she said, raising her eyebrows playfully. "Admit it. Don't try to be polite. You've seen horses that eat more neatly than I do."

"I saw a goat once that had bits of grain stuck all through its beard," he said.

George snorted. "Baaaah," she groaned, imitating the goat.

"A little lower," he said, grinning. "And then the farmer would say, *Madame, if you come any closer, they're liable to go after your shoes.*"

"How do you do that?" George laughed, almost taken aback at how uncannily well he'd captured the farmer's voice. "That sounds *exactly* like the farmer who lives by the mill."

"I do enjoy doing impressions," he said with a shrug.

"You mean they're your secret second skill," she said, raising her eyebrows. "If you weren't a composer, you'd be a great actor."

He sighed sadly, giving a half-sarcastic shrug. "If I could endure touring."

She sighed and patted his hand. "Was this a hard winter?"

Fryderyk looked at her with a heavy, bitter sigh of his own.

"Every winter is hard," he said simply, sullenly. Slowly, he gave half a smile. "Although I am getting better as the spring passes, just like I do every year."

George gave him an encouraging little nod. "I can see it. Your color's much better than it was when I came over in January and you played for me."

He raised an eyebrow. "I was distracted that day, wasn't I? I wish I could remember why..." Sarcastically, he tapped his chin. "Ah, yes," he said. "I think someone was lying underneath the piano while I was playing..."

George chuckled and shook her head. "I just couldn't help it," she said. Fryderyk just gave a chuckle of his own. George sighed, casting around for another topic. "Do you... do you like touring?" she asked, returning to the comment he'd just made.

Fryderyk shook his head emphatically, wrinkling his nose. "I don't like traveling," he said. "I'm a creature of habit... and a creature of comfort. I prefer my own bed and my own schedule. And I'm far too absorbed in the work of creating my new pieces to race around to Vienna and Berlin and London to perform for the adoring crowds. I'd much rather earn my bread giving lessons to maintain the freedom of going home by eight o'clock at night."

George just smiled.

"What a beautiful day," George sighed a moment later, looking out at the trees as they drove past, riding away from the busy shops and crowded-together apartment buildings of the compact, congested city to a more open part of town; past parks and fountains, city greens and boulevards. They passed under an apple tree in full bloom just as a breeze ruffled the branches, sending white blossoms cascading through the air. With a chuckle, George reached out the window to catch a few. Smiling, she playfully put one in Fryderyk's buttonhole.

Gently Fryderyk caught her hand. And a beautiful stillness touched George's heart as she silently let him hold it. Slowly, their entwined hands found their way onto the seat between them, where they remained. George sat silently, looking out the window and enjoying the day, enjoying his company, slowly relaxing as she responded to the move he was making. And this, all of it, felt right. So right.

Or did it? Again she shook her head as the thoughts crowded into her mind; the demanding words and disappointed faces of her grandmother and mother. Her grandmother would be frowning at

50

her, the sad little wrinkle that always showed when she was concerned deepening between her silver eyebrows. *Fix your cravat, my dear... and don't bother with your needlework. Go outside, my lad.* And her mother would roll her painted eyes, long, loose hair rippling as she tossed her head in disgust— *What is wrong with you? Don't listen to her... you've had enough lessons for one day... isn't the boy next door cute?*

George swallowed. She sat up straight. And she promised herself that if Fryderyk was tired, he could rest his head on her shoulder... not the other way around.

Fryderyk looked up as they turned a corner, the world opening up even more as they gazed out upon the spacious stillness of the pond and the church that stood just a breath away from the hustle and bustle of the big city.

"We're here," he said. "There's the pond. Here, please, Piotr," he called. Slowly, the carriage came to a halt.

George opened the door and stepped out. The blue lake sparkled in the spring sunshine, and the tall, white steeple of the church rose on the far side. A number of willow trees grew by the edge of the lake, shading a bench from the brightest light.

George took in a deep breath of sunshine and turned back around. *Help him,* her grandmother seemed to insist. *He needs help and can't help you, and you don't need help, but you can help him.* She extended her hand with a little smile, and, grasping it, Fryderyk carefully exited the carriage, his walking-stick extending searchingly before him.

That's not what a lady does, George's mother immediately sneered. *She helps her man, yes, but she doesn't disrespect him and his desire to be a gentleman toward her. Ladies are not gentleman.*

George gritted her teeth. And she chose not to respond.

Blinking the thoughts away and returning to the moment, she looked at Fryderyk again, who was releasing her hand from the careful grasp he'd taken of it as he'd leaned gently upon her strength. He gave her a half-smile, dipping his head with an embarrassed little chuckle as he transferred his weight to his walking-stick.

"Thank you. I know, I should be the one helping you—"

George shook her head with a nonchalant shrug. "I've never been much for traditional roles." She gave him a roguish wink, and he chuckled. "But you knew that already."

"I've never known a woman who could tie a cravat so well," he admitted. "Her *own* cravat."

"I've got to say, I've gotten pretty good at making men's fashions becoming to me," she said. A thousand memories rose in her mind— the forward-thinking tutor who had recommended she wear boys' clothing while horseback riding, her grandmother's adoring coos as little Aurore had paraded by almost more like her own brother, the way her mother had shaken her head at the whole thing. Of the brother and father who, long ago gone to rest as they both had, had nothing to say on the matter. And all the years since, in which the trousers she wore had become a combination of dressing for comfort and convenience and dressing to make a statement.

"Shirts and trousers are… freeing," she summed up. "I can move in them… and I can use them to show the world that women are more than our pretty faces." She looked down at the elegant dress she'd chosen today; the dress that covered a corset which restricted her to a very sedate saunter and seemed to contradict

52

what she'd just declared. "Although for *very* special occasions," she said, raising her eyebrows almost teasingly, "I won't say *no* to a dress."

Fryderyk shook his head with an embarrassed little half of a smile. "Now, I'm not trying to be rude, but I… I just never… never even thought of a woman wearing trousers. And I honestly… didn't know what to think at first."

"And what *do* you think, if I may ask?" George asked with another roguish wink.

Fryderyk just chuckled. "They are shockingly… scandalously… becoming." He shook his head. "And what I think doesn't matter— what you wear is entirely up to you. You don't make remarks about my clothing."

"You always look nice," she said. "Shall we sit down?" She gestured to the bench near the water.

"If you like."

George glanced at the ground, observing that it turned into a gentle hill strewn with stones and sticks, the ground visibly uneven in a few places. She offered him her arm.

"It gets pretty lumpy," she said, nodding at the terrain that lay before them. Fryderyk nodded and took her arm with a grateful smile, choking up on his walking-stick and accepting her help. Cautiously, she led him around the most uneven spots, glad that she could provide the support he needed; use her strength on his behalf.

Attentively rising to meet a need, her strength firmed up within her, ready to roll up its sleeves and take action. All too often in the past, it had risen in a painful, striving flex, a constricting fist clenching within her heart like a tangled ball of yarn, but in this moment, although it was ready to help, it was neither angry nor painful. Carefully, she settled Fryderyk onto the bench and sat down next to him, brimming with the joy of helping him. And with pride. She was behaving as the perfect gentleman. While also accepting chivalry from him. In this moment, no part of her mind; no figure from her past, was sniping at her to do more or do less; to man up more or to be more ladylike. In this moment, she, and the action she had taken to help someone she cared about, coming as it had on the heels of her grateful acceptance of the help he had offered her, felt balanced.

"Thank you," he said again.

She smiled. "You're welcome. Don't want you to fall and crack your head open…"

"Yes, once was enough," he said.

She stopped, her remark of comic sarcasm going sour in her mouth.

"What?"

Fryderyk shook his head. "When I was sixteen, back home in Poland, I went ice skating with some friends and fell and hit my head. I don't remember all of it, but everyone said the doctor was very worried at first. That was an awful winter; a few weeks later I caught a bad cold and the glands on my neck swelled up. Doctor had to put leeches on my neck."

George shuddered. "Well, that is something. Glad you lived to tell the tale."

Morbid jokes were just not doing it for him. He sighed. "Yes. So far."

George's heart pushed her forward, insisting that she put her arm around him, but she restrained herself and patted his hand instead. She shook her head. "I'm sorry. I'm not being very funny."

Fryderyk sighed. "I just pray I live to see another season." He shook his head. "My parents went to church, and I did as a child. I haven't been for a long time, but I do pray, and I know God is there. There's a lot I don't know, and a lot I'm not sure of, but I know He's there. I know He's good. And I know that He loves us."

George nodded and took his hand. "Yes, Fryderyk. He's always there. He's our ever-present help in trouble." She swallowed. "There's a lot I don't know, either. But I know… that God loves us. And that we… are given to one another to show love to one another… love that reflects the love He has for us. To come to know Him more through our relationships with one another. I know that there is a plan. And I know…" She held out her hand. "That we are more than this." George sighed. "Life… in the everyday… it's hard. But we have hope. Hope in… more."

Fryderyk nodded. "More."

George smiled. And she squeezed his hand. "And we, here and now… are here to look out for one another. To lift one another up. And I hope, in some way, at least… I hope a good day in the sunshine will make all the difference."

5   Connection

He nodded, then gave a heavy sigh. "Days in the sun... I used to take long walks in the sun with a beautiful girl named Marja Wodzińska." He swallowed. "I was engaged to her."

George looked at him. "Was?"

Fryderyk shook his head with a sad little shrug. "Yes... *was*. We would have married; we would have loved each other, but her parents insisted I keep in good health. That was... too much to ask that winter. They made me break it off." George felt a twinge as Fryderyk's voice broke. "I think about her all the time and what we might have had together... I would have worked so hard to be a good husband, and I know we would have been happy together. She would have had all the love I could give, but I can understand her parents' hesitancy; I've never been physically strong..."

George bit her lip and took his hand again. He took a deep breath that was almost a sob, and, without warning, laid his head on her shoulder. George's heart began to pound. Suddenly, this was very intimate. Her strength quavered inside her, flexing to meet his need. And yet, something else, too, rose inside her. Something different. Something... tender. And yet different from the motherly love she had always extended to the beaus with which she had once lived and loved. Something she wasn't entirely sure of. Because she could not make sense of it.

"You're very strong," she whispered, gently putting her arm around his thin shoulders. "You let her go."

Fryderyk shuddered, and she felt him nod. Wiping his eyes, he slowly sat up. She patted his back and he gave her a watery smile, which she returned. Wistfully, he sighed, looking away reflectively. And George let herself imagine the memories he was gazing into.

Fryderyk shook his head. And suddenly he blinked, his expression changing as he abruptly backed away from her, clearing his throat.

"I'm so sorry, this is completely improper, I'm being so rude—" Hastily he stood up and began straightening his jacket.

George smiled and shook her head. Gratitude for his vulnerability and pride at stepping up to support and comfort him chased one another around her mind, barking like confused dogs.

"I don't mind. I understand. Love is… love is hard. And it's important to have someone to talk to. I… I'm honored that you decided you could come to me."

Fryderyk wiped his face with his gloved hand. "Sh… shall we go?"

George shrugged. "If you're ready."

He nodded. "If you don't mind. This has been… this has been lovely, and we've spent two wonderful hours together. I'm just afraid I'm getting tired…"

She nodded, standing up again beside him. "Thank you so much for inviting me. I had a lovely time."

George took Fryderyk's arm again and guided him back to the carriage, her strength and his walking-stick keeping him steady as he cautiously contended with the uneven ground over which they were walking. He was visibly drooping, weary at the end of a long day outdoors and from the sudden outpouring of unexpected emotion; unsteady on his feet even with the help of her arm and his cane. Carefully, solicitously, gallantly, she helped him back into the carriage, getting in beside him and closing the door behind them. *Well done*, her grandmother said again, even as her mother scowled, arms folded, at the messy, disrespectful ways in which her daughter was interacting with this charming young man.

"You want another cookie?" George asked.

Fryderyk looked up with a smile and another little chuckle. "Oh, if you have any more. Yes, please."

They each had one more while they drove. Silently George looked at him as they passed under the springtime trees… He was worn out, even by this. He was weaker in body than she had realized. Silently, she sighed. All the more reason for her to help him. Make Grandmother proud. No matter what *Maman* would say.

"The trees are beautiful," Fryderyk murmured softly.

"Yes, they are," she said. "Such pretty blossoms." She looked out at the western sky, where the sun was slowly moving toward the horizon, the shadows lengthening as late afternoon passed into dinnertime.

"What do you like to eat for dinner?" she asked him.

"I like chicken," he said. "And fish. But I'm terribly allergic to pork, and I can't drink anything strong. I wish I could eat ham and kielbasa and drink coffee and wine, at least now and then. But I'm stuck with oatmeal and milk and pastries, and the occasional gingerbread cookie— the same things every day. So many foods give me indigestion it's ridiculous." He sighed, shaking his head. "Makes me wish eating wasn't actually necessary."

George shook her head, offering what she hoped was a sympathetic sigh. And after they had shared a reflective pause, she continued. "I cook a little. I learned from my grandmother. My mother never really had the opportunity to cook with me, and I didn't have any big sisters around to teach me."

Fryderyk nodded. "I'm the second of four children. But Emilja, who's number three... she's gone ahead of us to be with our Lord. A cough a bit like mine took her from us when she was fourteen... all at once in a terrible fit."

George felt her breath catch; felt herself suddenly blinking back tears she bent her head to hide as her heart seemed to break. *You've lost a sibling too*, her soul cried out, wishing to throw itself into the arms of Fryderyk's soul, comforting him in his loss even as she sought comfort in her own. *Do I tell him now?* she asked herself. *Do I tell him about Louis?*

Her heart ached as she thought of her baby brother; the brother she had barely met during the few months he had lived in this world. The brother whose hypothetical future no one would ever know; who might have become a soldier like their father, a doctor, a teacher, the heir of their mother's never-opened hat shop, or a professional aristocrat like his paternal ancestors. The brother whose life and career choices would also have been shaped by the fact that he was blind. The brother she thought of only occasionally... but whose absence ached like a hole in her heart every time she went near her memories of him.

She thought of Louis. And she bowed her head, her eyes filling with unshed tears, as she pondered the question, the ethical dilemma, that always rose when she was asked how many siblings she had— should she mention him? Or simply say, as she had so many times before, that she had been the youngest child in her household? Was it dishonest to say nothing of him? Or, in her silence, was she being respectful of her family; keeping private the loss that was her parents' even more than hers; that no one but her parents, gone though they were as well now, had the right to decide if and when to speak of? She swallowed, the unanswerable question aching inside her mind as it always did. And silently, she decided that now was not the time. Maybe someday… but not yet. Not today. The serious turns their conversation had taken showed the trust Fryderyk placed in her, trust she knew she could place in him, but she could comfort him today… and wait for the day when she would ask him to comfort her.

She shook her bowed head, bringing herself back to the conversation. "I'm sorry. So… so very sorry."

Fryderyk sighed. "Thank you. We both have consumption— although the kind we have is not contagious— I would never go anywhere, would never welcome students into my home for lessons, if I thought I was going to infect others. It's not something we caught; it's something we were each born with. But because it's not an 'illness' so much as a 'lung problem,' it can't be cured. It feels like I've seen every doctor in Poland, but although they've guided me toward helpful strategies that have made my day-to-day life easier, they haven't been able to take it away from me."

He swallowed, looking away into the past. "I'm from near Warsaw, actually; I was born in a village called Zelazowa Wola about fifty kilometers from the big city. I came here to France in '31 when I was twenty; I'd been touring throughout Europe, in a manner of speaking, at least, when the fighting broke out. At last… Poland was rising up to take back her freedom from Russia.

"My best friend Tytus, my traveling companion and roommate, hurried home to enlist, and I was left alone in Vienna, wishing I had never left home at all. I had intended to go to Italy, but things were… uncertain there, as well. So, I chose Paris. And it was on my way to Paris…" Fryderyk paused, biting his lip. "That I learned that the freedom fighters… had been brought down. And that I couldn't go home." His voice broke. "My passport says that I'm 'in transit to London via Paris'... and I am just passing through. I've just been here... for rather a long time."

George sighed, heart too full for words. Too full... and yet, not quite ready to tip itself into Fryderyk's waiting hands, sharing every painful detail of her complicated childhood and youth as he had just done. She trusted him... and yet, now was simply not the time. She sighed. And gently, she took his hand.

"I hope you get to go home someday," she finally said.

He nodded. "I hope so, too."

They drove on in reflective silence, the late-afternoon light growing soft and golden. "What's your day like?" George asked a few minutes later.

"My day?" he asked, looking quizzical.

She shrugged. "What do you do all day?"

He smiled. "Well, now that I'm not roommates with Tytus or with my other friend Julian anymore, it's just me and Valdeck, except for the days that Estelle, my cleaning lady, or Céline, my laundress, come by. I get up and get ready for the day, and then sometimes I teach piano lessons all morning. Then it's out to lunch, and more lessons in the afternoon. Evenings, I write. My adherence to this kind of schedule is admittedly a bit more sporadic in the wintertime; too often I'm in no condition to teach. I've been getting to feeling better now that spring is arriving, but lately I've been sleeping in until I wake up on my own, eating a boring breakfast of oatmeal or bread and some milk or hot chocolate, and then writing and playing all day, and sitting quietly around the house with the cat. I'm usually in bed by nine.

"I... I have a confession to make," he said, looking down at his lap as his voice filled with embarrassment. "The time you visited me not long after Marie d'Agoult's party, when I said I couldn't see you in the evening because I had things to accomplish, I meant sleeping. But on the other hand, sometimes I play the piano all night. I've woken up on my piano bench more often than you might think." He shifted in the carriage, getting more comfortable, and glanced at her with a little smile. "So, how about you? What's your schedule? Get up every morning and write fifteen pages before breakfast?"

George chuckled. "Well, some days I do. But I don't get up 'every morning,' per se. Sometimes I go to bed at six in the morning and get up at noon. I go through writing phases; phases when that's all I can do, stay in bed and write frantically— or anywhere in my apartment, really— sometimes I even find myself writing on my back porch in the middle of the night. And I can't do anything else until it's finished."

Fryderyk looked at her reflectively. "Do you find that you change a page and change it and change it and then when you decide it's finished it's exactly the same as when you first wrote it?"

She thought. "Guess I can't really say that. I have deadlines, so I can't be a perfectionist, and even if I didn't have any, I don't think I would be. For me, the writing just… happens. It's hard to describe, but somehow… I tap into some other part of my mind, and… I find myself holding a new novel. Besides which, I have editors. My job is to get the story done, and then they tidy it up the way they do and make it presentable." George shook her head. "So, no," she said. "I don't really find myself fighting with it line by line."

He chuckled. "That's what I do. I need to remember that it's usually best the first time I write it out. But I continually torture myself 'fixing' it. I sometimes spend six weeks on a single page."

George felt her eyes go wide. "Six *weeks*?"

"Usually," he said simply.

"Well," George said, "it's worth it. If I live to be a thousand, I'll never hear music as wonderful as yours."

Fryderyk looked at her, one eyebrow quirking in puzzlement. "A thousand? But... you won't."

George chuckled, even as her own mind filled with puzzlement at his literal take on her words. "Just a figure of speech."

Fryderyk shook his head with a little smile; a smile that turned into a yawn. Silently, George gave a wistful smile of her own. He was worn out.

They were turning the corner that led to her apartment. George looked out the window. "We're almost to my house. Thank you so much for a wonderful afternoon together."

Straightening up, he smiled and nodded. "Thank you for the same. I had a very good time."

The carriage stopped and she got out. He followed her, leaning heavily on his walking-stick. "You're a good friend, George."

She grinned and put her hand out. He shook it heartily. "You're a good friend too, Fryderyk." She gave a breathy laugh, her longing for him suddenly pushing her forward. "So, I don't suppose you'd like a kiss?"

Fryderyk blushed, and she immediately regretted her joke. "Today was so perfect," he almost stammered. "I wouldn't wish to harm the memory of our beautiful afternoon with... well... certain actions."

George nodded, biting back the embarrassment, the shame, the regret she felt at the look he was now giving her. In her impetuousness, had she ruined everything? Ruined the drive?

Ruined his day? Ruined any and every chance she would ever have to be the woman he might want to kiss?

She swallowed. "Fair enough."

He looked at her. And his face softened. "It's all right," he murmured, softly shaking his head. Drily, he chuckled. "I just appreciate your asking first."

George just tried to smile.

The sun was setting. Her friend was yawning. Reluctantly, George curtsied and turned away; walked back up to her door. Slowly Fryderyk got back in the carriage. He waved to her, and she waved back as slowly, the carriage drove away.

George sighed and walked back into the apartment. What a wonderful, lovely afternoon they had spent together. He was funnier and more tender than she'd ever known. There was so much about him to care about... and she did more than ever.

He saw her as a friend... and, it was clear, nothing else. George shook her head with a little smile, thinking of her sweet, sensitive new friend. She was glad that he saw her as a friend. She could return the sentiment.

George had blissful dreams that night; dreams that took her once more on the carriage ride she had shared with Fryderyk. And even as the dreams faded, she smiled as she remembered how he had been the one who'd asked her out, not the other way around. That said a lot. Especially considering his shyness. That *really* said a lot.

It was strange, though. And she wondered about how she felt. And about how it had gone. How he had... behaved. The scene played over in her mind; the way his face had crumpled, the moment when he had folded sideways to rest his head on her shoulder, a sob catching in his throat. Needing her. Relying on her. And yet… maybe not as a sweetheart— because he had been wilting in grief over being separated from his old girlfriend. His real sweetheart? The sweetheart… whom he still revered inside his heart?

She shook her head. And she wondered… what she really, truly ought to be doing. Whether it had been right to go out with him in the first place. What he really thought of her; what he intended. How she ought to respond to the mixed signals that may have been nothing more than an innocent, trusting loss of composure in the presence of a faithful friend. May have been nothing more than a moment that was never going to matter again.

Then she thought of how she had behaved. Of the kiss she had so impetuously offered him; at the scandalized horror with which he had rejected it. Of the shock she'd given him. And the agony of shame into which she had retreated. But from which he had drawn her again with his forgiving smile, with his half-sarcastic thanks that she had at least asked first, with the way that he had gone on as though she'd never done such an embarrassing thing. He seemed to be willing to forgive and forget. And maybe she could forgive herself and move on… move on with a renewed dedication to honoring his boundaries. Even as she navigated the hopes that someday, those boundaries would change.

She wondered where this would go. And what was going to happen next. And whether, head-over-heels in love as she was with his heavenly music, she should resign herself to being nothing more than his friend.

She would be a good friend; would treat him the way he wanted to be treated. Because she cared about him, more, she now realized, than she'd ever cared about any of the other men she'd courted… whether or not he and she were even courting anyway. Cared enough to put him and his needs first. Even if she had nearly ruined it by shocking him with the offer of an unwanted kiss. The unwanted offer that she gave breathless thanks did not seem to have ruined everything forever.

He was a good friend to her, too. But the day had not yet come for her to speak of Louis. Maybe someday… but not today. Picking her way through the complexities of silence and candor, she was still not sure how to put this part of her story, the existence of her precious, departed little brother, into words.

Is Fryderyk the one? she wondered as she prayed for peace; prayed for wisdom. *The one who truly needs me; the one who can make me the happy, feminine woman that part of me longs to be? The one who can save me from myself?*

6   Just Friends

Two days later, George was writing in her sitting room, fresh gingerbread cookies she'd made for no apparent reason cooling in the kitchen, when there was a knock on the door. Setting down her pen, she got up to answer it.

George smiled. "Oh, Fryderyk! How lovely to see you again!"

Fryderyk walked gracefully inside, elegantly removing his black cloak. As it swirled through the air, she thought she caught the sheen of a satin lining.

She took his cloak and top hat, hanging them up beside her own manly top hat and gentleman's-style coat.

"I had such a nice time the other day," Fryderyk said, adjusting the cuffs of his black jacket, then straightening his collar and cravat. "I'm so glad you wanted to come."

George turned back toward him with a smile; a smile that he returned with absolute sincerity, undisturbed by the shirt and trousers she'd chosen to wear today.

"Thank you so much for inviting me. Won't you sit down?"

He smiled at her oddly. "Uh, of course I will, if I may. Thank you." He moved a notebook off a chair and sat down across from the chair she had chosen by the coffee table. Fryderyk swallowed, his gaze dropping to his lap, where he was picking a tiny piece of lint off the cuff of his velvet jacket with a gloved hand.

"I'm sorry, by the way," he said slowly, "about how I acted. Talking about Marja, I mean. And, ah, invading your personal space." He swallowed. "I'm sorry it got so awkward. I didn't mean to do that— it came out of nowhere, you might say. Surprised... surprised even me." His gaze flickered upward, his brown eyes meeting George's for a heartbeat. "I guess I just needed… a friend."

George smiled, reaching out to take his gloved hand, which felt just as thin and cold as ever. "A friend," she agreed.

Suddenly there was a loud barking from the other room. Without warning, a small ball of shedding fur came pounding down the hall, almost somersaulting, then skidded on the hardwood floor, nails scrabbling loudly, bounced off the wall, and bounded into Fryderyk's lap. The composer sat there stiff with terror, beginning to cough as the tiny animal exuded clouds of itchy fur.

"Down, Marquis!" George ordered, pointing at the floor as she jumped up and stomped toward the little white dog, ready to grab him and forcibly remove him. Realizing he was in trouble, the dog meekly hopped off Fryderyk's lap, retiring in a puff of hair to a cushion under a chair in the corner. Fryderyk sat frozen in terror, breathing heavily as he clutched his chest. In the instant since the dog had appeared, his already-ivory face had gone three shades paler.

Feeling her own face going hot with shame, George frowned in concern, bending toward him tenderly. "Are you all right?" she asked quietly.

Fryderyk didn't answer. Just began coughing, burying his face in his handkerchief as his thin body shook with the force of the coughs that were overwhelming him.

Silently, George watched him. And waited, twisting her hands nervously together, as he endeavored to stop coughing.

Do something, her mother seemed to demand, Sophie's painted eyes widening in worry as she watched Fryderyk coughing, the visible part of his face growing red. *A woman always helps the*

68

man she cares about.

Help him, her grandmother seemed to insist, raising her silver eyebrows and snapping her crisp, white apron. *Lift his burdens. Stand up for him. He clearly doesn't have the strength to help himself.*

Help the poor thing, the angel commanded. *You know how much you like him.*

How can you best help him? another voice seemed to ask. *Stepping up to meet this need with graciousness and respect?*

George shook her head. Still, she dithered, torn, her striving strength held back by her unwillingness to patronizingly pounce on him as though he were a helpless, suffering child. As she watched, silently biting her lip and twisting her hands, wordlessly praying that it would stop, Fryderyk's words came back to her— the words he had spoken of his little sister Emilja. *A cough a bit like mine took her from us… all at once in a terrible fit.* At the time, George had not known how someone could have died in a coughing fit. But now, as she watched Fryderyk struggling to bear up against the gale that raged inside his lungs, threatening to fell him completely, she wondered if she understood.

Finally, she could bear it no longer. "Can I get you a drink or anything?" she begged.

Fryderyk managed to look up at her, a vein visibly throbbing in his red forehead. And with half a fleeting smile half-covered by his handkerchief, he gave a grateful nod.

George raced to the kitchen as Fryderyk continued rocking with the force of his coughs. Something she could serve him in an instant… something that wouldn't have to cool… Seizing upon the milk pitcher, George grabbed a cup and filled it, then ran it to him, moving easily in the slim trousers that didn't slow her down.

Fryderyk took it in a trembling hand, offering a quick glance of gratitude, slowly raising his face from the handkerchief in which it had been buried, and managing to get a little milk down without spilling it down his front. Finally, his breathing slowed, his coughs ebbing as his desperate gasps finally became deep, steady breaths.

"Thank you. I'm all right," he whispered, shaking his head and giving the cup back to George as he stuffed his handkerchief into his trouser pocket. Slowly, he leaned his head back, resting it on the back of the chair, rubbing his sweaty face with his hands. "Oh, that dog…"

"You aren't deathly allergic to dogs, are you?" she moaned as a wisp of fluffy fur drifted through the air on a draft. "I'm so sorry if I—"

Returning his gaze to her, he raised a thin hand. "No, no," he reassured her, shaking his head wearily and giving her a pale shadow of a reassuring smile. The redness of suffocation had faded, leaving him paler than ever, his thin face as white as the lonely moon. "Happens all the time. It's those chronic lung issues I told you about. He just surprised me, and that's how my lungs do everything— the hard way."

George just nodded. Her mind was ringing with a silent scream of, *Oh, my goodness, I thought you were about to die*, but another thought rose gently in front of the words, softly holding them back. Because if her most fundamental goal, even more fundamental than her goal of actively helping him, was to at the very least not make things worse, then telling him that she'd thought he was about to keel over was the first thing she needed to avoid.

She swallowed. And she let those thoughts remain silently

contained within her pounding heart.

George let out a sigh, setting the half-empty cup on the coffee table with a loud *click* and returning to her own seat. "I'm sorry, Fryderyk; Marquis just gets excited— he couldn't harm anybody. He's being *very bad*," she said with emphasis, aiming the last at the cowering dog, who was now trying to look as cute as possible.

Lowering his gaze, Fryderyk began methodically brushing the fur off his jacket. George paused, silently watching him. And her very soul seemed to hold its breath as she realized the magnitude of what was happening; the stakes of this moment. This was the test, she thought with an internal twinge, trying not to bite her lip. The test of how much he liked her. He could thank her for the visit and stagger out right now... and never see her again.

But... slowly, he smiled again. "Well, I'm just going to have to make friends with this fuzzball," he said, offering a hand to the dog, who was still sheltering under the chair. "Come here, fluffy." Marquis positively grinned and trotted up to Fryderyk's knees, jumping up in his excitement at being petted.

George sighed in relief, her heart calming as she released her anxious breath, her tense shoulders relaxing. The dog had not ruined absolutely everything. "I wonder what would happen if Valdeck and Marquis met one another," she said with a broken chuckle.

"Fur would probably fly, as they say," Fryderyk said, raising his eyebrows.

"I really do wonder," she said again, tapping her chin thoughtfully. "Maybe we can take them both to a park sometime; let them run around."

Fryderyk shook his head, wrinkling his nose. "I don't know what Valdeck would do. He's an indoor cat. Like me... so to speak. That's what my sisters always said about me."

George chuckled again, then nodded. "He probably disdains animals that like playing outside." She drummed her fingers on her knees, thinking of what to say next. "Would you like some— oh, of course, you already have your milk."

He nodded with a wistful little sigh. "Thank you. I'm sorry, I'm just so sensitive; I can't help choking on everything."

George bit back four or five replies that meant well but would have sounded terrible. She settled for a sympathetic smile.

Fryderyk shook his head with a sarcastic little smile, glancing at the glass on the coffee table. "Always milk. I can't manage anything else. No wine, no coffee… Sometimes I do get tired of drinking the same thing every day. But there is some comfort in routine." He shrugged his narrow shoulders. "I don't know… I'm tired of it, but it's still my favorite, somehow. Anyway, I know I couldn't handle anything else, so what's the use of complaining?"

George nodded. "You're so patient," she said slowly, haltingly putting her thoughts into the best words she could. "You deal with so much. Day in and day out. I don't mean to make personal remarks, but I see how hard it must be for you sometimes. I admire how strong you are in the face of all this."

"Strong," Fryderyk said with a slightly bitter scoff. "I can barely lift some of the larger books I own. When I'm sick, I can't always walk up the stairs." He shook his head. "I hate that I can't do the things I'm supposed to be able to do— I can't go and fight on the battlefield, I can't help my friends, I can't be a gentleman and help a lady— you helped me into the carriage, when I should have helped you— I can't do anything. It's not fair. And every day… every day, I feel bad about it. Every day, I wake up ashamed that I could never protect my loved ones in an

72

emergency; never fight for my country. Ashamed that everyone else… everyone else has to look out for me, because I can't look out for them, or even for myself. All because I'm not strong."

George felt tears prickling in her eyes, again forcing herself not to bite her lip. "It's a different kind of strength," she said slowly. "Inside. A… patient strength. A strength… that doesn't give up. And I just want to say how I admire you for it."

He gave a grateful smile. "Thank you. It is hard some days, and it's nice to have you appreciate it."

"I appreciate everything about you," she said. He looked at her oddly. George paused. She was going too fast. "You're such a dear friend," she said at last, intentionally softening her voice. She looked at him again. The dear, sweet, fragile person she cared about so much… What was she doing? "Would you like me to get you anything else?" she asked a moment later.

He thought. "I don't think so."

"I made cookies again today," she said in a tempting tone of voice. "Gingerbread, and they're still hot…"

He paused, then smiled, a tiny dimple showing in his fair, thin cheek. "Maybe a cookie. I thought something smelled good."

She smiled and got up. "I'll go get them. And I'll get you some more milk." George went to the kitchen, returning with a plate of four gingerbread cookies, two glasses of milk, and her composure. She put it all on the coffee table, then pulled up her own chair.

"Thank you, George." Fryderyk smiled and took a cookie. She took one, too, glowing with gratification to hear him say her name. They sat in silence, eating and sipping their milk. Fryderyk smiled as he finished his cookie. "These are wonderful."

"Glad you like them," she said. She winked. "I thought you would."

A little while later, Fryderyk stood up. "Well, I just wanted to see you again," he said. "And to thank you for the lovely carriage ride."

George stood up and offered her hand. He shook it with his cold one. Spending this time inside hadn't warmed him up, and it wasn't even that cold outside.

"Thank you for coming over," she said sincerely. "You're welcome any time."

"We'll have to arrange another meeting," he said, putting his hat and cloak on. "Soon."

She smiled and opened the door for him. "Soon. Yes. I really enjoyed seeing you, Fryderyk."

He turned, gave her another little smile and a wave, and went on his way.

George shut the door with a smile. He had actually come to see her… Feeling delightfully sappy, she hugged herself and sat down again. So what if they were only ever friends? She just wanted to see him and for him to want to see her… and she longed to hear as much of his music as he would play for her. As long as he liked her, enjoyed being with her, that was enough for her.

George enjoyed the next week in a whirl of writing. She recorded every detail of their times together in her diary; every detail of her feelings. She wanted to preserve it all.

She wrote about him in her diary, yes. But if he was reflected into the novels she continued birthing night and day, it was subtle. None of her male leads revealed themselves to be genius pianists, developed chronic respiratory concerns, or unveiled a penchant for gingerbread cookies. None of them turned out to be Polish.

74

None of them mourned a sister gone too soon or a sweetheart estranged by circumstances. And none of them had a beloved pet cat. And yet… part of her wondered what her own heart and mind would do. As art had imitated life within her books so many times and in so many ways, would a facet of Fryderyk one day walk across her pages?

"My carriage ride the other day with Fryderyk was amazing," George gushed to Claudette over cups of coffee at a café in Paris.

Claudette gave a playful snort. "Good for you, you crazy romantic, you. He didn't faint or fall into a heap?"

George shook her head. "No, of course not. He did… feel a little, ah, sad… about his sweetheart back home in Poland, but I was a good friend, and—"

Claudette facepalmed. "George, you do realize he's firmly categorized you as a platonic buddy, don't you? If he can tell you how much he misses his girlfriend back home, he's definitely not looking at you as a potential successor for her."

"Yes, I do realize, and I don't care," George announced. "That doesn't change how I feel about him."

Claudette sipped her coffee. "I hope you still feel that way in six months."

George went out to get the mail. She gathered the day's letters into her hands, shuffling through them to see who had written to her. And her heart skipped a beat as she recognized a familiar seal; a familiar scrawl. *Félicien Mallefille*, announced the return address. Why was he writing to her?

George hurried inside, tossing the other letters onto the kitchen table and tearing open Mallefille's letter with shaking fingers.

And, the empty swooping sensation inside her stomach seeming to fill with the heaviness of lead, she read what he had to say.

I have not forgotten you, my dear, my life, my sweet, my George. Not in Dresden nor in Milan nor in Budapest could I forget you. You may have tired of me, but I have not tired of you. And I shall roam the Continent until I find the balm of Gilead to heal my broken heart... or you return to me.

George heaved a bitter sigh, crumpling the letter into a ball and pitching it across the kitchen. Couldn't that impetuous rogue see that she had moved on? Couldn't he let her go? And couldn't he find something else to chase?

She shook her head. At least from a distance, he and the uncomfortable aggression she had once mistaken for passion were not a threat. And, she supposed, every letter he wrote had the potential to bear the designation of being the very last one he ever wrote to her. Eventually, she hoped, she might give up. She certainly wasn't going to write back. If she did, she would only fuel the fire of his pining. Her silence would say it all.

Every morning, George prepared herself for the day, more often than not donning the highly-atypical uniform of a shirt and trousers. She knew she wasn't normal— wasn't ordinary, wasn't typical. And yet— She shrugged, the crisp fabric of her shirt and jacket crinkling as she moved her shoulders. This was normal for her. This was how she dressed most days. This was what made her comfortable. What did she care for society's "normal?"

She looked at the women around her, the women who, in the rough years since the fall of Napoleon during her childhood, since the July Revolution of only six years ago, had gotten through so much change. France had fought against the world— Napoleon and his men against the combined power of most of the other nations of Europe. And under Napoleon, little Aurore Dupin's papa Maurice had fought courageously along with many other fathers, brothers, uncles, nephews, and sons. All while many mothers, sisters, aunts, nieces, and daughters were left at home… left in a nation that still needed to be fed, clothed, and stocked with manufactured goods. A nation in which, soon enough, the women rose up, taking their places in factories, shops, and domestic work in the homes of others.

Women who had grown during those years, sharing the collective experience of working while the men had been off to war; women whose voices had been growing louder since the Revolution of the 1780s and '90s, despite the limitations levied on them by the contents of the Napoleonic Code. Women who had found themselves in the adventure of work. And who did not want to be shoved back down into the smallness of the kitchen, the garden, the nursery, the convent, and the sickroom. Women who had not all been married off at sixteen with the expectation that they would have borne their husbands a good eight children by the time they were thirty.

Women like Mary Wollstonecraft, whose *Vindication of the Rights of Women* had shaken George to her core, freeing her from the blinding normalcy of the expectations of conventional society for what a woman would do with her life. In her breathtaking work, Wollstonecraft created a profound, sophisticated rebuttal of the many theorists of her age who had believed that a full classroom education was not right for the female of the species. Only when women in every rank of society were educated equally to their male counterparts, declared Wollstonecraft, raising the next generation into knowledgeable, cultured individuals, would the world step into the ideal future that glimmered so invitingly on the horizon. As human beings, not mere property of their husbands or fathers or ornaments to society, women deserved the same fundamental rights as the men they walked alongside. And the moral foundation of society demanded that women be given the place that they were so ready to take.

Aurore had grown up amid the aftershocks of this sea-change. Had seen her grandmother Marie-Aurore de Saxe, Madame Dupin de Francueil's, capable leadership of her own estate, which she had passed down to her granddaughter; had seen her mother Sophie's ambitions of one day opening a hat shop. And although she had inherited their pain, she had also inherited their ambition, their hunger to seek everything that the world had in store for her, and their courage to do what was necessary, dress the part, in order to gain access to what was out there. So every day, George tied her cravat around her neck and wrapped her waistcoat around her torso. And in that way, she protected herself from the slings and arrows of the world.

7   Doubt

Marie d'Agoult threw a party. George attended the celebration that evening, randomly deciding to go in a dress. She mulled about the room, walking through the crowd of guests with a glass of champagne in her hand, greeting this one, then that one.

"Did you hear about how Prime Minister Molé got the Assembly to pass the budget for next year before the parliamentary recess?"

"I don't know how he managed that—"

Silently, George approached the two men who were speaking, following the sound of discussions of political intrigue.

"What's that about the budget?" she asked.

The two looked around, eyes falling on the petite woman who stood there across from them in a flattering gown, taking a distinct interest in matters of state.

"Nothing you need to worry your pretty head about," one said patronizingly, offering what he must have thought was a magnanimous smile. "They'll sort things out."

"I'm sure they will," George said calmly. "Especially as the Chamber of Peers backed Molé up last month and rejected the proposals on government bonds." She took a sip of champagne, waiting for their response.

"Indeed." Both men lifted their own drinks to their lips at the same moment, their eyes meeting. A moment later, they had melted into the crowd.

George just watched them go.

They spent time together, the two friends. And yet... not all the time that was available to them. And George felt herself biting her lip as Fryderyk occasionally bowed out of spending a particular afternoon with her, as he was already doing something with another friend or colleague. Found herself shaking her head in disappointment when he had to cancel or reschedule a visit he had agreed to. Found herself sighing when she was the one who found herself double-booked, caught between an afternoon visiting at Claudette's or walking in the park with Fryderyk; tossing and turning as she waited for his answer as to which day next week would be best for them to spend together.

Why do I feel like this? she asked herself as she carried on through the days and nights, wearing herself out as she floundered in uncertainty, her emotions swinging from tearful frustration when two activities in a row had to be canceled to euphoric elation after a blissful, perfect afternoon spent walking in the park together or immersed in his music. *Like an idiotic teenager, losing sleep over him and jealous when he spends time with other friends of his without me even though we're not even a couple—jealous in spite of myself as an adult, feeling like I'm twenty years younger than I am… I must be in love.*

George shook her head as the thoughts filled her mind. And silently… she smiled to herself.

And yet… she sighed. She pondered. And she wondered. Because he… was so different. So different from any of the others; from anyone she had ever known. He'd been thrown into a panic by the dog running into the room and jumping onto his lap that one memorable time, even aside from the coughing fit that the dog and his fur had caused. The exquisite sensitivity that made Fryderyk such an artistic genius… was like nothing she'd ever seen. And he was like no one she'd ever met.

80

But what made him different? There were so many kinds of people; so many kinds of minds— so many different kinds of strengths and weaknesses. *I wish there was a word for how you think; how you process and understand the world*, she thought. *You're not simple— you're a genius— but you are very unique... and you have unique vulnerabilities, too.*

She shook her head. And she deepened her resolve to be the friend he needed her to be.

Love... George sighed. There were so many different kinds of love. The breathtaking infatuation with which Fryderyk's music had initially swept her off her feet, the caring friendship into which they had settled, the breathtaking passion she had shared with Jules, failed to find with Casimir, and struggled to extricate herself from with Musset... the motherly tenderness with which she had then looked after her many beaus day in and day out, long after ardent embraces had faded into pats on the hand, consoling hugs, and the gentle stroking of hair as this or that beloved struggled to sleep through the long, weary nights.

There were many different kinds of love. And George herself had given and received many different types of love. But what kind of love did she have for Fryderyk? George sighed again. And she smiled. Because the depth and breadth of her love for Fryderyk remained to be seen. But she knew... she knew that she loved him. And she hoped... that he loved her.

Every night, she still wrote. Distracted as she was by Fryderyk and what the future might hold for them, she still turned her mind to her craft, taking time as the sun went down to focus on the works that were life to her. Every evening, George set aside the thoughts of the day, the worries about politics, her past, present, and future, the world in general, and certain members of her social sphere, and entered the mirror-world that lay deep within her own heart and mind; the shadow-realm of distant memories, hopes, dreams, griefs, and deep, aching longings. In that shadow-realm, she sought to put together the pieces of her own long-broken heart; the pieces that life had scattered out upon the floor of her future, leaving her to spend this phase of her adulthood picking them up. Methodically, she gathered them up, patching and pasting them into her stories as into the fabric of a damaged stucco house; as into the intricacies of a mosaic. Slowly, she put the pieces of her own heart, mind, and history back together. But still… she wondered if she would ever be whole.

The days went on. And uncertainty slowly rose within George's heart, filling her mind like the high tide submerging the shore. Uncertainty as to the future, as to her developing relationship with Fryderyk, as to what was right. Uncertainty… that found her, almost without noticing it, reaching for dresses each morning, rather than shirts and trousers.

Don't wear those, her mother seemed to sneer when George glanced at the comfortable shirts, waistcoats, and trousers she had until very recently worn every day. Sophie curled her red lip, tossing her long, dark hair as she glared derisively at her daughter. *They're not beautiful. They're not lovely. They don't reflect the woman you are. And if you are trying to court this Fryderyk, trying to get his attention, at least, he won't find you beautiful in a shirt and trousers. He won't see the woman you are.*

George sighed. And glumly, she turned her attention to the second voice she now seemed to hear inside her mind. Standing across from Sophie, George's grandmother tapped her foot impatiently, her arms folded.

Wear what makes you feel like yourself, her grandmother said. *Your shirts and trousers make you look strong. And you are strong. Stronger than he is. So be strong. And dress strong. Don't change yourself for him... for anyone.*

But you love him, the angel of domesticity insisted. *And isn't that what love is... becoming our best selves for those we care about? What if your best self... has never been the* you *that wears trousers? What if the real* you... *is happy in the kitchen? Is nothing like what you would have expected? Is everything... you've been running away from for all these years?*

George just shook her head. And with a heart full of uncertainty, she walked away from her voices.

George was strong. But she was uncertain. And the more she imagined what a romantic relationship with Fryderyk might look like, the perfect romance she'd never had, the more she wanted to make it work... no matter how much work that required of her... or how much she would have to change herself. For Fryderyk, she would become her best self. Even... even if she had no idea if he ever even wanted to be a couple with her. Even if that was a conversation... that she bit her lip in trepidation to imagine actually having one day.

Nervous of upsetting the apple cart of the tenuous friendship she and Fryderyk seemed to be forming, George was careful, tying herself every morning into the feminine attire of the perfect woman; the happy housewife. Willing to make herself a little uncomfortable for the sake of their relationship, whatever exactly it was, she sacrificed her comfort, fitting herself into the mold of the classic, traditional woman, provider of love, safety, support, and security, the loving companion and potential future nurse she had been to Jules and Musset. Fryderyk mattered to her. So she would try… to make herself into what he needed her to be.

Help me do this right, she continued to pray. *Give me wisdom. Help me be a good friend to Fryderyk. Help me be what he needs me to be.*

"I feel like I'm going to do everything wrong," she confided in Claudette one afternoon as they played cards at Claudette's apartment. "Feel like I'm some kind of hypocrite, and when he sees everything that's true of me, he won't like me anymore."

Claudette played one of her cards. "I'm happy because I know who I am," she said.

George just sighed, looking down at her hand of cards to consider her next move. Maybe that was the problem.

Good girl, sighed the angel of femininity. *You're doing great. You're doing something right for once. You're on the right track. So, keep going. Be what he needs you to be. Show him you love him by unselfishly doing what he needs; adjusting yourself to meet his needs. It might not be easy, but it'll be worth it. And this time… this time, things will work out. This time, you will find true love. This time… you'll find someone with whom things will work out long-term.*

George shook her head. *True love?* she asked with a silent scoff. *I think you're getting ahead of yourself. We're just friends. And for now… for now, whatever I might hope for someday, I think I'm all right with that.*

But even Fryderyk's good friend could not wait forever to see him again. One morning in early April, George baked some muffins, then went out to her backyard and picked a bouquet of lilies of the valley from her tiny garden plot outside the apartment building. She tied the flowers with a red ribbon, put the muffins in a basket, and wondered if her friend was at home.

She'd find out. George chose a formal dress, put a hat on, grabbed her basket, and started walking.

"I wonder who that is, Valdeck," she heard Fryderyk say a minute after she knocked. The door opened, and he welcomed her with a smile. Today, he was wearing a white shirt and black waistcoat. "Oh, hello, George. Come on in." He almost seemed to blush as he said her name, but she smiled as he said it without replacing it with *Aurore.*

George grinned and marched into the apartment, raising the hem of her heavy skirts just slightly so she could make it over the threshold without tripping and breaking her neck. The apartment wasn't quite as dim as before. Maybe he was feeling better.

"How are you?" she asked quietly, setting her basket and the bouquet on a nearby table. Although the room was brighter, it was still really warm.

He shrugged. "All right." She heard a *meow* and looked down to see Valdeck striding imperiously into the room. He walked over to her, rubbing against her leg.

"So, you do like me," she said, bending down. "Come here, boy." Very gently, she tried to take hold of him. He kept moving. She sighed and stood up. "I guess not. Sweet, shy little cat."

Fryderyk nodded. "Yes. Shy." He twisted his hands together and looked down for a moment, biting his lip. "And sensitive. Spooks easily. Like me. Sudden noises scare me, you know, like someone coming into the room without warning. Makes me jump when someone behind me taps me on the shoulder or when someone I didn't know was in the room suddenly speaks. You know, just little things like that."

George nodded, taking notes on her mental notepad a kilometer a minute. "Those are good to know, Fryderyk," she said. "Thank you. I'll definitely work on those things."

He shook his head, raising a hand. "You don't have to— Don't feel bad. Being full of energy and surprises is the way you're built, and I'm built completely differently."

Slowly reaching out, she gently took his hand in both of hers. It was very cold. But she smiled when he didn't pull back. "We're not trapped by the way we're built, Fryderyk. We can both try new things… for each other." She smiled. "I want to be the friend you need. Will you help me?"

Slowly, Fryderyk smiled. And he laid his other hand on top of hers.

"Just be you," he said. "Just be you."

Just be you… George pondered his words. *Just be you…* Could he mean that? Did he know what he was asking for? And if she did… would he like her anymore?

She got brave. And she decided to find out. One day George's heart pounded as she arrayed herself in her favorite waistcoat and trousers, tying an elegant cravat around her neck and setting off the look with a top hat. She put on her gloves. And she went to meet Fryderyk at a local café.

He smiled when he saw her. He bought their tea. They sat down at a little table on the covered patio in front of the café. And they talked. About their writing, about their pets, about their friends, about the weather. About anything and everything… other than what George was wearing. At one point, the wind almost blew George's top hat off, and Fryderyk reached out across the table to gently tuck a strand of hair behind her ear. But he didn't say anything.

George smiled as she put away her outfit for the night, washing up and changing into her nightgown at the end of the long day. She had done it. Worn what made her truly comfortable; shown him the fullness of who she was. The woman who wore trousers because they set her free.

And he… had said nothing. Nothing at all. George grinned as she remembered that silence. And the acceptance within it.

Fryderyk said nothing. But the voices in George's head and heart had plenty to say.

George's mother sneered at her, folding her white arms and tapping her foot disdainfully. *In saying nothing, he doesn't mean what you think he means. What man could ever love such a manly, unladylike woman? I can't believe you went out in public like that, with everyone on the street walking by and seeing you… I'm ashamed of you. Your grandmother was ashamed of me for things I don't want to keep you from— now I'm ashamed of you for not following in my footsteps. As a confident, feminine woman. A lovely, lovely lady.*

If you're going to man up, do it properly, my lad, her grandmother insisted, flapping her starched white apron. *Help him; don't let him help you. You can't have the freedom of walking like a man and the romance of being wooed as a woman at the same time. You are a woman. But if you take on the exact same freedoms and privileges as the men, you'll take the same responsibilities and burdens, too. You can't walk beside him dressed the same as he is and expect him to carry your bags or open doors for you and buy you tea and flowers and little cakes and take you out to dinner. That's not fair. That's a double standard, and you can't have both. You know you can't.*

George shook her head. *I don't like him for the things he does for me*, she replied. *Besides the fact that we're not courting, anyway— even in all the kind things he does for me, which I'm very grateful for, and do my best to return in kind, he's not 'wooing' me. And as we figure out together what* fair *looks like… as we figure out ways of helping each other… I'll carry his bags and open doors for him, too. Maybe we'll take turns.*

George went to bed. And she continued pondering what Fryderyk had told her about himself and the way he functioned. *I spook easily… sudden noises scare me, like someone coming into the room without warning, someone behind me tapping me on the shoulder, or when someone I didn't know was in the room suddenly speaks.*

She'd seen those traits, those quirks, in action, as well as others, such as his literal-minded take on various figures of speech. Traits, quirks, that she had never seen in any of her other beaus. *What was it that was different about him?* she wondered. *How could it really be described? And what could it be called?*

She sighed. And how… as his friend… could she best help him?

Not trapped by the way we're built… Try new things…
George's own words followed her around as she went through her
days, visiting Fryderyk and receiving his visits; alternating
between trousers, cravats, and top hats and ladylike dresses;
vacillating between being the gentleman who helped Fryderyk
with everything and feeling a mysterious, strangely pleasant ache
deep inside her heart when he did something for her. And she
wondered… was *she* trapped?

And if so, by what?

"Why is all of this easier when I'm around you?" George asked
Claudette as they went shopping for gloves.

Claudette looked up from comparing two types of gloves.
"What do you mean?"

George looked down at the shirt and trousers she'd worn today.
"I mean, wearing what I want, doing what I want, being who I am.
I'm not afraid I'll scandalize you when I show up for lunch in
trousers."

"That's because you know me so well, and you know I care
about you for you, exactly as you are," Claudette said. She made
her decision and took her chosen pair of gloves up to the counter
to pay. "New friends… don't know you yet. And you don't know
them. That familiarity… has to develop. And that takes time. And
patience. And trust."

"Time. Patience. Trust." George bit her lip, absentmindedly
choosing a hair-ribbon to buy. "Just what I'm worst at."

8   Trust

George thought of Fryderyk. Sweet, gentle, a perfect gentleman… and a friend. A friend with whom she could, tentatively, be herself. The man… She sighed. Finally, after so many years of searching, was it possible that she had finally met the man who could free her to be herself? Make her whole?

Then she thought of the others— of Mallefille, of Musset, of Didier, of Jules, of Casimir. Thought of what they had given her. And what she had given them. She had had no father growing up. But with them, one by one, one after the other, she had sought something. But what? *Belonging*, her heart told her. *Acceptance. Love.*

George nodded. That sounded right. She had sought belonging. And yet… and yet… something had always held her back. Anxiety… fear, almost. Because… because life had hurt her. Hurt her so much. And if it could rip away her papa and her baby brother in an instant, turn her *maman* away from her, lock Aurore away in a convent for two years, how could she trust that anything was ever going to go well under any circumstances? And how could she trust anyone?

She was broken. Broken by life. Wrapped in the armor of masculine clothing, fighting to free herself from the tyranny of a world gone mad, she was full of pain. And fear. Fear that it would happen again. Because again and again they had left her; again and again the relationships had ended.

Again and again, she had failed to become the good woman who kept her man; failed to help the men around her, the fragile boys, half-broken by life themselves, who clustered to her as

90

moths to a flame, clinging to her as to their own mothers. None of them could be trusted, not really. And again and again, she had seen, life had shown her, that she was not lovable. Because of course, it was going to happen again. Of course, she was going to be forgotten, abandoned, left behind, unwanted. Of course, she was going to be rejected, neglected, hurt, just like always, all the way back to the beginning.

She was looking for belonging. She knew that. But she wondered... wondered if she would ever find it.

He only wants to be friends, George's mother seemed to taunt, raising a disdainful eyebrow. Scornfully, Sophie folded her slender, graceful arms, tapping a haughty foot as she regarded her daughter with contempt. *And you know that. Because you're too much for him. Who you truly are, the powerhouse in trousers, is too much for him. Or... or maybe, are you not enough? Not true woman enough? Not what he really needs? He likes you, but not in the way you're looking for. And you're going to have to accept that... or find someone else.*

George swallowed. And she nodded. *Maybe you're not entirely wrong*, she conceded. *But our story is not over. And together... we'll find out where this will go.*

Be gentle with him, her mind told her. *Men are fragile*, her memories insisted. *Your papa was your grandmother's son, and had to be treated as such. Men are fragile. They break. And they disappear.*

When is Papa coming back from death? a lonely little voice asked from deep within her heart. And George seemed to see the four-year-old she had been when they had gotten the terrible news that Papa had been killed, whatever that meant, after falling from his horse. The four-year-old who had patiently waited for him to come home… and was somehow still waiting, all wild, dark hair and big, brown eyes. Fathers were fragile. Breakable. Mortal. And so was every other man.

"I'm scared," George said.

Claudette looked up from the volume of Voltaire from which she'd been reading one quiet afternoon at George's apartment.

"Of what?"

"Of the future," she said, biting her lip and looking down at the hands she held twisted in her lap. "And what might happen."

Claudette glanced down at the book. "Do you mean politically, or—"

"Relationally," George blurted out. "With Fryderyk."

Claudette closed the book with a knowing smile. "I should have known that was what you meant." She reached out, gently touching George's hand. "My friend, what will happen will happen. All you're responsible for is your half of it. All you have control over is your half of it. Which is a lot," she said, "but that's what makes it exciting, too. The mystery… the unknown… the strange give-and-take that forms any relationship. The outcomes… that you're simply not going to know until they happen."

"I just keep waiting for something to happen," George said with a sigh. "For Fryderyk to suddenly up and leave; for this bond, whatever exactly it is, to bust up and turn into betrayal… just like it always does. I'm waiting for something to change, and I feel so on guard, watching for the signs, waiting for the words, listening for the change. Any day now, I just know he'll thank me for what we've had and say he doesn't want to see me again. Any moment now, he'll say he's going back to Marja Wodzińska back home in Poland. Any time now, he'll tell me that I'm too much... that I'm not enough. Any day now, he'll disappear from my life, just like all the others."

Claudette squeezed George's hand. And she looked up into her face. "George," she said quietly, "any man who would say you're too much or not enough... is not good enough for you."

George wiped away the confused tears that were gathering in her eyes. And slowly, she smiled.

She stuck things out. That was her gift... but was it also her curse? George shook her head as she thought of it. So many times in the past, she had stuck things out, staying with this one or that one just a little longer, determined that she could heal him with her love, willingly trusting that he really could become more than he was at present. Each time, she had been faithful, loyal. Each time, she had hoped, trusted. And each time... she had had her heart broken. Each time... she had been wrong.

"You are brilliant," Fryderyk mused one day. George bit back embarrassment as she saw a copy of *The Master Mosaic Workers*, her latest novel, on his kitchen table. She didn't say anything. But her mind whispered, *Just wait. Just wait 'til you see what I really am. You won't like it— you won't like me anymore— and you'll leave me just like all the others did. No matter how loyal I am.*

But those words had no place in this conversation. So she remained silent.

And yet... she was honored. George's heart warmed as she pictured Fryderyk going to the bookstore, selecting one of her works from the shelf, purchasing it, and taking it home and reading it. Smiled as she imagined her words filling his imagination; wondered how he pictured the characters who had become some of her best friends. Wondered what the stories she had written meant to him; how the messages she had conveyed had touched him. Whether, quite simply, he liked her books. Because if he did... that boded well as to what he thought of her as a person. But if he didn't... that might reveal his opinion of her as well.

Every morning, George prepared herself for the coming day by putting on her armor of a shirt, a waistcoat, a pair of trousers, a cravat. But armor... George straightened her top hat. Armor, like the protective gear she was putting on, didn't just protect one from the dangers and struggles of life. Armor empowered one to go out into combat. And she went into battle every day of her life, confidently elbowing her way into the boys' club of the world of careers, slaying dragons, fighting against the suffocating smallness of what the world around her thought women could do.

Every day she actively rebelled against the ideas, old as human society itself, that women could not, should not, live and love on their own terms, making their own decisions and earning their own money, wisely choosing the combination of career, marriage, and motherhood that worked for them as individuals. And she spent her days fighting against a world that told her that a woman without a husband, without children, was a failure. And that it was wrong to be happy outside the confines of the kitchen and the nursery.

She sighed as she adjusted her cravat. And she remembered. Remembered the little four-year-old she had once been, pretending a soup bowl was a helmet, tromping around in her papa's big army boots, playing "war" and killing off the enemies of France from the fortresses she had constructed from furniture (or, sometimes, that her mother had constructed for her as a playpen). Being her father's heir, his protégé, his little lad. And then, some years later, being her grandmother's laddie. And now... now, buttoning up the body of a woman inside the uniform of masculine attire. She gave half a chuckle. Just as long as she wasn't wearing a soup bowl on her head.

She could almost hear the voice of that four-year-old; the four-year-old she had once been. *Be what Papa wants you to be, and he'll come home from the war for good*, she seemed to say. George shook her head. Only... she hadn't been. And he... he had not been able to.

She was a woman. But not the one she wanted to be. But if she gave up her masculine attire and habits, became a feminine woman as the world defined that job description, she would be giving up the independence that was life to her, the decision-making power her grandmother had taught her to wield with wisdom, the authority to make her own choices, the right to earn her own money and spend it how she chose. And those things were too precious to her. Even as she agonized, day in and day out, over how authentic she was truly being.

Time went quickly, when George and Fryderyk were together. Sipping tea at a café, strolling in the park, meeting at a museum or a restaurant, visiting at his apartment or hers, sharing in her art or in his, sitting side-by-side on his couch as he lauded his favorite scenes of *Indiana*, *Valentine*, or *Mauprat*; sharing in the singular intensity that they found together as he played his piano for her. The hours seemed to fly by in a rush of delight that George wished to grasp in her hands, pulling them close, forcing them to pass more slowly so she could savor every beautiful moment. It was so intellectually stimulating to talk to someone who truly understood the creative process; who deeply knew all the joys and sorrows of being an artist. Someone to whom she could relate like no other. Someone... like Fryderyk. And she treasured every moment they spent together.

"So... tell me," George said over a cup of tea one lazy afternoon that had suddenly become wonderful when Fryderyk had decided to come over. "What's it like to be the greatest composer who ever lived?"

Fryderyk blushed into his glass of milk. "Oh, stop it. Mozart, he was the greatest composer who ever lived." He shook his head. "It's not so different from being the greatest novelist who ever lived," he said with a wink. George felt her face grow hot as she cracked a smile.

Fryderyk sighed. "It's... it's a calling. And it... it just... pours out of me. All my thoughts; all my feelings. And I try to write it all down; make it perfect. And somehow... other people enjoy listening to it. And that earns me money. And gets me fans..." He shook his head. "Fans who want more and more and more. Fans who want concerts."

He shuddered. "I hate giving concerts. I'm just not built for them. Every single concert I've ever given has scared me almost to death. Takes a week for me to recover— put me on stage in front of an auditorium full of strangers staring at me and expect me to play well, and to enjoy it— that's the worst way to spend an evening I can imagine. Their stares, their breathing, their faces…"

He shuddered. "Best way to make me absolutely petrified and so confused and distracted and just plain disoriented that I can't even find the notes. And other artists *enjoy* giving them? Frankly, I can't imagine how that's possible. That's one reason I envy Franz Liszt, truly— how easy he finds it to give concerts; how much he enjoys doing them." Fryderyk shook his head. "Concerts are a nightmare for me, so to speak," he said again. He paused, and George watched a smile slowly spread across his face like the dawn touching the hillsides. "But to create… to create, rather than to perform… just myself, and my piano, and a pen and paper… that's all I need."

George smiled as the same joy filled her. "Just myself and a pen and paper… that's all I need, too. And… life. Little bits of my life that make their way onto the page; memories, ideas, things I've learned. Sometimes it's hard to tell where my life ends and my story begins. It's all so… real."

Fryderyk nodded. "Real. Yes. It is. More real than anything else in the world. And when you're in the midst of it… it's all that matters. Like nothing else exists."

She took his hand. "Exactly." She smiled again. "I'm glad you understand. Not everyone does."

Fryderyk smiled. "I was going to say the same thing."

He understood. Fryderyk… as a fellow artist, he understood. Understood the joys and sorrows of the life of the artist; understood the calling to create; the strange magic of releasing one's very soul in one's art form. He understood her. And she understood him.

George smiled. Finally, after so many years of searching, had she finally found a friend, a companion, who truly "got" her?

George sat on Fryderyk's couch. And taking a deep breath, she began to read. George read her newest manuscript to her friend, holding out her very heart to him in shaking hands, offering the words, the worlds, born from her very soul. And even as her soul seemed to bite its lip, afraid that he might drop the precious gift she had placed in his hands, she chose to trust him.

She read. Over the course of an entire afternoon, she read him her work-in-progress, introducing him to her beloved characters, taking him along on the adventures the friends she'd met on the page were navigating together. She read. And he listened. Losing herself once more in the story she seemed to have nearly forgotten the moment she'd given birth to it, she scarcely glanced up from the page, but each time she did, Fryderyk was gazing raptly at her, as lost as she was in the dream in which they were sharing.

Breathlessly, she came to the end of the story. And slowly, wearily, she set her manuscript aside, shuffling the pages into a neat stack. Silently, she looked at Fryderyk. And they both smiled.

"Thank you," he whispered. "That was... amazing."

George reached out and took his hand. "No," she whispered to the fellow artist with whom she'd just shared her heart. "Thank *you*."

He smiled when he saw her. His eyes lit up. And every day they spent together seemed to bring him as much joy as they brought her. George watched Fryderyk carefully, gauging his enthusiasm; his responses to her presence and the things they did together. And fleetingly, part of her heart whispered a question… was he in love with her, too? And whether or not he was… would she ever find out? Could she ever get up the courage to ask him?

"I'm glad you're here," Fryderyk said softly one day as they sat together in a café, drinking tea. "With me. Glad that you're… my friend."

George smiled at him over the rim of her teacup. "I'm glad you're my friend, too."

Fryderyk gazed wistfully into his teacup, giving a thoughtful sigh. "It's hard, sometimes," he said softly. "For me. Just… in general. And I…" He bit his lip. "So far away from family, and not having a roommate anymore, I don't always feel… secure. And I look around and just feel… so uncertain. Like I'm not entirely sure I'm all right… on my own, like this. I've always felt safer when I have someone here with me. With my parents, with Tytus or Julian as roommates, I just felt better about things than I ever did alone. And I was so grateful to them, to Tytus and Julian and Wojciech and my other friends, for bearing with me with everything I need from them."

He looked at her. "You, my friend… you make me feel safe. I go about my week knowing I'm going to see you, and knowing you'll say something wise and encourage me, and I… I just feel better about… everything, now that you're here. And I'm grateful. Because you…" He sighed. "You make my uncertainties certain. And I'm certain I'm secure, I'm safe, I have someone near who cares about me. And that… that is so precious. Something I never would have asked for from you but that I can never thank you enough for giving me."

George smiled. Gently, she reached out and took his cold hand.

"I'm glad I'm here," was all she could say.

He needs me, George said before the voices of her mother or grandmother could say anything. *He really does. As a friend; as a companion. As someone who can help him feel secure. Maybe it's a little outside the exact norm, the sort of companionship he needs, but I can... I can do him good. And he can do me good. And this... whatever it is... can just be what it is. What it is is all right. And we are all right.*

9   Questions

"**W**e saw a play together the other night,"
George sighed happily to Claudette over
cups of chamomile tea one evening they
had spent visiting at George's apartment.
"Fryderyk and I."

Claudette nodded. "Really? Did you have him safely home and
tucked into bed by nine o'clock?"

George rolled her eyes. "Ten o'clock," she ceded.

"So he's becoming more flexible, then."

George sighed. "Little by little."

Claudette sipped her tea. "Well, baby steps are still steps in the
right direction, I suppose."

George just smiled. Long enough, dreamily enough, for the
smile on Claudette's face to turn into an affectionate chuckle.

"You know you're staring into space, don't you?"

George sat up straight with a slight startle. Shaking her head as
she chuckled, she blinked, then closed the mouth that had
somehow drooped open.

"My parents always did used to say, when someone else saw
how lost I was in my daydreams, that even if I sat mulling things
over in total silence much more than most children did, it didn't
mean I wasn't thinking…. that it was just in my nature."

"Three guesses as to whom you're thinking of now," Claudette
said, taking another sip of tea. George just chuckled again.

Claudette looked up. "But it wasn't a date, your carriage ride
with Fryderyk? You're not courting?"

George felt her face grow warm in a blush. "No, no, we're not
courting," she said, shaking her head. She sighed. "We're not."

Claudette looked closely at her. "And you're still all right with that?"

George felt a slow smile spreading over her face. "I like him too much to let that get in the way," she said.

Claudette took her hand. "I'm so glad to hear that."

They celebrated their art together, George and Fryderyk. And somehow, they created space for one another. Space that both freed and cocooned them, where they were truly free to be who they were. Space created by the understanding that could only be shared by an artist and an artist.

Every time she visited him, Fryderyk played yet another one of his pieces for George, and she read to him from her novels, published and still in-progress, rediscovering along with him the words that she had emptied out, sentences, pages, and plots that had seemed to disappear from her mind the moment they had jumped from her fingertips to the waiting page. Words... that were too deep, somehow, for the part of her mind concerned with memory to capture, to hang onto. Words... that to find healing, she had to let go of. And she had. But now, with Fryderyk, she gathered them up again. She examined them. And slowly, she continued to heal.

And yet... they weren't courting. At his apartment and at hers, meeting for tea or for a stroll in the park, going to the theater or out for dinner, their social lives intertwined, their time together serving as bright spots throughout their weeks. And George... she spent time with her beloved friend... the friend whose eyes lit up with love every time he saw her. The love... of sweet friendship.

Wistfully, she pondered what they had; what they were sharing. And gently, she acknowledged a weary echo of disappointment… disappointment colored with a gentle tinge of peace that she did not recognize. *Maybe… maybe I don't have to be "swept away," like all the other times, like in all my other relationships*, she considered. *Maybe real romance… real love, romantic or not… is slower… more gentle. And maybe… I can be all right with that.*

But Fryderyk wasn't George's only friend. After reading her manuscript to him, she read it to Claudette, receiving a different, if somewhat overlapping, set of admiring comments, astute observations, and probing questions. George noted Claudette's comments with a smile. And she was so grateful for both of her friends.

Over the spring and summer of 1837, George and Fryderyk continued to see one another every week or two, Fryderyk seeming to breathe easier, grow stronger, with every day that passed. The color returned to his cheeks and the light to his eyes as he began to walk with what was almost a spring in his step, the wan, skeletal thinness of his face and hands fading as he regained the weight the winter had stolen from him. Each day, he coughed less. Each day, he had more energy. And with each day, each week, that passed, he and George did more things together.

"I just don't know…" Fryderyk said, biting his lip as he dithered between one style of white gloves and another on a shopping trip he and George had taken together. "They're both so nice… George, what do you think?"

George smiled. "I think… they are both very nice. And I think… that you are the only person in the world who really knows which ones you like better. The only person in the world who can make that choice for yourself."

Fryderyk looked at her. Slowly, he smiled. And with a nod, he made his decision.

"I'm feeling better... about things," George announced to Claudette as they walked Marquis in the park together.

Claudette adjusted her hat, endeavoring to keep it from blowing off in the breeze. "I'm glad. What changed?"

"My perspective," she said simply. She sighed, reaching out to squeeze Claudette's hand. "I'm so grateful for my friends... all of them."

Claudette gave her a knowing smile. "So am I."

I've gotten to know Fryderyk, George recorded in her diary. *Observed him like a detective; learned his quirks and needs. Why he never walks into a room left foot first, I may not have figured out, but it feels like our lives themselves are working together as we work to balance each other out and support one other's vulnerabilities. In offering each other our own unique strengths, we're almost harmonizing, making larger, more beautiful chords than we ever could have alone. We're both a work in progress. And so is our friendship.*

Romance... love... George pondered them. And she pondered Marja Wodzińska, the specter who still floated wispily above them, a diaphanous ghost of memory who entwined herself between George and Fryderyk; the precious memory who still brought tears to Fryderyk's eyes. And for the thousandth time, she wondered... where was Marja inside Fryderyk's heart? And by drawing closer to him... was George breathing the fragrance of flowers intended for some other altar? Was she preparing herself to stomp all over the domestic bliss of a long-intended betrothal; a beautiful marriage that might someday take Fryderyk home to Poland? And by even hoping for more, hoping for the wrong thing, was she being a terrible friend?

Friend. George shook her head. And as best she could, she rededicated herself to being the friend that Fryderyk needed... even as he reached out to her as the friend she needed.

George was incredibly grateful for Fryderyk's friendship. But with him... even with him... could she be herself... be everything that she was, just as she was? Whatever this was that they were sharing... it wasn't perfect. It had its ups and downs. And its downs included regularly being interrupted by a dithering indecision that seemed to be as much a mysterious part of him as the agonizing loyalty with which she had struggled for so long and in so many ways was of her. And even when he didn't cancel or reschedule, as he so often did, he still deferred to her as to when and where they should meet, leaving all the decisions to her in a way that felt less chivalrous than childlike and impassive; less generous than timid and slightly helpless.

Musset made me make all the decisions too, she reflected in her diary. *But that was different. Musset... he was lazy. Not interested in going to the trouble of doing his best. And he... he was burdened with pain no one else could help him with; pain he tried to ease with his many addictions. And he put everything on me.*

Jules also looked to me. But he was little more than a child; he was nineteen when we found one another. Making his own decisions was still something he was coming into. And he was happy to let me make them. But that was a season of life, both for me and for him— since then, he's grown into his adulthood, and the things for which he looked to me then, he no longer needs.

But Fryderyk... he seems a bit different. When he looks to me, he seems nervous. Anxious. Unsure. Almost afraid. Like he wants me to lead him; as though he's more comfortable being told what to do than to decide for himself. Like that makes him feel safer. Maybe there is something of a child in him. And yet... the bottom line is that he needs me. They all needed me. And loyally, I will always be there to be needed.

There was joy. But even despite all the joy, it was still difficult... difficult to find that elusive balance; difficult to trustingly hold her heart open after it had been burned so many times. Because despite their friendship, a creeping fear whispered to her that she could not be herself with him. And that Fryderyk, deep down, was not as reliable as George might have hoped.

There you go, George's grandmother seemed to say when Fryderyk canceled or rescheduled a visit, shaking her old, gray head of carefully-powdered hair piled high in the style of another era, *you see, he breaks his promises, he can't be trusted, just like all the others, just like your mother.*

So she held back. Protecting her heart from further disappointment, she held back. Held back from trust. Withheld the loyalty and faithfulness that had always gotten her burned; had convinced her to stay in the shipwrecks she'd hoped to turn into stories of true love, stay just a little longer, because things would surely turn around. Even... if they never had.

When Fryderyk canceled or rescheduled an outing, she bit down her frustration, fighting not to be disappointed... and striving to continue caring. *Not again,* she sighed wearily, and yet not with any real bitterness or resentment. Simply with fatigue. Because… because how could she truly get her hopes up, after the thousand disappointments in love and romance that she had already endured? Her heart… it was too tired to hope for everything it had once dreamed of. And it was too weary to be disappointed. So she was kind. She was patient. And she… tried very hard to be a nice friend. Even if that was all Fryderyk would ever want. Even… if she would never get up the courage to ask him if he wanted more. And she struggled not to give up; not to let herself stop caring out of sheer exhaustion that she knew she would have to keep from slipping into disillusionment.

Politely, she let Fryderyk help her here and there, offering chivalry and gentlemanly care of her own to him, but always with that stubborn flex aching inside of her, the gentleman inside her itching to take action and serve him, the disappointed woman unwilling to let Musset, Casimir, Didier, Jules, Mallefille fail her again. Being a woman had brought her little but disappointment. But could she find what she was looking for in the role of the man?

I don't know what to do, she prayed. *Fryderyk is back and forth and up and down… I can hardly keep track of him sometimes. And I'm not… I'm not even sure who he really is. I'm certainly not sure who I am, much as I'm working hard to figure that out. And I'm not sure if Fryderyk will ever want to court me. Not sure if he, possibly, considers what we have right now to be "courting." Not even sure… if he has someone else. And I'm not sure what You want us to do; what You want us to be to one another. Are we… are we really just supposed to be friends?*

"I know I said I was feeling better about things," George said one day at Claudette's apartment as she and her friend unloaded the many bags of shopping they'd brought back from a day on the town. "But now I'm not so sure."

"What's going on?" Claudette asked, brushing a speck of lint from the new top hat George had chosen.

"Time. Patience. Trust. The things I need the most but have the least of."

Claudette shook her head with a sigh, taking her friend's hand and offering a sympathetic half-smile.

"You'll figure one another out," she said. "I know you will."

"You look lovely today," Fryderyk said one day as George visited his apartment. She looked down, almost choking on the tea he'd just served her as they sat across from one another at his kitchen table. Looked down at her cravat, her shirt, her waistcoat, her trousers. The completely masculine outfit in which she had attired herself.

"No, I don't," she mumbled into her teacup, feeling her face burning with embarrassment; her stomach twisting with confusion. "I'm the weirdo in trousers... but I don't know how to be anything else."

Fryderyk gave her a soft smile. "I don't want you to be anything else. I like the weirdo in trousers. She's my best friend."

And there was nothing George could do but laugh. Even as she shook her head in confusion; in a painful uncertainty. But even with the uncertainty and the confusion... could she feel her heart opening?

Fryderyk looked away with a sigh, then gave George another wistful little smile. "I don't know how to say this, but... I've never met a woman like you. Never. You're so different from my mother; my sisters. From what I would expect a woman to be; to do. But I like you," he said quickly, reaching across the table and taking her hand. "So much. You're mysterious… you're fascinating." He shook his head, and George continued listening, wondering where he was going with this. "And you're… liberated. My mother, my sisters, Marja, even, they're from… a different world. A world where they've gone along with… and hopefully found joy in… what's expected of them. Home, marriage, children. That was what I saw growing up. And it seems to work for them. They're happy, I think, and they're not unfree, but they're… conventional.

"But you," he went on, "you didn't choose those things. You aren't conventional. You're an artist, a career person, just like me. You… had the strength to say *no* to what you knew wouldn't work for you and claim what you wanted in life, whatever society said."

"No, I didn't choose those things," George said. "I could have; I nearly married Casimir Dudevant and became Baroness Dudevant, but he was dull and boring and all he wanted to do was play cards and drink with his buddies and hunt and have me admire the dead things he dragged home. He wanted to bring home game and have me cook it and have a gaggle of children and raise them together because that's the standard thing to do and be a cookie-cutter, picture-perfect example of ordinariness, even if we didn't relate to one another personally. To be a team, and maybe a functional team… but not much beyond that. His dreams of what marriage… what love… could be were so small compared to what I dream of."

She shook her head, envisioning Casimir putting his feet up by a cozy fireplace, surrounded by a picture-perfect family on a cold winter's night. That was what would have made Casimir happy… but being the wife in that perfect picture would not have made her happy.

"He wasn't a bad person, but… marriage to him wouldn't have been the right choice for me. And despite what everyone told me about what a wonderful match he was and what a wonderful marriage we would have, I would have regretted it."

"My world was a more rigid place," Fryderyk said. "That's what I've always known. As a boy, I was raised to hope for a life of marriage and children, and my sisters were, too. We grew up in a world where women were expected to marry young, have lots of children, and stay in the kitchen, and men were supposed to support their families by following their fathers into the family career field. If I do get married someday, I'll be the breadwinner, and my sister Ludwika, who's already married, is a homemaker. And I don't think she's unhappy in that… but I also see… that you wanted more. More than being a wife, a homemaker, a stay-at-home mother. And part of me hardly knows what to make of that… but it's fascinating. You wanted *more*."

"I did," George agreed. "And I got it."

Fryderyk shook his head, giving a thoughtful little sigh. "I don't know if this is too personal, but… where did you get your name? *George*, I mean? I know your given name is *Aurore*."

George smiled. "When I first started out on my own as an author, I was with Jules Sandeau. And after we published *Rose et Blanc* together— I did most of the work, but the credit went to him— I wrote my first novel of my own, *Indiana*." She gave a wistful sigh as she remembered the feeling of holding her firstborn novel in her arms.

"I had recently broken up with Casimir, and I didn't want to raise any hell by putting my own name on the cover of my book, but I can think of a number of my fellow female authors who write under male names. So I chose the first name of *George*, and the surname *Sand* commemorates my partnership with Jules. And this name… it's opened doors for me. And it's freed me from the distractions of a feminine name that would limit my scope and get so many of my readers hung up on the fact that I'm not just an 'author;' I'm a 'lady writer.' It's the name that set me free to live the life I wanted to live. And I love it for that." She gave a wistful chuckle. "I can honestly say it makes me smile every time I hear it."

10 Uncertainty

Fryderyk nodded. He paused, releasing what was almost a dry chuckle. And he went on. "Sounds like you and Jules worked well together— at least for a time. But I have to ask… have you ever had a beau who was threatened by you and your choices; your successes in these things?"

"All the time," George said simply. "I've known many artists… Félicien Mallefille… Jules Sandeau, as I said… Charles Didier… Alfred de Musset…"

"You know Alfred de Musset?" Fryderyk asked.

George raised her eyebrows. "Saying I 'know' him is putting it mildly. Unless we're speaking in the biblical sense."

Fryderyk gave the ghost of an embarrassed chuckle. "Understood."

"I've lived dangerously," she said, shaking her head slightly. "And I've been spoken of as dangerous. Like a lioness."

She looked at him; at his embarrassment, at the hint of a blush that had colored his fair cheek at the oblique suggestion that his friend was a promiscuous homewrecker, at the silent question of *how many* that waited on his lips.

"What about you?" she asked. "Are you threatened by me? What I've done? How I've lived? Whom I've… 'known?' What do you say… am I good, bad, crazy, too much?"

Fryderyk gave a heavy sigh, looking away. And George waited in the silence for his decision, his verdict, biting her lip and feeling her stomach twist within her as she watched him weighing the choice that was before him. Eyes opened by this revelation, would he run away from her now? Was this the end of what had never had the chance to become anything anyway?

He looked at her again. And silently, calmly, unblinkingly, she looked back. "No," he said finally, giving a little shake of his head as he offered her a small smile. "You're... free. And maybe... a little bit dangerous. Or your life may have been in places. But you... you don't threaten me, my wonderful friend. You're not crazy, and you're certainly not too much. You... protect me. If you're a lioness, I'm like your cub. You may be dangerous, but only to keep me safe."

"A lioness and her cub?" George asked, raising her eyebrows. "Goodness, Fryderyk, I know I'm six years older than you are, but you're not asking me to be your mother, are you?"

Fryderyk blushed again. "No, no, nothing like that," he stammered. "Nothing like that. But just to say... you make me feel safe. And if anyone doubts you or feels threatened by you... well, they haven't lived through the things that have inspired the choices you've made to get yourself to the life you want to live. Choices that are your own... that you've made because they were right for you. You're strong, and powerful, and surprising, and very different from any woman I've ever met, but... I'm glad I know you. And I'm glad... you're *you*. I'm glad you're my friend George."

George smiled and squeezed his hand. "Thank you, Fryderyk," she said. "I'm glad I'm *me*, too." She sighed. "So, yes, to sum up, other beaus of mine have seemed threatened by me being myself. But that... is why I'm not with any of them now."

"I'm glad you told me," Fryderyk said simply. "Honestly. I appreciate your openness; your honesty. That's the basis of any relationship— open communication. No secrets. No judgment. And no surprises."

Slowly, George smiled, her heart seeming to grow lighter as

she realized that he really meant it. "No," she said. "No surprises. I promise."

Fryderyk smiled. "I'm glad your choices have made you happy. I want… you to be happy. Happy in your career; in what makes you feel alive. It doesn't matter to me if you don't cook or you can't sew a button onto a shirt— or if you can, but you don't choose to, because those things don't bring you joy. I hope you can always focus on the things that make you the happiest."

George returned the smile. "Thank you. I want you to be happy, too. I'll let you in on a secret," she said, dramatically lowering her voice. Fryderyk leaned forward with a curious little smile. "I love cooking and embroidery, and one of my favorite things to do each summer is to make huge quantities of plum jam in my kitchen of the estate I inherited from my grandmother."

Fryderyk's eyebrows rose. "You inherited an estate from your grandmother?"

George patted his hand. "Someday I'll tell you my whole life story, just like you've told me yours."

He just nodded.

George smiled. "So, cooking, embroidery, jam-making; they may seem rather feminine, but those things make me very happy." She winked. "I just want to be sure, that if and when I'm enjoying domestic pursuits, it's on my own terms." She looked expectantly at Fryderyk, but he just grinned. "I am happy," she said again. She squeezed his hand. "And you… are one of the parts of my life that makes me happy."

He was all right with her. George shook her head in grateful amazement as her heart grew lighter still with every thought of the conversation she and Fryderyk had just shared. Her past didn't frighten him, didn't offend him, hadn't sent him running away screaming at how ridiculously, terrifyingly improper she was. Maybe she still had a lot to figure out. And maybe what they might one day be to one another remained to be seen. But in this moment... George smiled. Because when Fryderyk looked at her... he smiled. He liked her. Truly. And she liked him.

George took herself out for a beer, nudging her way past all the other waistcoat-clad patrons to the bar and ordering something for herself. And she stood there sipping it, watching the men around her chatting and teasing, fading into the hum of life that surrounded her. She was completely invisible, blending perfectly into the crowd. And here she stood, the only woman in the bar, silently drinking alongside the men around her; the men who did not question the appropriateness of her presence. Dressed like a man, she was invisible. And she was beyond being questioned. Standing here in her waistcoat and trousers, she was free. Free to do exactly as she chose.

She read her stories to Fryderyk. And she read them to Claudette. On quiet afternoons and long, lingering evenings, she shared her works and words with Claudette, smiling as her friend listened raptly, gladly accompanying George through this journey of the mind. As she told George many times, the actress knew a good plot when she heard one. And even if Claudette was a little biased... it was good to hear.

George made her way into the bookstore. There they were— *Indiana, Valentine, Lélia, Jacques, Simon...* the precious book babies who had flown the nest. And she smiled as she saw them.

Shyly, the clerk, a woman a little younger than George, smiled at her.

"Women don't usually write books," she said meekly, nodding at the display of George's books, "and if we do, it's usually under a man's name... but we can sell them."

George nodded. "I suppose that's frequently the case," she conceded. She tipped her top hat, offering a bow. "Madame George Sand, at your service."

The clerk's eyes went wide. "Madame Sand?" she whispered.

George grinned. And she shook the woman's hand. "At your service," she said again.

"So all of the Sand books... are yours," the clerk said, shaking her head in amazement.

"Every single one of them," George concurred. "I had a dream," she said. "A dream that went far beyond what society said a woman could or should do. And I followed it. It was difficult," she admitted, "in places... but so, so worth it." She looked at the clerk, whose eyes were shining. "What about you?" she whispered. "What's your dream? The dream that's too big for our world... the dream that will change the world?"

The woman just looked at her. But behind the sigh that escaped her lips, the glimmer of unshed tears in her eyes, George caught a glimpse of the powerful dream that awaited its moment. Silently, the clerk looked at George. And she smiled.

George smiled back. And she placed Victorine Chastenay's *Memoirs, 1771-1815*, a gripping account of the author and her family's survival of the Reign of Terror, on the counter.

"I'll buy this one."

Every morning, George put on her shirt and trousers. The shirt and trousers that disguised her from the world; that freed her to go where she wanted to go and do what she wanted to do. The shirt and trousers… that concealed her.

She glanced idly into the mirror as she slipped on her trousers, buttoned her shirt, wrapped her waistcoat around her torso, straightened her top hat… as she disappeared into the camouflage she put on so faithfully. The camouflage she needed. Because she was not a lovely woman who wanted to flounce through town with her hair streaming becomingly over one white shoulder, lifting her skirts daintily to keep from tripping on her hem in her tiny little shoes. She was not particularly beautiful. She was short. And she was curvy; when she was old, she would probably be rather stout.

But that was all right. Because living up to societal standards of fashion-plate beauty wasn't important. Physical appearance was never going to be the most important thing, and she had many other more important things going for her— her talent as an author, her sparkling wit, her powerful intellect, her courage, her daring, her devastating intelligence. All of which were far more valuable than being pretty. Women who were only pretty, after all, had clearly lost something of themselves in the soul-sucking toil of styling themselves to please the men around them. George neither thought of nor cared what the men around her thought of her appearance. They were not her audience. Except… that what they thought mattered the most. And that her success in playing to them as an audience was reflected in how well she was able to blend in with them.

George shook her head as she straightened her waistcoat one more time, turning away from the mirror and the singular vision it showed her. Who cared what anyone thought of her appearance.

For her purposes, it suited her much better for no one to ever think of it at all.

George didn't go to Nohant that summer. She missed it, remaining in Paris as the days grew warm and then hot, but she knew... that as her mysterious bond with Fryderyk continued to deepen... she was needed here.

Fryderyk heard from home, now and then, and he shared with her the letters he received from his family in Poland— his father Mikołaj, his mother Justyna, and his sisters Ludwika and Izabela. Glowing with joy at every word he received from home, he shared their words with her; the wisdom of his father, the love of his mother, the local gossip curated by his sisters. George smiled and listened as he translated and paraphrased his mother's Polish letters, reading his father's French ones over his shoulder as he narrated them. And she smiled with the joy, the relief, it always brought him to hear from home.

George... she never got letters from home. Her parents were gone; her grandmother was gone; her baby brother was gone; her elder half-siblings, one on each side, were not an active part of her life. She had friends. And they filled her heart with love. But she wondered... how she wondered... how it would feel to have that— the easy back-and-forth across the Continent; the delicious anticipation each party would experience as they waited for news from home or from abroad... How would that feel?

Home. George bit her lip. *Home*... had meant so many things over her life. Had meant the little garret she had lived in briefly with her mother; had meant her grandmother's estate; had meant the convent in which she had spent two years as a teenager; had meant a handful of apartments all over the Continent, love-nests she had shared with the fellow artists with whom she had lived and loved. And now… now, where she stood as a contented literary spinster, carefully considering a friendship that might or might not ever blossom into anything else, what did it mean?

She shook her head. Home… was her. Right now, she was her own home, making her home wherever she lived. Her memories were her family. And her books were her children.

She didn't receive letters from home. But she did get mail. Did receive correspondence from friends, acquaintances, colleagues, and even the occasional ex.

Mallefille would not stop writing. George sighed when she got his letters, glancing at the postmark to see what city he was in now— Rome, Berlin, Vienna, Munich, Geneva, Prague, Milan, Amsterdam, Copenhagen, Lisbon. All over the Continent he was roving, searching for the elusive balm that would allow him to get over her. He didn't promise revenge or threaten to harm her; only caught her up on where he was and what he was doing… and promised to be back someday.

George read his letters. She sighed. And she threw them in the fire.

Always, George wrote. Day and night, fighting through horrendous migraines and squinting as her eyes went fuzzy, sustained by coffee, chocolate, and the occasional cigar, shaking out her aching, cramped-up hands and arms even as her mind continued to write, churning out sentence after paragraph after page, she wrote, releasing her very soul, the soul no one else would ever understand. The soul that had been too much for every family member who had turned away from her; every man whose fond embraces had one day turned to ice; every friend who had tried so hard to understand her. Maybe only she could understand herself. But maybe… her stories would change the world.

George opened her armoire. And she gazed into it; at the collection of dresses, shirts, waistcoats, trousers, shoes, boots, and hats that she had amassed over the years. And softly, the angel of domesticity that lived inside her heart spoke up.

What are your options? she whispered, her pink lips brushing against George's ear and making her shudder. *What do you really want? And what does Fryderyk need?*

George sighed. She looked down at the shirt, waistcoat, and trousers that she had chosen today. And she thought of the accepting silence with which Fryderyk had not chosen to comment on her choice of outfit as they had taken a stroll at the park earlier today. The silence… that was kind. Polite. And yet… What did Fryderyk want from her? What did he need? Did he need a friend; a friend in trousers? Or did he need something more? Did he need…

She lowered her head with another heavy sigh. And she thought of her mother and how hard Sophie had worked, struggling to keep house, striving to maintain the homes she had shared with George's father Maurice. All for love. Love… that had turned to grief when Maurice's horse had thrown him on the road, killing him instantly in a way that George had never fully understood, taking him from them forever.

Love had turned instantaneously to grief. And it had taken with it, so it seemed, Sophie's hopes for her life; for the domestic bliss she had only ever begun to take in her grasping fingers. The domestic life that George really had little idea of how to run, outside of the panoramic, businesslike, almost industrialized version that was her grandmother's management of her grand estate almost in the manner of a company. Because… had she ever seen it? Or had she only ever seen the lack of it? The longing in her mother's voice and eyes for more; for peace, for warmth, for security, for the knowledge that in standing at the stove in an apron, she was creating a haven in which all could be right in the world for her dear family, even if only for a little while?

Haven. Home. George shook her head. And the plots of so many of her novels spun once more through her head. Complex and sad creatures were her heroines, wounded by life and searching for healing. Until… one by one, the leading ladies of George's works found their way into the hearts and arms of sensitive, caring men; men who held the keys to their broken hearts. And in the arms of those men, these characters found wholeness.

George watched her characters go by; took note of the choices they made. Saw that somehow, this thread was always the same; the *happily ever afters*, happy endings of domestic peace and homey security that seemed to bring George a moment of peace each time she wrote another one, and yet ached in her heart as she saw the dream yet unfulfilled within her own life. Again and again the story played out, in a dozen settings, a dozen iterations. And again and again, it escaped from her yearning grasp like swirling smoke, bringing her nothing but disappointment.

And she wondered why.

Her heroines found their greatest joy, ultimately, in the arms of men who loved them, cooking and cleaning and loving in the cozy, nestlike warmth, the safe, snug, secure cocoon, of the domestic haven they had created.

So why couldn't she?

Reaching into the wardrobe, George pulled out a comfortable, feminine dress she hadn't worn for a long time. And she laid it out to wear tomorrow.

She hoped for the future. And she remembered the past. The past that haunted her, no matter what she did, no matter where she went. The past that taunted her, questioned her, utterly refused to shut up and leave her alone.

What is my daughter thinking, living as a lonely literary spinster? her mother seemed to sneer, tossing her dark, wild hair in derision, her lip curled dismissively. *You can't marry books. You can hold them in your arms, but they don't have arms to hold you. If you keep going like this, you'll have a whole family made of nothing but ink and pages, but you'll still be alone. You will always be alone.*

George shook her head. *I don't know what will happen*, she responded. *But neither do you.*

11 Balance

They met for tea; they met for lunch. But when they met for an activity, George and Fryderyk were not always alone. They visited with Liszt, with Delacroix, with Wojciech Grzymała, a friend of Fryderyk's and fellow Polish expat. George sat back and enjoyed listening to Fryderyk and Wojciech converse in rapid Polish, their eyes lighting up as they welcomed the breathtaking joy of being able to speak together in their own language. And when they resumed their conversation in French, she delighted in the stories they swapped of "back home—" Polish school days, name days, and holidays of years gone by.

Amiably, Wojciech both accounted for and ignored Fryderyk's quirks, making sure his friend did not sit in a draft, closing the curtains on a sunny day so the sun didn't get in Fryderyk's eyes, swapping plates with him at a restaurant when the peas, the potatoes, and the chicken got blended together into a muddle by the chef. Wojciech was patient, kind, protective, persevering, everything that George strived to be. And she smiled to meet another friend who truly "got" Fryderyk.

Is this what it's supposed to feel like? George wondered one September morning as she put on a graceful blue dress, smoothing the fabric that flattered her small, curvy form, arranging the flounces of the heavy skirts that trailed behind her, slipping her feet into the itty-bitty shoes that made her trip along like a tiny little pony. *Being a girl? Being a woman? A… traditional, feminine woman? Not the boy, the young man, Grandmother wanted me to be, not the wild floozy Mother didn't want to keep me from becoming if that was what I wanted, but a model, domestic woman? The woman I should be? A woman who stands by her man, who is angelically feminine, who is happy? Really happy? Is this...* She looked into the mirror, at the curled hair and white shoulders that looked back at her. *Is this... me? The real me? The me I've been looking for all my life? And... am I being authentic?* she asked herself. *Really and truly? Is all of this... really me?*

She looked behind her, at the top hats on her shelf and the suits in her armoire. And she closed her eyes and wondered. *Which is the real me?*

Out on her own, she was living her best life, an independent literary spinster who made all her own decisions. And yet... she delighted in the joy, the satisfaction, of a pie well made or a handkerchief skillfully embroidered. Again and again, she shook her head, worn out by the continuous dichotomy with which she continuously, constantly struggled. Independence... domesticity... they were completely at odds. And no one could really have both. Even if some part of her wanted both. And so she leapt back and forth over the chasm that separated them, jumping from cozy domesticity to forthright independence and back again. Even if it was going to drive her crazy.

She put all her soul into the struggle of seeking true balance. And yet, she was never satisfied that she was succeeding. Never satisfied that she had found it. Never satisfied that she was doing enough... that she was not being too much.

What am I really looking for? she prayed. *Really and truly? And when will I finally find it?*

124

George shook her head. And in a thousand little ways, she tried. Gave and received, forced herself to take turns with Fryderyk as to who was being the gentleman, helped him reorganize the contents of all his bookshelves as he helped cook dinner at her place, made herself accept what he did for her while gearing up to administer her next dose of gentlemanliness toward him. And she went home tired with the struggle of it.

Don't be passive, her grandmother scolded whenever George accepted Fryderyk's periodic invitations to a meal he bought for both of them; whenever she took his hand and gingerly allowed him to help her in or out of a carriage, whenever she hesitantly let him help her on or off with her coat or walked questioningly through a door he was holding open for her.

George set her jaw, the angry fist inside her heart, the constricting ball of yarn that was now so tangled that she could barely breathe growing tighter still. And half the time, she politely rebuffed the kind gesture he was offering, or else responded within seconds with a gesture of her own that was at least as grand. Because passive was the last thing she wanted to be. The trouser-wearing literary spinster who paid all her own bills was not passive. And she never would be. She was not weak.

She shook her head as he took the initiative to do kind things for her. And she wondered… what could she accept from him? Was it wrong for her to fail to do everything for herself every single time; inappropriate for her not to provide him with the gentlemanly gestures he wanted to offer her? Was it, contrariwise, rude of her not to accept his chivalry? Or could she… as his friend… gratefully accept the clear effort he was making as he took action for her with such intention?

George shook her head again, gritting her teeth as the questions pounded inside her skull. Because there were no answers.

Fryderyk set aside the letter from home he had just glowingly shared with George one quiet afternoon they'd spent together at his apartment. She smiled appreciatively. She swallowed. She took a deep breath. And slowly, she asked,

"How is Marja?"

Fryderyk's hand tightened on the edge of the letter, crumpling the edge of the creamy white paper. He swallowed. And he looked up with a sigh.

"I'm not sure," he said simply. "I haven't heard from her… for a long time."

Silently, George nodded. Part of her question was answered.

Seeing him once or twice a week, George noticed Fryderyk begin to change as the summer of 1837 slowly, gently faded into autumn. Often, he seemed to have a headache, and, subtle as it was, she could see him slowly losing the weight and color he'd gained over the spring and summer. His cheekbones stood out more, and his clothing hung differently. His hands looked bonier; felt more fragile when she touched them. And they were always cold. But when she asked him, softly and wistfully, if he was all right, he said that he was.

He coughed more often, harder, his ivory face disappearing behind a handkerchief as he discreetly cleared his lungs. And several times during her visits, she noticed a blue dressing-gown hanging on a doorknob. Had he taken it off when he had heard her knock? George never chose to mention it.

As October went on, passing into November, he became worse than ever, moving more and more slowly, coughing almost constantly, and wearing out after even the slightest exertion. Just now, he was lying back in the easy chair in his living room under a blanket, almost drowsing even though he'd barely stirred outside that day. Holding back her concern, George tried to focus on the Bach biography she was reading out loud.

"Johann took jobs playing the organ in nearby cities from the time he was in his middle teens…"

Fryderyk started coughing. George bit her lip, letting her eyes flicker to his pale face, the lower half of which was covered in his handkerchief, and tried to keep reading. "…finally establishing himself for a number of years at the Blasius Church in Mühlhausen."

He wasn't going to stop. George set down the book and hurried to Fryderyk's chair, resting a comforting hand on his thin shoulder as she struggled not to say anything that would make it worse. He rocked back and forth in the chair, his face growing red behind the handkerchief as he coughed so hard she was afraid he would gag, a vein throbbing in his forehead.

"Let me get you some milk," she said after waiting what she judged to have been too long. Moving quickly in her slim trousers, she ran to the kitchen, splashed some milk into a glass, and delivered it to him in a panting rush.

Gasping, Fryderyk accepted the cup and managed to sip at it. George watched in painful concern as slowly, the storm of coughing passed, leaving him lying limp in the chair, sweaty and exhausted.

"I think… I need to lie down," he whispered, pushing the blanket aside and struggling to sit up. George took the half-empty cup he weakly offered back to her and put a supporting arm around his shoulders as he rose, her strength flexing lovingly as she helped him stand without even thinking about what she was doing. He laid his head on her shoulder, letting her take some of his weight.

"Do you want the couch, or do you want to rest upstairs?" she asked softly.

"The couch is fine," he said, his tired voice barely above a whisper. George led him to the overstuffed green couch, where he sat down heavily. The redness of the coughing had faded, leaving him very pale once more. Slowly, he turned his body so he could lie down on his back, bending his knees so George could sit, too.

His thick brown hair was falling into his eyes, and his fair face was covered in sweat. "Are you all right?" George asked quietly, taking his cold hand. Reaching over, she gently brushed his hair out of his eyes, and, as she returned her hand to her lap, he took that one as well, meeting her eyes with a little smile.

"I'm all right," he replied even more quietly. "Just tired. Coughing like that always wears me out... and winter's coming."

George nodded sadly. "It is. I know it troubles you."

"Yes. It does," he said, nodding as he rubbed his forehead. "And it's already coming. I always get sick in the winter. I get the grippe, or my lungs get worse, all my respiratory problems, and I lose weight that I can't afford... I'm glad I'll have a friend with me this year." He gave her another weary little smile.

She returned it, gently squeezing his cold hands. "Oh, yes. You'll have your friend with you. I'll stick around and cheer you up. I'll always be here when you need me."

He's pathetic, her mother seemed to say as George left

128

Fryderyk's apartment for the night, her friend settled comfortably on his couch for the moment. *He's going to die. And you know that. What do think you're doing, taking up with someone like that? Is it because he needs you? Because goodness gracious, he does.*

George sighed as she seemed to see Sophie roll her dark eyes. *We don't know what's going to happen,* she said. *We don't. But please... just leave me alone and let me take care of my friend.*

George set her teacup down with an angry huff. "I hate the third week of the month," she grumbled.

Claudette looked at her from across the table at the café at which they had met. "I was wondering what was wrong," she said mildly. She looked at George pointedly. "If you were feeling all right." Claudette nodded at the flouncy, ribbon-bedecked dress that George was wearing today. "What with you wearing *that*."

"I'm *not* feeling all right," George spat, folding her arms over the bodice that lay smoothly over her painfully-tight corset. "I'm feeling extremely annoyed right now. This week of the month is always frustrating, because my laundress always picks up my dirty laundry on the fifteenth and brings it back all clean and pressed at the very end of the month, so I never have enough to pick from during this particular week." George gave a heavy sigh. "Ugh, why don't I have as many boy clothes as I have girl clothes?"

Taking her last sip of coffee, Claudette stood up. "Let's fix that," she said briskly. "Right now. George Sand, you and I are going straight to the men's shop across the street and I'm going to buy you a pair of trousers. Come on."

George looked at Claudette. "But I wasn't—"

"I'll buy them for you," Claudette insisted in a businesslike tone, pulling George out of her chair. They paid for their coffee; then Claudette linked arms with her and led her to the front door, pulling her away from the café and across the street. "And a new shirt, too. We are not running the risk of you having to dress like this again if your laundry is late. Let me fix this problem for you."

George shook her head. And with a grateful smile, she allowed herself to be led into the menswear shop to allow her friend to fix her problem.

Her new outfit stowed proudly in a bag under her arm, George said goodbye to Claudette and continued on her way through town for a fresh stack of notebooks and a few new pens, which she was carrying enough cash to purchase. She headed into the stationery shop, the bell tinkling as she entered.

"What can I get for you, *mademoiselle*?" the shopkeeper asked, stepping out from behind the counter and offering a deep bow. "We have a lovely selection of fountain pens just right for writing home to Mother… practice that pretty handwriting."

George gritted her teeth. "Thank you," she said shortly. "I know just what I need today."

Fryderyk always told George when his family wrote. He updated her on their lives— how the political climate in Poland was continuing to undergo subtle changes, although, thank God, they were still safe, general family news, even juicy bits of local gossip. George smiled as she heard the news of his mother, his father, his sisters. But there was never a word about Marja. Not a single word.

Broodingly, she let her imagination summon up image after

130

image of what this young woman might look like— short, tall, blond, brunette, curvy, gangly. What her personality might be like— chipper, reserved, funny, studious. How much she loved Fryderyk— and how much he loved her.

George shook her head and sighed. And silently, she continued to wonder.

He's not yours, her mother and grandmother seemed to agree. *And he never will be.*

George just shrugged, shaking her head with a sigh. *I just don't know*, she replied. *I just don't know.*

The autumn of 1837 wore on. Cold winds and rain stripped the bright, glowing leaves from the trees, beating against the houses until the windows rattled. Shivering even as she encouraged him to wrap up warm, George kept all the fireplaces at Fryderyk's apartment burning when she visited.

Late one night, the rain turned to snow, sparkling on the brown grass, gleaming on the rooftops. Winter was beginning. George sighed to herself as she wondered how Fryderyk would do this winter. Just another reason to be glad she was with him now. She was happy to help take care of him. And she would probably have to.

Wear the other one. The red dress that shows off your curves. Show him how beautiful you are. Loosen up. Live a little. Be like me. Be my daughter. After all, I want what's best for you.

George put on her gloves, straightening her top hat and adjusting her fluffy cravat. And she shook her head.

No, Mother, she said inside her head, even as she fought back a blush at the revealing dress Sophie seemed to be wearing in her imagination. *I don't want to be like you. And I won't.*

"How do you get your head to shut up?" George asked abruptly.

Claudette looked up from the sip of coffee she'd just taken. "Without alcohol?" she asked. She paused. "No, alcohol sometimes makes it worse." She set down her cup. "What do you mean?"

George shook her head with a heavy sigh. "Well, you know I'm a crazy author, right?"

Claudette squeezed her hand. "Just my favorite crazy author in the whole wide world."

George gave half a chuckle, half a grateful smile. "Well, as a crazy author, I have… processes, and… experiences… that other people, people who are of less of a crazy-author bent, might struggle to relate to."

"Are you talking about writing until six in the morning and sleeping til noon?" Claudette asked. "Because lots of people do that. And wonderfully countercultural as you are, you are not the only woman in France to wear trousers or to write under a man's name."

George shook her head. "Well, what I'm referring to is, my mother and grandmother… or my memories of them and my ideas of what they would say to me, what they would want for me and from me… they won't shut up. Won't stop henpecking me with these bossy demands, telling me what to do, what to wear—"

"George Sand, you're over thirty years old— your mother cannot tell you what to wear, even if she weren't dead."

George choked on her coffee, a shocked laugh turning into a

132

painful hiccup. And she used her cravat to wipe up the coffee she'd spilled on her friend's table.

"Sorry," Claudette said.

George gave a real laugh, shaking her head as she wiped her mouth. "It's fine. And you're right… being that she's gone, and so is Grandmother, they can't tell me what to do. And I don't have to listen to them. But I just… I just feel like I need to be… loyal. Although loyalty is what's burned me every time. With Mother and Grandmother and with all the crazy artist boyfriends I've had over the years."

Claudette sighed, any hint of the riotous humor of a moment ago gone. "My friend," she said softly, "you can honor someone's memory without being obedient to them. And you can be a good friend… a loyal friend, even… without doing everything the other person wants."

George looked up from her coffee. "You can?"

Claudette nodded. "You can."

12   Home Cooking

"George," Fryderyk asked one winter morning as they visited at his apartment, "may I break off this scintillating conversation for just one moment and start getting things out for lunch? If that's all right with you, of course?"

George looked at him over her half-empty cup of tea. "*May* you? Of course, you may— why are you asking me?"

Fryderyk swallowed, seeming to shrink slightly as he made his way into the kitchen to start heating up the chicken and potatoes he'd prepared yesterday.

"I don't know… I suppose because…" He shook his head. "Because I don't know how to do anything else? Because I'm so used to asking permission that it feels normal? Feels rude if I don't?"

George frowned. "But why would that be rude? And why would *that* be normal? Did I miss something?"

Fryderyk sighed, stirring the pan of mashed potatoes that he was reheating on the stove, inside of which the wood that was burning transferred a gentle heat to the range on top. "You missed my childhood," he said softly. "Well, you didn't 'miss' it; I just mean… you weren't there. And you didn't see it. Didn't watch me grow up; didn't see what was normal for me. And what continued to be normal even as I became a teenager; a young adult. What I got used to."

She cocked her head. "Which was what?"

He shook his head, beginning to fill two plates with fluffy mashed potatoes, adding a piece of chicken to each plate without letting the chicken and potatoes touch. "A lot of 'May I?'" he said simply, a reflection of simple, childlike trust appearing on his face. "And a lot of 'No, you may not, because you're too sick.' Between my parents and all my doctors, I was always being told, very lovingly, what I should do or not do... mostly not do. That stays with you, George. And even now, one small part of me still thinks it feels funny not to have someone to listen to."

George accepted one of the plates, taking it into the kitchen and silently appreciating the care with which Fryderyk had made sure that her chicken and potatoes were not touching, either.

"Well, you're an adult now," she said slowly. "And you have been for quite some time. You're twenty-seven years old, aren't you? So don't go thinking you need my permission, or anyone's permission, for anything. All right? Don't listen to me— listen to yourself!"

Fryderyk gave half a small smile. "I'll try."

George shook her head as she embroidered a sampler that evening at home. Fryderyk had literally asked her if it was all right for him to get things out for lunch. Asked her... like a child would ask. Asked her... as though she was his mother, his aunt, his teacher, or some other loving figure in authority over a child. Asked her... as if he really wanted to know. Asked her... in his own apartment.

But why? What was the matter with him? And why did he think that that was necessary; that that was right? Why did he think that any adult should ever ask permission for anything?

She remembered his face. And she knew. That simple, childlike trust... the trust he now placed in her.

She shivered. The trust he now placed in her. The trust that a young boy would place in his mother. But George... She shook her head. She didn't want to be a mother. She certainly didn't want to be Fryderyk's mother. And he certainly didn't need her to be.

They were going to have to sort this out.

Give me wisdom, she prayed. *And bless him with understanding. We have got to sort this out.*

He understands, her mother seemed to sneer. *He honors his mother and what she would want for him, because he knows she wants what's best for him, like I want what's best for you. He's ready to listen. So why won't you?*

George just shook her head.

Thick snowflakes fell like goose-down outside George's sitting room window one early December afternoon in 1837, cloaking the trees and bushes. George sighed, setting down her embroidery, pushing aside the blanket that had been tucked around her legs, and stretching as she rose from the armchair in which she had been cocooned for the past two hours. She had best look in on her neighbor. See how he was doing on this winter day.

What if… what if she brought him dinner? With a smile, George went to the kitchen, shaking out her long skirt as she went, and got out a soup pot. She settled into the cozy rhythm, chopping vegetables and heating broth as the snow continued to fall cozily outside the window, trying to make a nourishing soup better than she'd ever made before. She'd gotten those Brussels sprouts for a really good price the other day at the market. Of course, this was a recipe for broccoli soup, but she'd substituted ingredients before… she'd just follow the rest of the instructions to the letter, and let it simmer for an hour… She settled down in the sitting room to continue her embroidery while it cooked.

Was this what it was supposed to feel like? she asked herself as the afternoon wore on. *Being the domestic angel who made soup for her beloved on a snowy winter's day; nourished him with her cooking skills and her endless love? Was this, standing at the stove stirring homemade soup, what being a woman, a ladylike, model woman who was not fierce or tempestuous, the sweet, gentle woman she should be, was really supposed to feel like? Was this, standing in the kitchen in a dress and an apron, what was going to make her truly happy? Was this what was going to usher her and Fryderyk into the happily ever after that George's parents had never gotten to share, and that she herself had sought with such poignant determination in the endings of so many of her own novels?*

Maybe, after so many years of searching, she had finally found someone who would fix her. The man with whom she could finally become the perfect woman; the woman who gloried in cooking and mending and cleaning. The peaceful angel of domesticity she should be.

George sighed. And the angel of domesticity that seemed to watch over her life seemed to beam a satisfied smile over her shoulder.

Finally, the soup was done. My, the smell was… strong. But strongly-flavored things always were the best, weren't they? Sweating but proud, George put a lid on it as out the window, the late afternoon deepened into the blue of a winter twilight, washed her hands and face, put the pot in a basket under her arm along with the almond cake she'd baked that morning on a whim, got her coat on, and set out through the blue of the evening for Fryderyk's apartment.

George walked quickly through the snowy streets of Paris on that quiet, early winter evening, not paying attention to the inquisitive stares of passersby curious as to what she could be carrying in that enormous basket that was steaming.

Arriving at Fryderyk's doorstep as the blue of evening faded into black, she balanced the basket on her hip and knocked heartily on the door. Lamplight shone through the windows— he hadn't gone to bed yet. Silently, George chuckled at her own lack of planning; how she couldn't technically have been sure of him being home and awake when she arrived. Thank her lucky stars that he was.

A minute later she heard footsteps and a thick cough, and a few moments after that, the door slowly opened. Fryderyk peered out into the winter night, wondering what late visitor could be calling on this bleak December evening; then his eyes lit up as he saw her.

This time, he really was wearing the dressing-gown. It looked too big for him. And yet, even though he had his dressing-gown on, he still had his cravat tied up to his chin. So modest. And so… George bit her lip as she got a good look at him. So pale. Maybe… maybe he was feeling less well today. But still… still pleased to see her.

"Come in, George," he said hoarsely, stepping to the side to let her in. She stepped inside and made a real effort to stomp the snow off her shoes and brush it from the hem of her skirt, then flung her damp coat onto an overstuffed armchair that seemed to have fairly delicate upholstery. Even though it felt good to warm

138

up from outside, she could still tell that it was boiling in the apartment. Valdeck jumped from the top of a chair and bolted up the stairs.

"Cat doesn't like me today," she said teasingly. "Guess I'm scary in my big coat. It's just me under here, kitty," she said as he disappeared like a ghost.

"He doesn't like competition," Fryderyk said. Making his way over to the armchair, he took George's coat and hung it up for her as she flashed him a grateful smile. Again, something inside her ached. She should have done that. And yet, something else ached as well. Because letting him… letting him do something for her "just because"… felt good.

She let that thought go, nodding knowingly at Fryderyk's words. "I'm flattered. Brought you something," she said, marching into his tiny dining room and heaving the heavy basket onto the table, managing not to spill the soup. "Would you get bowls and spoons, please? I made you some soup."

Fryderyk smiled as he saw the pot of soup on the counter. "Oh, soup? Thank you very much, George."

He fetched a bowl and spoon for each of them from the kitchen cupboards, along with a ladle, then sat down at the table. Accepting the ladle, George served him a generous portion of soup.

"There you go. Tell me what you think."

He smelled the soup, paused, and gave an extremely polite little smile. "I don't seem to have much appetite right now— I actually just had a bit of dinner. Maybe later…"

George gave him puppy-dog eyes as she ladled a healthy portion of soup into her own bowl and sat down across from him. "Oh, come on; let's have some together. Please? I made it just for you." After another slight pause, Fryderyk slowly nodded and picked up his spoon again.

"*Bon appetit*," George said, then shoveled in a huge bite. Fryderyk took a small, delicate sip from the side of his spoon.

Both were gagging in an instant.

Fryderyk leaned across the table and grabbed a glass of milk he'd already poured for himself, draining it in two noisy, frantic gulps.

"What did you put in there?" he coughed. "Oh... my..."

George grimaced, trying to get the awful, sticky residue off her tongue. It was so bitter...

Sniffling as her nose began to run, she choked out what she remembered putting in. "Beef broth, potatoes, Brussels sprouts... it shouldn't be undercooked. I let it simmer for an hour."

Fryderyk nodded, a look of understanding mixing with the still-fading disgust and the glimmer of an eye-roll she watched him clearly resist with great intentionality. "So that's what it is," he choked. He shook his head, offering a half-pitying little frown. "Oh, dear, George, you don't cook Brussels sprouts for an hour. They get really... strong." He gagged again and put his napkin to his mouth, turning faintly green.

Still struggling to divest herself of the terrible bitterness that coated the inside of her mouth, George put down her spoon and got her hanky out of her handbag to wipe her nose. "Oh, Fryderyk, I'm sorry, I didn't mean to, oh, and I wanted to make such good soup for you, I spent all afternoon... I can never get anything right; I've tried so hard... the soup is so terrible, and I've been trying so terribly hard, I like you so terribly, this is terrible..."

George buried her face in her handkerchief, feeling it burning with shame. There it all went— her dreams of idealized domesticity, the happy kitchen angel who wanted nothing more than to nourish her man with delicious homemade soup. Delicious homemade soup that had turned into poison. Instead of nourishing him, she had half-killed him with the disaster she had come up with. Shame, shame, on the domestic goddess and her epic failure. Shame, shame, on her dreams of giving. Shame, shame, on her hopeless, grasping search, her hapless attempt at the acquisition of a *happily ever after*.

"Well, the soup is terrible," Fryderyk agreed, trying to laugh. Gently, he patted her shoulder, the delicate touch of his thin hand so light she could barely feel it. "There, there," he said encouragingly. "The soup is terrible, but you made it because you care... and I do feel very cared for. Oh, dear, this is very awkward. I suppose I'm a terrible host." They shared weak grins. "This is just a terrible list of terribles," he said with half a chuckle.

Oh, what a mess. George sniffled again, then burst out laughing. "Terrible list of terribles, that's what it is," she said, shaking her head as she grinned pathetically.

Fryderyk smiled. "Now, that's better, isn't it? Let's just put it away now and... and open the window. Oh, my. We need to air out that terrible smell." Slowly he got up, giving a grunt of effort as he heaved the window open a few centimeters.

"Open the window and throw it out!" George crowed, gesturing grandly with both arms as she began to grow slaphappy. "Can't give it to the cat—"

"No, definitely not," Fryderyk said, shaking his head as he returned to the table. "I love him too much." But his love for his cat aside, he joined in in harping on the ghastliness of the soup.

"You know; this gives me an idea for a new piece. We'll call it— Ode to Indigestion. Only, it's not much of an ode—"

"It's a funeral march!" George cried, collapsing and slapping the table in her mirth. "Soup that's so bad you'd rather die!"

"Speaking of which, where *did* you get this terrible recipe?"

"Well, I did use a few substitutions," she admitted, wiping tears of laughter from her eyes.

"Such as the Brussels sprouts, I'm guessing."

"Well, I like to improvise in the kitchen," she said. "Maybe next time I'll bring you flowers. Well, it should have been— it was meant to be broccoli soup, but when I went to the grocer, he's such a pleasant little fellow, he said that Brussels sprouts are in season and they're more plentiful this year than broccoli, and so I figured I could substitute it. Obviously I can't."

Fryderyk could not hold back his amazement at her foolishness. "Obviously— obviously you can't— substitute Brussels sprouts for broccoli…" he guffawed, pounding the table as hard as she had. "Just like you can't substitute garlic for orange peel…"

"Or sauerkraut for whipping cream!" George howled, too amused herself to be offended. "Or lemon juice for anchovies!"

"Or almonds for potato!"

Now Fryderyk was gasping for breath. As much fun as this was, George knew she had to bring it down a little. And she had better get up and close the window, too. As lovely as the chilly breeze was, coming into the close, overheated apartment, she didn't want him to get a chill.

She took a shuddering breath, her laughter gently ebbing. "Almonds, that reminds me; you'll never guess what I brought for dessert."

142

He raised his eyebrows as his uproarious laughter slowly subsided. Slowly, he caught his breath.

"Ah… I think I'm full."

"No, no, you'll like it," she said, getting up and approaching the window, outside of which the cold, winter night had deepened into a quiet black. She stood there for a moment with her eyes closed, letting the frigid air waft over her, then finally closed it. Silently, she remarked to herself how easy it had been for her to close. Easier than it had been for him. But… She bit her lip. Did that mean that she could not say he was strong?

Turning back to the table, she took a pan wrapped in a dishcloth out of her basket. "Look, almond cake. Just for you. Let me see if I can find a knife to cut it."

"In the second drawer," he said, pointing. She served the cake and they shared it, Fryderyk offering more compliments than she could have hoped as he enjoyed the incontrovertible evidence that she really could cook— or, more specifically, bake. Maybe the goddess of domesticity was not such a failure after all.

13   Freedom

"You know…" George said a few minutes later, looking down at her empty plate, "there was something I actually wanted to talk to you about. Something I think we need… to discuss."

Fryderyk looked up. "What?" he asked.

George picked up her fork, scraping the tiny cake crumbs on her plate into a little pile in the exact center. "There was something you said a visit or two ago… that kind of concerned me."

He bit his lip. "Was it the thing I said about Salieri possibly having murdered Mozart? I know that's just a conspiracy theory, but the evidence is too strong to ignore—"

George put a hand up. "No. Not that. The thing about you wanting to ask permission for things… feeling like you need permission for things. Or as though it's rude not to ask if you may. Wanting to have me to listen to… or wanting me to tell you what to do. Like I'm in charge of you… like I'm your mother or something."

Fryderyk looked at her. And he bit his lip again.

"I'm sorry," he said softly, looking away.

"Don't be," she said quickly. "I know there's a reason. A good reason. But… I think we just need to, well, talk about it. And maybe you can help me understand a bit more."

Fryderyk sighed, wistfully looking away into memories George could not see. "Well… there's a lot to it. A lot of reasons. And a lot of time. Like I said, I've always had problems with my lungs, and my parents never wanted me running around outside. And I

144

always had doctors everywhere. So, I just became so used to looking to them; to listening to them. To waiting for what they would say and asking before I tried anything new. Because I... I honestly didn't think it was safe to do otherwise. They were the adults, and they knew best, and I didn't want to get hurt. Maybe..."

He shook his head with half a little chuckle. "Maybe some small part of me is still afraid that I'll get hurt if I don't double-check everything first. And... I would never say that you're my mother; I already have one, but you're here, right with me, and you care about me, and I trust you..." He took her hand. "I trust you completely. And I know you would never let anything bad happen to me. Just like I won't let anything bad happen to you. So, I think," he summed up, "deep down, I'm just so used to listening that I don't know how to do anything else. And you... you are someone for me to listen to. Someone I want to listen to."

George sighed. "Well, Fryderyk, I'm grateful that you trust me, and I would certainly never let anything bad happen to you... except maybe my cooking." She winked, and they shared a laugh. With a sigh, she continued. "But I'm not here to be your adult; to be your mother. And you know that. I will always help you when you need help, and you can always turn to me when you need me, but you... you are an adult. And you know that. And the only adult you need to listen to is your own self. So... don't listen to me— listen to yourself." She squeezed his hand. "All right?" George winked again. "My decision not to have children was intentional. You are not going to be my child, and I am not going to be your mother." She raised an eyebrow. "I just hope that doesn't disappoint you."

Fryderyk shook his head. "No." Gently drawing her hand to his lips, he kissed it. Slowly, he nodded. "All right."

George smiled. "All right." She sighed. "Thank you for getting into that, Fryderyk." She shook her head, not sure what else to say. "Thank you."

Fryderyk nodded with a little smile. And George set about cleaning up the dining room and kitchen, putting the empty pan from the almond cake back into the basket she'd brought it in; leaving the terrible soup to cool on the counter. Silently, she smiled. That had been a challenging conversation. But they had walked through it together. And maybe, now… maybe, he could see a little more clearly the privileges and responsibilities it was up to him to take in hand. And maybe she, armed with a greater understanding of why he did what he did, could help him truly feel safe.

Fryderyk yawned.

"It's getting late," George said, looking at the clock on the wall. "After eight o'clock. I've been here almost two hours."

"I was in bed when you arrived," he admitted, yawning again. George bit her lip as she took a closer look at him, suddenly realizing that although his neck was covered by his cravat, rather than wearing a shirt and trousers under his dressing-gown, he was wearing his nightshirt. And as he stood there with her in the kitchen, fighting back another yawn, she watched him shifting his balance again and again as though he were struggling to keep his feet.

She sighed, shaking her head in anger at herself, half-wishing he had chosen not to answer the door at all. In bed? Then she shouldn't have come at all. He was so weak, and she'd forgotten, and selfishly made him get up and host her and be up and busy for

146

two hours when he needed to be resting… Well, what was done was done, but she knew she had worn him out enough. Laughter may have been the best medicine, but too much of anything was still too much.

She tried to smile. "What with how late it's getting, maybe I should be going."

"I hate to make you leave," he said with a little frown, but she shook her head.

"Oh, no, I'm the one who disturbed you by coming so late— you were so kind to let me in at all. We've had our visit, and it's been lovely to spend time together; thank you so much for letting me come in and stay so long."

"And thank you for the soup," Fryderyk said. "Even if it was… terrible." They both grinned, but restrained themselves to small titters of laughter. He yawned again, and George's stomach tightened as a subtle shifting of Fryderyk's weight from foot to foot turned into a distinct stumble as he began to sway on his feet. Biting back a gasp of fear, she crossed the room in a heartbeat, ready to catch him if necessary.

"Here, let me take your arm," she said, linking arms with him as she had with her grandmother all those years ago. "Why don't I see you upstairs?" she asked. "Being… being that you're not feeling your best? Just to make sure you get settled in safely before I go." *So you don't fall straight back down the stairs and crack your head open like you did that time you went ice skating as a teenager,* she silently finished.

Fryderyk looked at her, tired eyes lighting up as a smile touched his thin face, revealing the elusive dimple in his cheek.

"Why not?"

Crossing the room a little shakily as he leaned gratefully on George's arm, Fryderyk walked with her to the foot of the stairs. Quietly, he let her put her arm around him, and actually laid his head on her shoulder while they walked upstairs together in perfect stride with one another. Again, she felt her strength flexing as she soared to the tough, independent side of the chasm inside her heart; the satisfaction of coming through, the joy of offering her strength on his behalf. Stepping up. Maybe she was becoming a proper gentleman. And maybe that wasn't a bad thing. And yet, there was also great tenderness… and such gentleness in the care she offered her dear friend.

Silently, George shook her head. Since when had she actually helped a man up the stairs? Most of the men she'd been with could have *carried* her up the stairs without a second thought—Mallefille using only one arm. But here she was, the one offering help. Here she was, offering her strength, her leadership, to meet Fryderyk's needs. Here she was, looking after someone she cared about. And here he was, not only letting her, but gratefully accepting her gesture of tender concern and loving support.

Tough and tender all at once, George was jumping all over the chasm inside her heart, the strange ball of yarn inside her heart tangling as it struggled to be tight and loose all at the same time. And through both lovingly offering her strength on his behalf and finally unleashing the long-confined angel of domesticity, she was helping him. And maybe… maybe, she was happy. Even… even if she had no idea where she was in terms of boundaries. No idea how this strange, sudden closeness might impact what was to come. No idea what was going through Fryderyk's mind as he accepted her assistance.

George glanced around the rather murky upstairs and stifled a

148

cough. It was dreadfully dusty up here. Odd, since the downstairs was quite neat. Slowly, they walked past the open door of an upstairs sitting room, where she noticed a second piano, and, at a welcoming nod from Fryderyk, continued into his dimly-lit bedroom, lined with shelves of books and knickknacks and shrouded with heavy, olive-green curtains. Carefully, George pulled down the heavy crimson comforter of the large, soft bed, which she hoped wasn't as dusty as the rest of the room. A small, red armchair stood in the corner, and an old armoire stood across from the bed beside a bureau, both full to bursting, she was sure, with Fryderyk's opulent wardrobe.

What color even is *this rug?* George silently asked herself as she took in just how dusty the bedroom was. *This can't be good for your health. But do... do I say anything?* Silently, she decided not to. But she wondered just how and when she might offer to take action to help him.

After lighting the candles that stood at attention on top of the bureau, Fryderyk bent and took off both slippers, carefully lining them up with great precision at the end of the bed. Then he took his dressing-gown off, and George hung it on the doorknob of his wardrobe for him. She noticed, however, that he left his cravat on. Though he was in his nightshirt, his neck was still covered up to his pointed chin. Slowly, almost painfully, he lay down, then half-sat up again to begin slowly and laboriously drawing the blankets up over his body.

The angel of domesticity pushing her forward in a heart-pounding rush, George scrambled to the tender side of the chasm before Fryderyk could say anything, stepping up to the side of the bed to pull the heavy covers over his thin frame, carefully tucking him in.

She was tucking him in. George could scarcely believe it. She was in Fryderyk's bedroom, literally putting him to bed… before nine o'clock. He needed her.

Fryderyk looked at her as she smoothed the blankets that she had pulled up to his chin. "You just said you don't want to be my mother," he said. "So why are you tucking me in?"

George looked back, her insides seeming to shrivel as she shrank back, shaking her head at her own hypocrisy; her utter failure to abide by her own decision. "Yes," she said slowly, "but I know you're not feeling too well today. And sometimes… sometimes exceptions can be made." With a breathy chuckle of embarrassment, she managed a wink. Straightening the covers once more, she stepped back with an awkward little smile. "Just don't get too used to me tucking you in," she said, "and I won't get used to it, either. You know I'm not trying to be your mother."

Fryderyk just chuckled, rolling his eyes playfully at her. "Thank you, my funny friend." He gave her a grateful little smile, then stifled a cough. "Thank you… for everything you've done today."

George smiled. "You're welcome."

The cat hopped up on the bed, and Fryderyk put out a thin, bony hand to pet him. Softly reaching out, George touched Fryderyk's other hand, which was freezing. Gently, he clasped her hand in his, his touch so light that she could hardly feel the pressure. And her heart broke with the frailty of the beloved friend who lay there so quietly, going to bed so very early.

George couldn't do this any longer. "Get some rest," she whispered through the lump in her throat, reaching out to gently run her hand over his thick, brown hair.

He looked up at her, a contented little smile on his thin face.

"Thank you," he whispered rather hoarsely. She could almost hear the junk plugging up his lungs.

"You're welcome," she replied, all she could get out. "Need anything else?"

Fryderyk shook his head gently. "Not right now. I... I enjoyed our visit." He fought back a wheezing cough, and his face crumpled as he pressed one of his ever-present hankies to his mouth. She took his frozen free hand in hers, gently rubbing it as he struggled to fight down another coughing fit. Beneath her fingers, she could feel every joint, every bone, of his long fingers, his narrow palms, his slender wrists. As Fryderyk contended mightily with his coughs, finally forcing them into submission, the cat curled up beside him in his own effort to comfort his master. "M... maybe something to drink," he said finally in an exhausted rasp.

"Milk?" she asked.

"Yes, please."

She frowned. "You'll be all right while I'm gone?"

He smiled. "I'm sure I will. I can shout when I have to, you know. Or Valdeck will come and get you. He takes good care of me."

"All right. Be right back." George hurried downstairs to make up for the pause she knew she would be taking. She made as much noise in the kitchen as she could, scraping the stepstool across the floor so she could reach the dishes, slamming cupboards, tinkling the glasses and mugs together as she chose one, stoking the fire inside the stove and thumping the pot onto the range to warm the milk, and pretending to have her own coughing fit to cover the fact that she was weeping as she waited for it to heat. The skeleton, the weak, dying skeleton who couldn't even get up the stairs by himself, who had to go to bed when the evening had barely begun… She could hardly believe that this was the same man she'd met at Liszt's party. If winter could do this to him, how long would he live?

Help him, she prayed as her mother and grandmother seemed to shake their heads sadly and hopelessly. *Heal him. Make him strong again. And get him through this winter.*

Realizing she'd taken long enough, George took a deep breath, blew her nose, wiped her eyes, took the pan off the stove, and carefully carried the mug of warm milk upstairs to him.

He was still breathing. That in itself was a blessing.

"Are you all right? Did you drop something down there?" he asked from where he lay against his pillows, his forehead crinkling in a concerned frown.

"No, I didn't drop anything," she said thickly. She was sure her eyes and nose were still red. "I'll be fine."

"Are you sure?" he asked, sitting up a little. His frown of concern deepened. He knew something was up.

"I'm just thinking about you, is all, you and your health," she said, trying not to let another flood of tears come. But she couldn't help it. The mug of milk found its way to the bedside table and sat forgotten as she sank down onto the edge of the bed and crumpled forward in tears, clutching her hanky.

"I worry sometimes, too," he said wistfully, reaching out to give her one of his hands to hold and pat her back with the other. "That's when I play the piano. That helps. And I pray. In the winter when my health gets bad, I get so I'm not strong enough to go to church, but I do pray."

She nodded, wiping her eyes. "I will pray for you, Fryderyk.

Every night. I care so much about you, my dear, dear… Fryderyk. You mean so much to me. I couldn't bear it if… if we couldn't be together anymore." She met his eye, biting her lip. "I'm sorry… I don't want to upset you…"

A gentle, calm smile touched his thin face as he softly shook his head. "You're not upsetting me. My dear George. You could never upset me. You bless me in so many ways, every day we're together. I just wish I could give more to you; you see how pitiful I am—"

"You're not pit—" she began, but gently, he raised his hand, and she paused to listen.

"My earthly body has been a terrible disappointment to me. Always. And I feel… like I'm always disappointing others."

Fryderyk paused, then slowly, another small smile crept across his pale face. "But… with you… with you, I've finally found a place I can be myself. As a musician, I have to perform…" He shuddered. "And each time I have to go on stage, I still get scared. And to perform… that's what people want from me— they want my 'musical genius' or whatever they might call it; they want to listen even when I don't want to play; I have to give and give and give. And I just… I just want someone to take care of *me*. And let me be myself."

George smiled, nodding as her tears passed. "You've given me the same thing. The freedom to just be… me. A woman who wears trousers because they're freeing, and doesn't have to be pigeonholed into one role or another. A woman…" She sighed, feeling a strange sense of truth rising in her soul as she spoke. "Who may never choose to be a mother, but has a lot of love to give. And…" She paused, opening heart almost seeming to break as the next words came. "The chance… to belong."

14   Faithfulness

Fryderyk sighed. "I long for someone to hold me, someone to care for me, someone to love me. Valdeck is a great comfort, but I need more. I get so lonely sometimes… I miss my family, my home in Poland, so much. Some days, I just want my *matka*, my mother. And my dear, dear, sweet friend… I long to have you care for me. Although," he added, raising his eyebrows, "like we were saying, not as a mother to me. As a friend. As a loving companion on whom I can rely; one solid, consistent thing in a world that sometimes doesn't make any sense. Someone who can help me feel safe; who can help me answer my questions. Who… can make my uncertainties certain.

"It can be hard," he said slowly. "It's… complicated. I'm sure you've noticed some… things about me. My… I don't know… *quirks*. Like how easily I spook, how I always eat the same things and keep the same hours because routines are the only control I can cling to in a crazy world, how crowds overwhelm me and I hate giving concerts, how I just don't get silly jokes that don't say what they mean, how I'm so sensitive it hurts. And I have so many stories of the ways I wear out my kind friends and roommates with all the things I need from them.

"I know I'm… different. I always have been. My parents helped me find strategies to manage daily life; strategies I still use all the time. But this 'difference' brings with it a whole set of positives and negatives. It helps me create my art… but it doesn't make it easy to travel or go to a festival or eat new foods or change the plans I've made. It's just part of who I am… always

154

has been."

George nodded. "Thank you," she said softly. "For being so open." She offered a small smile. "I have… been curious. But I… I get it. My experience isn't identical to yours, but from an artist to an artist, I can truly say… that I understand. I understand *you*. Artists… we're not typical. I'm certainly not. And as you've said, the things that make you unique also help you create your art. Even… if it's not always easy."

Fryderyk looked at her. "It's not."

She sighed. "So… please, tell me more. I want to help and support you in any way I can, but I need you to tell me what's helpful and what you need from me."

Fryderyk shook his head with a little shrug of his thin shoulders. "There isn't really a word for it— *artistic temperament? Extreme sensitivity?* I notice everything, I feel everything, everything comes at me full force— too hot, too bright, too loud, too itchy, too much. *Too… too much* is probably the best way to describe it. Everything is too much. So much of the time. And it's hard to find a balance between protecting myself from the 'worst' of it while also participating in life outside my apartment. But I'm glad," he summed up, "to have a friend like you. Someone who 'gets' me. And truly cares about me for me."

George clasped his hand. "Of course, I do. Likewise, I'm glad to have a friend like you— a fellow artist who appreciates me for me." She sighed, the words he'd just spoken still spinning inside her mind. "Again, thank you for being so open. And I want to be the friend you need me to be… always."

Fryderyk swallowed. "Thank you… best friend." He gave half a wistful smile. "Makes me wonder, though, what Marja would have thought of me as a husband. What we might have had together. Even if we never will… because that potential future is one that is definitely not going to happen. And I'm probably never going to see her again. Her parents will marry her to someone else. And I sincerely hope she will be happy."

He gave a reflective sigh, then slowly smiled, a glow of contentment transforming his face so if it were not for the fact that he was in bed at nine in the evening, George never would have guessed that he was sick.

He squeezed her hand. "And then there's now."

George looked at Fryderyk, her heart beginning to pound as her stomach flip-flopped. Was he about to ask her to begin courting?

"You make me so happy," he continued. "But I just… I don't want to disappoint you. In any way."

George gazed down at him, her eyes brimming with happy tears of absolute rapture. "I could never be disappointed in you," she whispered. "You just play your blessed piano whenever you like, and I could never be disappointed." She paused, a thin chuckle rising in her chest to emerge as an odd-sounding wheeze. She swallowed. And she looked down at their entwined hands. "Are we courting?"

George could see Fryderyk looking at her, but she didn't make eye contact; didn't take her eyes off the ivory hand whose long fingers were laced with her own. She heard Fryderyk sigh beneath the sound of the pounding of her own heart. And she heard him swallow.

"I… I didn't think we were," he said slowly. He paused. "Did you… did you want to be?"

Slowly, George raised her eyes to his. And she allowed a smile to touch her face. "Yes," she said simply.

Now Fryderyk was the one who looked down, pondering the two hands that remained entwined. He gazed at them, biting his lip. And slowly, he released a sigh.

"You know how much I care about you," he began softly, and George bit her lip as she struggled not to wilt, internal voices of anguished disappointment that she had lost out in love yet again arguing with voices that told her she should be grateful for the friendship they had. Slowly, Fryderyk looked up at her, and she made herself meet his gaze. "Don't you?"

They always reject you, whispered the angel of domesticity with a sneer. Swallowing back a thousand feelings, George commanded the angel to shut up. And she looked at Fryderyk, who was waiting for her answer; waiting for her to confirm that she knew how much he cared about her.

She looked at him. "No," she said softly, gently shaking her head. She swallowed. "That's why I'm asking. Asking… what kind of care you have for me. What kind of relationship you want this to be… what kind of friends you want to be… what you want us to be to one another? I want to know… so I know what the future holds. So I know what to hope for." Loudly, George swallowed again. "I'm in love with you," she declared.

"You are?" Fryderyk asked softly.

Convulsively, George nodded. "Yes," she choked out. "I am."

Fryderyk returned her gaze, gently squeezing her hand. "I really have tried to show you how much I care… tried to let you know that you're one of the best friends I've ever had. And I'm so grateful for everything you do for me." He paused, looking away again, and George made herself continue to listen, drooping inside as she tried not to let her frustrated disappointment bubble up into actual anger. "But courting... if we courted... what would be your hopes and dreams for what that would look like... what that would mean? Are you asking me to marry you?"

George shook her head. "All I want is to be with you," she said sincerely, and she found that it was true. Somehow, only half a heartbeat after what was arguably a sound rejection, she was alight with the hope of what mattered the most. "I don't care about the details. As long as I can be with you; as long as I can continue hearing more and more of your beautiful music and sharing with you in what it means to be an artist. As long as it never ends... we don't have to court if you don't want to." She sighed, slowly beginning to release her hopes and dreams of courting, grasping instead onto the artistic companionship, the deep friendship, that they had already established. "So what do you think?" she asked softly. "Can we have more of what we have now? Whether or not it ever changes?"

Fryderyk nodded. "I don't want things to change," he whispered. "Not even by calling what we have 'courting.'"

George looked at him. "So... we're not?" she whispered.

Fryderyk shrugged his thin shoulders. "I just don't know yet. It's a big decision. One I'm not quite sure I'm ready to make. Even... with you. But don't doubt that I care, my friend," he said, squeezing her hand. "Never doubt that I care."

George sniffled, then found a wistful smile. "I don't doubt that," she said, shaking her head. And that was true.

Fryderyk smiled. "I don't want you to change. And I don't want the beautiful friendship we have to change. I like being together with you."

George wiped away tears, both happy and sad, as she nodded.

158

"And I like being together with you. Being with you... who sees me for who I really am; who understands me as an artist to an artist... sets me free."

"Free," he repeated softly. He looked at her with a wistful sigh. "That's the only time I feel truly free... when I'm composing; when I'm playing. When I'm... at one... with my art. Maybe my earthly body is a terrible disappointment to me, but in music... in my music, I can fly if I want to. There's nothing that holds me back. Nothing but me... and it."

George nodded. "I know what you mean. I feel the same way— I'm only truly free when I'm writing. It sweeps me away... to somewhere else... where I can be myself. Where I can... find myself. And it's somehow... bigger in there— bigger than the outside world. It's almost like I'm dreaming my way through it... but when I'm done, I have a story. And it's such a beautiful place... it's like I never want to leave. So I go back, and back, until I can't keep track anymore of how many novels I've published... because that is where I can finally feel free."

She ran her hand over his hair again. "So, let's set one another free. I need you, Fryderyk. As much as you need me."

They sat in silence for a moment, basking in the loving friendship that had brought them together.

"You're such a blessing to me," Fryderyk whispered. Now it was his turn to run his delicate fingers through her hair. Again, she felt her heart opening. And she chose... she chose to accept his words. Chose... to receive them. Because she knew... that they were true.

"You're my blessing, too," she murmured. Fryderyk gave her a sleepy smile, then stifled a yawn. Since they'd been talking, he'd become even paler than before. George checked her pocketwatch. "It's almost nine-thirty. I didn't mean to keep you up so late." She turned to the forgotten mug of milk and found that it was still a bit warm. "Here. Have your milk and settle in. I'll be back in the morning."

He took the cup in his thin hands, slowly sitting up to drink it. He moved slowly and deliberately, so cautiously that it frightened her. Was he really afraid that he would spill it?

Finally, he finished the milk, and she set the mug back on the bedside table for him. She'd do his dishes tomorrow.

"I'll see you in the morning, then," she said, gently touching his hand.

Slowly, his fingers closed around her hand, and he drew her hand closer so he could kiss it. She didn't move; just sat still and smiled. He was saying *yes*, to everything that truly mattered.

If he had kissed her hand, did she have permission to kiss his head? George bent forward, brushed aside his silky hair, and brushed her lips against his forehead. He became very still, but she could hear him smiling.

"All right," she whispered, standing up. Oh, he had the sweetest, sappiest little smile on his face. She squeezed his hand one more time. "It's getting late. You need your sleep, and I have some things to do at home. So, I'll see you tomorrow, all right?"

He smiled and lay back among his pillows, settling in comfortably. Gently, she tucked him in again. Valdeck purred from where he lay beside Fryderyk and lay his head down.

"Good night, George. And thank you… thank you for everything."

"Good night, my dear friend." Releasing a heavy sigh of pure joy, George gave Fryderyk another smile, then blew out the

160

candles that stood on his bureau, quietly leaving the room and closing the door behind her. She tiptoed downstairs and found her soup pot, still mostly full of what was now cold, terrible soup, wincing and grinning at the same time as she set it in her basket alongside the empty pan from the almond cake. Everything gathered up, she let herself out into the dark winter night, locked the door behind her, took a deep breath of the cold, refreshing night air, and floated home.

George went to bed with sweet dreams already dancing through her head. *She had found him,* she thought with a sigh of relief. The man she could trust, the man who could do it, the man who held the key to her heart, who could finally free the maternal goddess of domesticity who had miserably twiddled her thumbs in her tower ever since before Aurore had even known what it was to be male or female. If she took care of him for long enough, cooked and cleaned and read and fussed and tucked him into bed at night, she would finally come to know what it was to be a woman.

She would, she told herself. Even if a twinge of disappointment still ached inside her as his words replayed once more inside her mind... the words with which he'd reassured her of his friendship— the friendship he never wanted to change in any way. Even... even with romance. The words with which he had thanked her for everything... except, perhaps, for the awkward, impulsive way in which she had asked him to become her beau... the offer he had declined in the kindest, politest way she could ever have dreamed of hoping for. If that was how rejection could feel, she knew she would spend the reflective moments of her future gritting her teeth even more at the heartless dumpings she had received time and time again from more fellow artists in her past than she could count.

There he is, simpered the angel, pink cheeks glowing as she sighed, her perfectly-curled ringlets of golden hair shimmering as she exhaled. *The man you've been waiting for. The man who can fix you. So you can finally settle down. So you won't have to be fierce any longer. And so you can finally be happy.*

George sighed in turn, opening her heart to the possibility that this relationship, whatever it turned out to be, would do her some good. And she smiled as another thought came to her. Finally, her aching, brooding questions about Marja Wodzińska were answered. Beloved memory though she might be, she was no longer an active part of Fryderyk's life. Without George ever having to ask it, her question had been answered. Marja, God bless her, was not standing at the window, waiting for Fryderyk to come home and marry her.

Even if… George looked down at her own hands; at the white fingers whose only ring was the one she'd inherited from her grandmother. Even if he was not ready to court her, either.

She did pray for him. George asked God to bless Fryderyk with a good night of sleep. She asked Him to bless Fryderyk with a healthy winter. And she asked Him to bless the day they would spend together tomorrow.

He's a good guy, she told her mother and grandmother before they could comment. *I love him. And we are going to help one another.*

Maybe he is a good guy, her mother and grandmother seemed to chorus, joined by the angel of domesticity and the little four-year-old, who nodded their heads in agreement. *But you've seen that he doesn't want to court you, marry you, or settle down with you in any capacity, so you're going to have to deal with that.*

George sighed, joy and pain arguing inside her heart as the conflict of so many unknown possibilities echoed out into infinity. And she nodded. *I will.*

15 Patience

"I'm confused," George said.

Claudette took a bite of the soup she had ordered from the restaurant where they'd met for lunch a few weeks before the Christmas of 1837.

"About what?"

"About myself." She looked down at her shirt, her trousers, her cravat, a strange uncertainty filling her. "Fryderyk... he's so weak. And he... he needs me to help him. A lot. Give him my arm as we walk up a hill together, pull out his chair for him, carry things for him, open doors for him. And there's this feeling inside me when I do those things for him... this feeling of strength. But it's not a good feeling— it's weird; uncomfortable. It's like I'm jumping from one side of a chasm to the other, where one side is all homey and domesticated and the other side is tough and independent. And when he does something for me— pulls my chair out for me, helps me in or out of a carriage— I have to force myself to accept his help."

Claudette shook her head. "I know you've never been much for traditional roles."

"Exactly." George bit her lip. "Fryderyk is... fragile. And he needs me. Needs me to be the gentleman. Just like my family needed me to step into the role that my papa left empty when he died... the role that I was never able to really fill. I was ashamed that I couldn't. And my grandmother still seems to chide me for it." She bit her lip again, remembering the unreasonable pressure that had been placed on her. "Maybe it was wrong of Grandmother to make those demands of me; to try to turn a girl of six, ten, fourteen, into a facsimile of her own father. But she did anyway."

George took a bite of soup. Claudette kept listening.

"I think of the boy, the laddie, that my grandmother tried to mold me into." She sighed. "It wasn't right. But... was there a reason? A real reason?"

"Your grandmother managed Nohant before she passed it on to you, didn't she?" Claudette asked. George nodded. "Well," Claudette said, "running an estate takes a lot of hands. There are a lot of moving pieces; a lot of kitchen maids and farm boys."

"Don't I know it," George said. She took another bite of soup. "Now I'm the one who directs all the kitchen maids and farm boys and laundresses and repairmen and all the rest."

Claudette nodded. "As the mistress of Nohant yourself now, you know firsthand how challenging it is to coordinate everything and keep it all running smoothly. But what might have your grandmother's perspective been? When you lived with her in Nohant, you... were a tiny, wonderful little girl. Not a big, strong farm boy. You could embroider and play music and read poetry aloud on a quiet afternoon, but you couldn't have helped with the heavy work of the farm. You just weren't... a boy. Weren't your grandmother's grandson. And in her own pain, her own need... she tried to turn you into one. No matter how wrong she was to do so."

George nodded as she thought. Of the disappointment she had been. And the disappointment... that she still was.

She shook her head. "I think of Casimir, Mallefille, Jules, Musset, Didier... how they treated me. What they needed from me. And how they never came through for me. Never offered their strength on my behalf— the outward strength that they had in abundance, far more than Fryderyk might. They relied on me, leaned on me, clung to me in dependence— they were little boys looking to find a mother in me, an editor, a nurse, a counselor. Not a partner; not someone who could walk side-by-side with them through all the storms of life, a true counterpoint whose strength matched their own. And they never did everything that they were capable of for themselves, let alone did anything for me. Never came to me to offer their help to me, only to beg for help from me. And I was never able to trust them; to rely on them for anything."

Claudette raised her eyebrows. "That's because relying on men for anything is a fairly big risk to take."

George nodded, wholeheartedly concurring. "It is. Fryderyk, though..." She sighed. "I don't know. It's mysterious, but he's... different. Maybe he doesn't have the outward strength that they had so much of. But he... he has something else. An inner strength that's determined to do everything he can for himself before asking for help instead of whining for my help every other minute or grouchily demanding for me to do more. He only ever asks for help that he truly needs, and he's always grateful. And he... does things for me. Makes an effort for me. Works hard, with intention. To help me in and out of my carriage, open doors for me, carry my bag. Things that the others almost never did. Things that aren't always easy for him to do... but that he does because he cares."

"Because he cares," Claudette repeated. She raised an eyebrow. "I suppose the next question is... being that it matters so much to him to do these things for you... do you care about him enough to let him?"

George shook her head. "Yes... and yet, I'm still working on actually doing it." She sighed. "The others... they were rather pathetic. Men as a species… are rather pathetic. And even Fryderyk has his iffy moments, uncertain moments, moments that make me scratch my head. Moments where he does in fact rely on me too much, or in the wrong sort of way, especially when it comes to making decisions or making sure I'm all right with something. But he does what he can to be helpful to me. He needs me in ways I'm comfortable giving," she summed up, "and I'll always be there for him. Just like I know he'll always be there for me."

Claudette looked at George. And slowly, she smiled. "I don't think you're confused," she said. "I think you know exactly what to do."

Fryderyk did rely on George. Trust her. Lean on her. And as he dithered; as he danced uncertainly between two equally good choices of top hats or two equally delicious dinner entrées, between visiting her apartment or inviting her to his, between attending this play or that concert, she reminded him… that he was an adult. His choices were his own. The only permission he needed to do anything was his own. And the only opinion that mattered in regards to the food he ate, the clothing he wore, how late he chose to stay up… was his.

He listened. And slowly… he began to believe her.

Look at him, George's grandmother seemed to say as Fryderyk paused mid-sentence to cough, struggled up the stairs, trudged slowly down a hallway, wearied after a short walk in the snowy park or an evening at the theater. *His body is not strong. And when someone else has a vulnerability that you don't, it's your responsibility to help them.* Her grandmother seemed to shake her head, the generational wisdom that had given her the strength to manage the estate of Nohant for so many years shining from her steely blue eyes.

Is it, though? George responded. *Of course, I'll help him when he needs help. But if I swoop in and rescue him every time it looks like something isn't easy, won't I be robbing him of the opportunity to do everything he possibly can for himself?*

And how dare you ever let him do anything for you? her grandmother's voice continued. She folded her soft, old arms; the fragile arms that belied a hidden strength with which she could box the ears of a misbehaving kitchen maid, and sometimes had.

George shook her head. *How dare I? Same answer. If I don't, I'll be rejecting his kindness. Things... that must be important to him to do for me. And even...* She bit her lip. *Even more so if it's not easy. I don't want him to hurt himself for my benefit, but can't I accept the honor of him making an effort for me? Even as I make an effort for him?*

Her grandmother's words faded away. And reflectively, George went on with her day.

"Do you speak any Polish?" Fryderyk asked out of the silence of the cozy early evening.

George looked up from the scene she was editing as they sat together on the couch in his sitting room. Two empty soup bowls sat on the coffee table, evidence of the delicious dinner they had shared.

She shook her head. "No— I only know about three words in Polish."

He smiled. "I was just thinking, I'd like to teach you some."

George nodded, returning his smile. "All right. I'd love to learn

168

a bit."

Over the next hour, he taught her a good dozen words in Polish, such as *cat*, *piano*, *mother*, and *father*, and about eight of them stuck. He smiled as he guided her through the pronunciations, his face lighting up as his native language rolled off his tongue.

"It feels so good to speak Polish," he said gratefully. "Feels like... like a little bit of home. Thank you for doing this together."

George squeezed his hand. "Of course."

"My house was bilingual," Fryderyk said. "My *matka* is Polish, and my papa came to Poland from France as a teenager. We spoke Polish at home, but they both speak both, and all of us children speak both. But *Matka* always writes her letters in Polish, and Papa always writes his in French."

"Which do you write in?" George asked.

Fryderyk smiled. "I can write in both, but I love it, just love it, when I get to write home in Polish. And when I hear Polish..." He gave a delighted sigh. "Best thing in the world. Feels like home. I think in Polish," he continued. "And my works... well, I've only written a handful of songs with lyrics, but all my works are written in one or the other. I might have a mazurka that represents the sun rising over the budding trees early in the springtime, and a polonaise about the same image, but one is written as my *matka* would describe it and the other is written from my papa's perspective. Her soft, sibilant Polish and his bold, throaty French are so different... and so are the pieces I write in their voices."

Fryderyk chuckled. "They taught us so well, my sisters and me. And I know people insist on calling me a 'musical genius,' but they don't know how much learning, how much education, how much work, has gone into who I have become. Speaking two languages at home wasn't always easy, but it expanded my mind; laid the framework in my brain from which my music would grow. In conversation, writing, and inside my own head, I use both Polish and French every day."

George smiled. "Thank you," she said. "For sharing it with me."

Always, George wrote. And again and again she crafted happy endings for her characters; happy endings that brought her an instant of peace, contentment, and satisfaction before going cold in her hands, crumbling into dust. She shook her head as she thought of it, weary heart aching with a sad, bitter frustration. *No matter how many times I write* And they all lived happily ever after*, it never works; it never comes true... What am I doing wrong?*

George and Fryderyk visited here and there through the early winter of 1837. Casually, they hung out together, Fryderyk popping over to George's apartment for a short visit and vice versa, the two of them meeting for tea or lunch— they coexisted in a comfortable, easy informality, anything but courting. It wasn't serious. And it didn't need to be.

It was beautiful. The artist and the artist, lives intertwining to form a perfect duet, challenging though it sometimes was, giving and receiving on equal terms. The ease with which they related; the trust that had grown between them, took George's breath away every time she thought of it. This was so different... so different from any of the other relationships she'd had. The genuine, care that they had for one another, the sincere interest they took in one another, the true friendship that had grown. This friendship... was

170

beautiful. And she wanted more. Even if this friendship was all they ever shared. Because in this friendship… she knew she had found the truest love she had ever known.

George and Fryderyk's meetings usually ended with a brief moment of planning; the determination of when they next intended to meet. Until one afternoon, they parted without making plans for their next meeting… and three days went by without him having said a word to her as to when he wanted to see her again. Then four, five, six. *He's probably just writing,* she told herself as she birthed another novel in the silence, and then yet another. *Just like I am.* But worry began to gnaw at the pit of George's stomach as the days of silence stretched out into weeks.

Is he all right? she prayed on the tenth day of mysterious, deafening silence. *Is something wrong? Please take care of him. Please make sure he's all right. And please let him get in touch with me.*

He's gone, her mother seemed to say on the eleventh day of no communication, shaking her head so her dark curls cascaded over her white shoulders. *And he's never coming back. He's abandoning you. Just like all the others. Because you bored him. You weren't good enough. And your soup was terrible. He's moved on to someone else. Or gone back to Marja. Or even home to* Matka *in Poland. You've lost him. Lost your chance. It's over. He doesn't need you. Never did, not really. And he doesn't care enough about you to bother to tell you what he intends to do next with his life. He doesn't even want to be your friend. He's leaving you, just like they always do. And you will always be alone.*

George swallowed, determined to fight fear with truth. *No*, she said. *That's not true. He'll be back when he's ready. And until then... I'll wait. Because isn't that what faithful friends do? And am I anything if not loyal?*

She missed Fryderyk. And yet, she wasn't cut off from all communication with those she knew... although she might have preferred to have been. Because Mallefille... kept writing. He was in Savoy now, having also visited Vevey and Lake Geneva recently. And he wanted George to know that he still missed her very much.

What did I do? she asked herself as she pondered Fryderyk's silence on the twelfth day since they had last spoken. *Was it the terrible soup? But we laughed about that. What changed? Should I reach out to him? And if so, when? And how?*
George buried her face in her hands, the weight of a thousand memories of other breakups seeming to weigh down her shoulders. *I killed it again, didn't I? I've been too much. Just like I always am. But how did I kill it? What detail am I missing? What exactly was it that changed? And how... do I change it back?*

Is he sick? she asked herself as she tossed and turned that night. *I know winter isn't kind to him. But if he's sick, he knows that I'm here for him, and he would certainly reach out to me. Wouldn't he?*
You don't know that he would, Sophie said, tossing her hair dismissively.
He probably would, George's grandmother said, *but what if*

he's not well enough to do so?

George sighed. And she rolled over again. Tomorrow… she would do something. Only… she was not quite sure what.

Check on him, insisted the angel of domesticity on the thirteenth day since George's last visit with Fryderyk, as large snowflakes drifted down from a gray December sky. *Find out how he is. And if he's not well, take care of him until he is.*

But that wouldn't be ladylike, Sophie cut in. *A lady doesn't bother her man with her questions. She waits for him to reach out to her.*

Now George's grandmother interrupted. *But the strong must look after the weak*, she said. *Fryderyk is weak. So what are you doing not taking action to find out if he desperately needs your help? What are you doing abandoning him in what might be his moment of need?*

George felt herself leaping to the tough, heroic side of the chasm inside her heart. And she strode into her kitchen to make muffins. She was going to find out how he was.

George made the muffins. And as she did, she continued to think. To wonder. And to doubt.

He's not failing to reach out to you because he's unwell, the angel of domesticity sneered. *He's turning away from you because he doesn't need you. Because he no longer cares about you. And because he doesn't want to see you again. You've scared him off because you're too much. And yet… and yet, you're not true woman enough. You never are. And you never will be. You can't do it, and you know you can't.*

What did I do on our last meeting that offended him? George wondered as she measured flour and sugar. *Hmm... We talked about Scarlatti... we went out for tea... and we came back to my place to hang out... and Marquis jumped up on him again. Only for a minute, but I saw him frown as he sat there picking each individual dog hair off of his black jacket. That must be it. That must be the reason... that he never wants to see me again.*

But doesn't he? her grandmother seemed to ask. *You know how much he depends on you. Even if he will never have romantic love for you, he won't reject the one who looks after him and keeps him safe. Go on. Take him the muffins and find out if he's still alive.*

So he's given up on you— good riddance, Sophie sneered. *He's gone back to Marja. And that's that. Now you can move on and find someone else... find someone who really loves you.*

George's grandmother sighed. And her expression changed. *He seemed to need you,* she said. *But on the other hand... maybe you don't need him. But I don't suppose you'll ever truly know until you find out.*

George turned away from the voices, putting the tins of muffins into the oven. And silently, she waited for them to bake. Finally, she was taking them out of the oven, wrapping them in a cloth and nestling them into an adorable little basket just right for presenting to the love of one's life. And with a veritable fire in her belly, she set off for Fryderyk's apartment, ready to take a risk.

She marched to his front door. And she stopped. Silently, George looked up at the apartment building, picturing Fryderyk inside, playing his piano, writing, reading with the dog, fixing himself a cup of tea... Stepping up to the door, she raised her hand to knock, her stomach twisting as her heart pounded, sweat beading on her forehead despite the December chill. Silently she stood there, willing her hand to move, struggling to force herself forward. She waited, the strong and the tender, certainty and doubt, battling one another into oblivion until rather than choosing a side of the chasm within her heart, she seemed to fall into its depths, flailing as she tumbled into darkness. She took a deep breath. And she turned and ran all the way home.

She shoved the muffins into the pantry. She had a good cry. And she wondered… what in the world she was supposed to do next.

16   Forbearance

It was a cold winter. And in her own way, George struggled. Her lungs were hale, but the cold and damp got into her bones, the oppressive clouds burdened her with frequent headaches, and the occasional head cold, slowing her down with coughs and sore throats, gave her more sympathy for Fryderyk than ever. Even as she wondered... how he was. And what he was doing.

She wondered. She worried. She prayed that he was, in fact, all right. And she waited. "I haven't heard from him in ages," she confided in Claudette on the fifteenth day of uncertainty. "It's been over two weeks. And I'm getting worried."

"You know where he lives," Claudette said. "It's only a mystery as long as you don't solve it."

Christmas came and went. George celebrated quietly, decorating her apartment, making Christmas sweets. And... thinking. Pondering. Wondering. Moping. Because again... she was alone at Christmas.

Move on, her mother scoffed on the twentieth day of silence. George blushed as she saw the embarrassing evening gown Sophie was wearing. *It's Christmas, my dear! And it's time to move on! Time to have some fun. Go to a party and find someone new. He's clearly not coming back. So celebrate your freedom by having a night out on the town and seeing where that takes you... seeing who you might find.*

George sighed. And she just shook her head.

Forget about him, the angel, Sophie, and George's grandmother all seemed to insist. *He's never coming back. What you thought you had was never as real as you hoped. And even if he honestly hoped to share in more with you, it's clearly not going to work out. You're wasting your time waiting for him any longer. So give up. And move on with your life.*

Either he's all right or he isn't, George mused to herself in the silence. *And until I find out... might as well be both at the same time. But when will I drum up the courage to find out which it is?*

The new year came, and George tried to prepare herself to welcome 1838 and whatever it would bring. *Should she write to him,* she asked herself on the twenty-fifth day since she'd seen Fryderyk. Or maybe to a mutual friend— Liszt? Delacroix? Although her fellow artists were honestly unlikely to know more than she did. Or should she just up and visit Fryderyk, invitation or no invitation? Or should she wait? Wait, possibly, for nothing at all?

She swallowed. And she closed her eyes. Maybe his silence... was his way of communicating that he, like so many before her, had left her. Had rejected her. Had moved on. The painful fear clawed at her, catching inside her throat. And she shook her head, feeling tears beginning to run down her cheeks, as she asked herself the question... if he had rejected her, did she even want to know? Which would hurt more... hearing him say the words that he didn't love her and didn't want to see her again, or never finding out at all? Which would break her heart for good... carrying the weight of never knowing how he really, truly felt, or confirming the worst? Could she go on forever in the impossible balancing act of maintaining both outcomes as being metaphorically true simultaneously, or would that break her? But if her heart was insisting she find out, how would she accept the outcome once it actually came? Did… did she even trust him enough to hear him say *no?*

Unwanted thoughts of Mallefille spun uninvited inside her mind; thoughts of the love they had once shared. The love that had unraveled into jealousy and frustration, grinding to a final, unhappy halt. And he had left, gone far away, taking his broken heart with him as he went to explore the rest of the Continent. It was over, what they had shared. But she wondered, shaking her head miserably… was it possible that what she had shared with Fryderyk was over… before it had even begun? Had their months of sweet friendship meant anything to him at all?

And the thought pierced her heart with uncertainty. Should she… keep looking? Should she… find someone else?

She wrote. George immersed herself in her writing once more, spending time with characters old and new. Amid their storylines she found consolation, distraction, a positive use of time and energy. And in this use of time, she found joy. Peace. Safety. A refuge from the world around her and all its confusing knowns and unknowns; from the maddening mysteries of real-life relationships, whose frustrating, tangled convolutions never went as neatly as they could in the perimeters of a carefully-measured plot. Losing herself in the safe, beautiful mirror-world of her imagination, she sometimes almost forgot about Fryderyk. Almost. But not quite.

Faithfully, George waited. Thirty days became forty, fifty, sixty. Slowly, sadly, the happy times she'd spent with Fryderyk became more a beloved memory of what might have been, rather than something she was actively looking forward to recapturing. And slowly, wistfully, she began to ask herself what the future held. But then— she was out for coffee one day in the early spring of 1838, disguised from the world in a waistcoat and trousers, when a familiar cough made her whirl around.

"Fryderyk!" she cried. He stood there just inside the entrance of the café, his face lighting up as he saw her. His face... that was so pale, so much thinner than last she'd seen him, his eyes hollow and ringed with dark shadows. He stood there bent like an old man, huddled into a coat that seemed much too large for him, a wisp of musical genius that could be knocked sprawling by the touch of a feather.

George ran to him, reaching out to take his hands in hers as her heart began to race, her breath coming in gasps of delighted shock. Frozen and skeletal, his hands sought hers, his long fingers intertwining with hers as they stood together like the only two souls in the universe, staring at one another in a silent greeting.

George caught her breath, taking half a step backward. "How... how are you?" she asked softly, biting her lip as she took him in again; his gaunt face, the frailty in which he stood there almost shaking with the brutal effort of leaving the house.

Fryderyk just shook his head. "A little better," he said hoarsely. "I... I've been pretty badly off," he admitted. "With pneumonia. I was stuck in bed for a couple of weeks, coughing up blood."

George's heart seemed to break. And it was all she could do to restrain herself from throwing her arms around her friend and holding him to her heart.

"I… I'm sorry," was all she could manage. "Are you… are you any better?"

He gave her a small smile. "Well, I'm out of bed, aren't I? Doctor says I'm finally out of danger. Got the 'all clear' to be up and about. It's… it's taking awhile to recuperate, but I am getting stronger. I'm definitely on the other side of the worst."

George nodded, feeling her forehead crinkling in a painful frown as she bit her lip, fighting back tears for what he had just endured. "Oh, I'm glad to hear that, at least." She paused, looking him up and down again; the way that simply standing there seemed to be actively wearing him out. She glanced into the interior of the café. "I want to hear all about it," she said. "Can we sit down, and talk? And you can tell me everything."

Fryderyk nodded. And they found a table where they could sit.

George looked at him. "I… I wish I could have been there. Wish I could have helped." She swallowed, a sudden ember of anger, of hurt, confusion, disappointment, even betrayal, kindling inside her heart. "At first I thought you were composing," she continued. "And then I— I thought you went back to Marja, or found someone else, or even went home to Poland. I thought… you didn't want to see me again. Thought you didn't need me." Fryderyk blinked in surprise, but she went on, offering the heavy, painful feelings she had carried inside for the past weeks.

"I've written two books in that span, but I certainly would have left them for you, if I'd have known you were sick. If I'd have known you needed me." She swallowed again, looking down at her hands, clenched in her lap. "Nothing is more important than my dear friend." She looked up at Fryderyk, unclenching one hand and slowly offering it to him. Slowly, gently, he took it in his, the wrinkle in his forehead deepening as he silently took in her words.

George sighed, then went on, her voice catching. "So why… why didn't you reach out to me, call on me, when you needed me, best friend? Don't you know how much I care? I would have come in a heartbeat. You know I would have." George blinked back tears; tears that started out angry, then faded into a pensive disappointment. And fervently, she squeezed Fryderyk's cold hand. "I want to help you. And I want to be there for you— I will always be there for you. Always."

She looked at him, allowing the ache in her throat to release; allowing two tears to slide down her cheeks. And she waited for what he would say.

Fryderyk gave a heavy, wistful sigh, looking down at their entwined hands. "I… I'm sorry, George," he said softly, his words coming haltingly, thoughtfully. "I do know how much you care. And I do need you. I never meant to shut you out, never meant to make you think I'd gone away and was never coming back, never meant to make you think I didn't want to see you. Never."

He shook his head, an expression crossing his face that she could not interpret. "I… I really was very sick. I don't remember much of my illness, I admit— it was mostly just me and the doctor, and I was drifting in and out of fever for days on end. But if I'd have known… if I'd have known you were worried, if I'd have known you were feeling hurt, if I'd have thought to myself of how you would have set aside everything to come and help me… of course, I would have called. And I would have been glad to have you there with me."

George looked at him through her tears. And she just nodded. The words *I wish I had been* were redundant.

Fryderyk gently squeezed her hand, blinking back what might have been tears of his own. "So, thank you, George," he said softly, his weary eyes lighting up with gratitude as a small smile touched his translucent face. "I… I can't tell you how much that means to hear. My dear friend."

George returned the smile, illuminating it with all the love inside her heart. She squeezed his hand back. But she said nothing.

Fryderyk gave a breathy chuckle. "I thought…" he said softly, "Once I was awake and thinking again, I thought maybe you would come bursting through the door one day."

"I almost did," George said with a breathy chuckle of her own. "I made muffins and everything… but I didn't know. I just didn't know… what you were doing, or if you would want to see me."

Fryderyk squeezed her hand, shaking his head lovingly. "Of course, I would have wanted to," he reassured her. "Of course, I would have. This, today, was my first day out of the house to test how I'm doing, and if I did well enough, I was actually going to come visit you later this afternoon."

George looked at him, the fear she had been carrying that he never wanted to see her again jumping to gratitude that he had missed her in their separation, then leapfrogging to a hope that he wasn't disappointed that she hadn't come to check on him.

"You were?"

He smiled. "I was. I've missed you, George."

She sighed, again resisting the urge to stand up and hug him. "I've missed you, too."

Fryderyk heaved a sigh of his own, then straightened up in his seat, looking at her with a different light in his eyes. "I'm just so glad to see you again."

She nodded, eyes brimming with more tears. "I'm so glad to see *you* again. Do you... do you want to order lunch together? And... you can come over today, if you want."

Fryderyk smiled. "Sounds good." And kissing her hand, he picked up the menu.

Pneumonia... coughing up blood... George bit her lip as she rode home from lunch in her carriage with the promise of a visit from Fryderyk late that afternoon, blinking back tears as she thought of it, her poor, dear friend beset by pneumonia. She imagined him lying in bed, tossing and turning, burning with fever. And she wondered... who all had taken care of him.

He didn't leave me, she told the thoughts of her mother and grandmother before they could offer their observations. *He was too sick to get in touch. But he's going to be all right.*

Too sick to get in touch, maybe, her grandmother replied, putting her hands on her hips and raising a silver eyebrow... *But you know what that means. It means he had someone else taking care of him. Even if it really was only the doctor, he could have called for you early on, when he was still well enough to summon the doctor, if he had really wanted to. But he didn't. He relied on someone else. And his heart is not yours.*

Now George's mother cut in. *Who sat at his bedside?* Sophie seemed to ask her daughter. *Wiping his feverish face with a cool cloth, bringing him water, making him soup and tea and oatmeal? Will you get up the courage to ask him? And even if you do, will he tell you the truth?*

George shook her head. The unkindness of those words slashed at her heart. And she fought to argue that they were not true. And yet... unkind and unnecessary as they may have been, they forced her to wonder... what was true. And what the future held.

Give me wisdom, she prayed as she had so many times before. *Help me find the truth.*

She wondered. And yet, she smiled as a sense of certainty settled over her heart, a welcome answer to her prayer. He hadn't abandoned her. And if he had had the strength to reach out to her, to ask her to come to his side, he would have called. And she would have come.

"How was your Christmas?" Fryderyk asked as they shared a brief visit at her apartment later that afternoon. George handed him his hot chocolate, then took a sip of her own.

"Quiet," she admitted. Reaching out, she patted his hand. "I would have loved to have spent it with you."

Fryderyk smiled. "I didn't get to celebrate Christmas at all," he said sadly. "I was in bed with a high fever, coughing up blood. Thinking back, I can't even remember for certain which day of my illness *was* Christmas. They've kind of blurred together."

George tried to offer a poignant little smile. "Well," she said, "we could make Christmas cookies together, if you want."

Fryderyk smiled. "I'd really like that."

"He's all right," George announced to Claudette over a game of cards at her friend's chilly apartment. "Or he will be. He's been sick, but he's on the other side of the worst now."

Claudette played a card. "Then why don't you look happy?" she asked.

George just shook her head.

184

Three days later, George spent time with another friend... but this time, her friend was the one who needed answers from her.

Pauline sat down in George's living room, wiping her eyes. "So, what do I do? Alfred has already asked me to marry him..."

Sitting down beside her on the couch, George took her hand. "You say *no*," she said gently. Pauline just gave another sob, burying her face in her handkerchief.

"But he's so romantic!"

"He's also a train wreck and a trash fire and a hornet's nest you don't want to touch with a three-meter pole! I know Alfred de Musset, Pauline— better than I ever might have wanted to— and I promise you that if you accept his proposal, you will regret it for the rest of your life."

George gazed down into the tear-filled eyes of the lovesick seventeen-year-old in front of her. Pauline García, the young Spanish opera singer, wiped them on her sleeve, then looked up at George again.

"But Alfred is such an angel to me... and he promised he'd change, because he cares about me so much, and I believe that he can—"

"He told me the same thing," George said, shaking her head. "And I suppose that he did... but he only got worse. Musset has problems... that I can't fix, that you can't fix, that no one but he can fix. His own battles to fight. And I promise you... he is not worth your time. I know only too well how appealing he can be, but he is not... worth your time. And no matter his good intentions... he can't keep the promises he makes."

George scooted closer, putting her arm around Pauline and letting her rest her head on her shoulder. "I know it hurts," she said quietly. "I've been there. Many times. But it's not the end of the world."

Blowing her nose, Pauline slowly looked up. "It's not?" she asked.

Softly, George smiled. And she shook her head. "It's not."

17   A Bond is Forged

Slowly, Fryderyk improved, regaining the strength that the pneumonia had stolen from him. And he and George resumed their casual routine of meeting for tea here and there; spending afternoons cooking together at her apartment or baking cookies at his. Together they gained. They grew. And they grew… closer.

And yet… *Marja Wodzińska*. The name followed George around inside her mind through the spring of 1838, dogging her through the days and nights. *No longer engaged… her family made us break it off…* George remembered the catch she had heard in Fryderyk's voice as he had said those words so many months ago; the sadness that had glistened in his eyes. The heartbreak he had shared with his trusted friend. And a small part of her still wondered, his reassuring promises notwithstanding, where Fryderyk's heart truly, truly lay. Especially in all that remained unspoken in terms of just who had nursed him through his illness. And a small part of her wondered if she… George shook her head. If she should be pursuing him in any way.

She knew they were no longer technically together. Knew that Marja's family had separated them; that the young woman was not waiting for Fryderyk to come home to her and make her his bride. And yet, the small part of George's heart that ached with uncertainty grew as the days and nights passed; grew into a swelling tide of doubt that eclipsed all other thoughts, hopes, and dreams. And the wisdom she continued to pray for had not yet made itself apparent.

A thousand times, she almost asked him— the simple question, *Do you love Marja?,* on her very lips. But a thousand times, something stopped her. Because what kind of a way to ask was that?

They were friends; a pair of artists who understood one another in a way that no one else could. But were they… *were* they… more? And would they ever be?

The question grew, the uncertainty chasing her through her days; tormenting her at night. Every day, every night, the voices of her mother and grandmother seemed to interrogate her, grilling her as to what Fryderyk really thought of her, insisting that he didn't really care, or at the very least, not in the way she might have hoped. And the question she could not answer chased her relentlessly, plaguing her hour by hour, as painfully as the questions she had asked in the absence caused by his illness. And again, the status quo of the two possible outcomes, that he was still with Marja and had separated from her, being true simultaneously was not good enough. She had to know for sure.

George got out her stationery. And she expressed her ocean of concerns to her acquaintance Wojciech Grzymała, good friend of Fryderyk's that he was, begging him for clarity.

Had I known that there was a prior attachment in our dear boy's life… I would never have bent down to breathe the scent of a flower intended for some other altar. … His happiness is sacred to me.

… I have no wish to steal anyone from anyone, unless it be prisoners from their jailers, victims from their executioners, Poland from Russia.

Perhaps you had better consider reassuring him that I am not currently in a relationship… I had considered it a fine thing that he abstained out of respect for me, out of shyness, even out of

fidelity to another. There was an element of sacrifice in all that,
and hence strength and chastity as properly understood. It was
that which charmed and allured me the most in him. ...He said, I
think, that "certain actions" might spoil our memories. It was
foolish of him to say that, wasn't it? And can he mean it? Tell me,
what wretched woman has left him with such impressions of
physical love? Poor angel.

...If his happiness depends, or is going to depend, on her, let
him go his way. If he is to be unhappy, prevent it! If I can make
him happy without putting an end to the happiness he receives
from her, I can adopt the same attitude. If he cannot obtain
happiness from me without being unhappy on her account, we
must avoid each other and he must forget me. ...I will be firm on
this, I promise you: for far as future is at stake, and if I have no
great virtue so far as I myself am concerned, I am ready to
sacrifice myself for one whom I love. You must tell me the plain
truth. I rely on you and expect it from you. There is no point in
your writing me a letter which I can show to justify myself.

Over the course of thirty-two pages George explained her
situation and dilemma; the ethical question of whether it was right
for her to have any involvement with Fryderyk while Marja
Wodzińska remained in his heart— and her uncertainty as to
whether Marja remained in his heart at all. She read it through,
making sure she had her thoughts in order in a form that would be
in some way intelligible. And she sent it off.

Two days later, a letter almost as thick as the one George had
just sent arrived in the post. And she smiled to see that Wojciech
had written back.

Have no fear that you are intruding upon an existing romance, he reassured her. *Countess Wodzińska has made it clear to our friend that marriage to her daughter is not a realistic prospect. As the fragility of his constitution has left him unable to pass a full winter in uninterrupted good health, the Countess fears to allow her daughter to marry, even for love, one whose early death would only leave her a young widow. Marja's family has already securely betrothed her to Józef Skarbek, and the two of them are happy. Neither you nor Fryderyk should allow your hearts to be troubled by the slightest bit of anxiety for Marja. All is well with her. And her future is secure.*

Fryderyk has no obligation toward her... and neither, he has told me, does his attachment to her remain. He remembers her fondly and wishes her well, but he neither pines for her nor loses sleep over what they might have had. Whether he will give his heart to you I cannot say, but it does not belong to Marja... He is free to give it to whom he chooses.

Do as your heart guides you... and treat our friend with gentleness. And if you establish a bond, whether the two of you bind your souls in the matrimony of the church or embrace at the altar of art, I implore you... remain faithful to him. Commit to him. And do not add to his pain. If you choose him, you choose him until death.

George smiled down at the letter, releasing a heavy sigh full of tension and worry, breathing a prayer of gratitude as the weight of so many weeks of mystery lifted from her shoulders. So there was no current romance still blossoming between Fryderyk and Marja. Nothing for her to intrude upon. Nothing... George felt her smile grow into a grin as her heart swelled. Nothing standing between them. Now there was hope… hope that what they had could grow into something deeper. Now that she knew that it was appropriate for her to ask him about becoming a couple.

Then a small cloud seemed to pass in front of the bright sunshine of her joy and hope. Nothing… but the fragile health that had prevented Fryderyk's marriage to Marja.

He didn't leave me, and he's no longer courting Marja, George thought before her mother or grandmother could offer a word of complaint. *And there's no reason for me not to ask him about courting… ask him again, that is. Although last time… he said* no. *But he's definitely not with Marja anymore. So there's nothing to bar me from bringing it up again when the moment is right.*

Sophie seemed to shake her head, curling her red lip in disdain. *Nothing but the fact that he's going to be dead before he's forty.*

George shook her head with a sigh. And she went to go make herself a cup of tea.

One breezy spring morning when the sun kept disappearing and reappearing among the fluffy clouds, George and Fryderyk took a carriage ride together. Dreamily, they rode along a lane of pear trees resplendent in fragrant blossoms. And softly, he laid his head on her shoulder; her shoulder that was suited up in a shirt, a waistcoat, and a jacket just like his.

She looked at him. And she swallowed. Finally, after so long, she was ready to ask him. He wasn't strong. No man was. So she would be. And now that she was free to do so, secure in the knowledge that nothing… and no one… stood between them, it was time to step up.

Except… She paused. For the conversation they'd had during

the winter… the conversation when she'd asked Fryderyk if they were courting and he'd said they weren't, holding up the perfection of the friendship he didn't want to ever change. If she loved him, was the best way of showing him staying eternally in the *let's-stay-friends* of the platonic companionship they shared, sharing the artistic bond that only they could ever truly grasp without ever hoping for more? Or, if she truly loved him, with a romantic love that seemed to outshine the very stars and delve deeper than the bottomless sea; to outdepth and outfathom the boundless universe itself… did she have to tell him?

She bit her lip, paralyzed with painful indecision. What if by asking, she changed everything? Ruined everything? What if he walked away from her?

Don't do it, her mother seemed to warn. *It won't be worth the heartbreak.*

Don't bother, her grandmother said. *You know what he'll say.*

But another voice, a voice whose source she could not identify, gently spoke up. *If you don't ask him, you'll never know. Some risks… must be taken.*

George took a deep breath. And to that new voice, she chose to listen. She moved a little closer to Fryderyk, and he sat up straight, looking at her with a smile. She offered her hand, and he rested his hand on hers. It was so thin, so cold… She put her other hand on top to try to warm it up.

"F… Fryderyk," she whispered, "can I ask you something?"

He looked back at her, eyes wide, face open, ready to answer any question… or at least any question but the one she was about to ask.

"Yes, of course."

She took a deep breath. She swallowed. And, heart pounding,

she threw caution to the winds and went for it, tossing her question into the universe like a coin into a wishing-well.

"Fryderyk... what would you say if... if I... asked you if I could have permission to court you?"

His face went blank. Her entire being seeming to contract, retreating into its protective shell, George bit her lip, stomach clenching as her heart and mind threatened to crack into a thousand spinning fragments of regret at her impetuous stupidity; her idiotic impulsivity. What had she done? Would this ruin everything? Would he even want to be friends anymore? Was this the end?

She held her breath, forcing herself to wait for his answer as she forced herself not to close her eyes, forced herself to keep looking at him, forced the expression on her face to remain politely neutral. And silently, the question hung in the air between them like a ghost.

Fryderyk paused. He took a reflective breath. He looked at her. And slowly, slowly, the biggest smile she'd seen spread across his thin face. He squeezed her hand. "I think I'd like that. I... I'm in love with you, too."

Fryderyk's eyes were shining. And George caught her breath as a warm rush of desire pushed her forward. *Kiss him!* the angel of domesticity seemed to insist. *You know you want to!*

But George paused. And with a silent smile, she shook her head at the angel. *Not yet*, she said calmly. *Not yet. I do want to, but he's not ready. And if he's not ready, we're not ready. But that's all right*, she summed up. *True love will wait. And this is true love.*

Returning to the moment, George smiled at Fryderyk. Silently, she opened her arms, and silently, he scooted closer. And they sealed their love with a hug.

The next morning, bright and early, George hurried to Claudette's house. She had some news.

"Oh, George!" Claudette said with a smile, opening the door just a crack and gathering her dressing-gown more closely around herself. "Come in, come in, before someone sees me like this!"

"I'm sorry; I just couldn't wait!" George sighed, floating into the room. "I have to tell you everything! And you're telling me that you wear all kinds of fantastical costumes on stage, but you're embarrassed about your nightclothes?"

"Everything about what?" Claudette asked, closing the door behind George and walking into the kitchen, which, unlike George's, was neat as a pin, kitted out with all kinds of exotic ceramics, the window looking out onto Claudette's backyard, bursting with flowers and singing with birds, flanked by heavy curtains of dark blue fabric twinkling with a delicate pattern of gold embroidery. "Is this about Fryderyk? Do you want some coffee?"

"Coffee would be lovely." Dramatically, George sank down onto the couch in Claudette's sitting room, a squashy, overstuffed piece of furniture upholstered in ornate, vaguely Oriental, textiles. "And for your information, we have a thing."

Claudette looked up from pouring the coffee into little Turkish-style porcelain cups. "You have a 'thing'?"

George grinned. "Yes! We're courting!"

Claudette shook her head as she handed George her coffee. "Well, congratulations, George— you scored yourself a Polish corpse."

194

George blinked. "Polish corpse?" She rolled her eyes. "Claudette, he may be a little short and a little skinny, but he is *not* a corpse."

"He almost was this past winter," Claudette said mildly, raising an eyebrow as she took a sip of coffee.

George just gave a dismissive *tsk*. "He is strong," she countered. "Really. Inside his heart. And that's all that matters, anyway."

Claudette sighed, shaking her head. "Courting? Really?"

"I think so... Well, almost. I asked if it was all right for me to court him, and he said it was. He wants to spend time with me, Claudette. We're going to the theater next week."

Claudette sat down next to George and looked at her with another sigh.

"You've already been to the theater with him. What makes this any different? And George... what do you see in him? He's all bones, he's afraid of everything that moves, he can't breathe for coughing, and he looks like he'll blow away on the next windy day. Even if you got him to settle down with you, he'd last what, two, three years? And then what? You spend the rest of your life missing him. Is it really worth it?"

George shook her head, gazing contemplatively down into her coffee cup. "I don't know... it's strange... I've always loved taking care of people, and... I don't know... it just seems like he needs me. Even more than Musset or Mallefille or Casimir did. Almost... almost like my father needed my grandmother."

Claudette shook her head. "You mean like a kid needs his mother? He *needs* a *doctor*," she said, patting George's hand. "I'm sure he can afford one."

"We'll just see where it goes," George said, sitting back and taking another sip of coffee.

Claudette just shook her head. "All I can wish you is the best."

So, you've done it, George's grandmother seemed to say.

George smiled. *Yes, I have. We're officially courting now.*

Her grandmother sighed, shaking her gray head as a sad warning seemed to shine from her wise blue eyes. *All right, then. Enjoy it while it lasts. But don't say I didn't warn you… amid all the good qualities he may have, there is something more of a child in him than there is in most men. And he will always need you. Need your faithfulness.*

George nodded. *Well, I will always be there for him to need.*

She turned to her mother, staring boldly into Sophie's painted eyes. *I didn't scare him off*, she announced proudly. *I can't have. He's mine.*

Sophie just shook her head.

The world shone, sang, danced, glittered. George floated through her days, lifting up prayers of gratitude, her feet barely seeming to touch the ground. Because she… was courting Fryderyk. His heart was hers. The sweet friend, the elegant gentleman, the genius composer, whose brilliance had stolen her heart the first time she'd heard his music. The loving patience she had offered in months of platonic companionship… had been more than worth it. He was hers.

He loves me, she announced to her mother and grandmother. *Really loves me. And we are happy… truly happy.*

Really? Sophie seemed to ask, raising a dark eyebrow.

Her grandmother shook her silver head. *Enjoy being his*

mother, then.

It won't last, her past told her. *Never has, never will.*
It will, she said. *This time, it will.*

George wished herself the best. And so did the angel of domesticity that lived inside her mind; the angel who dreamed of the prince on the white horse who would one day arrive to make her the woman she dreamed of being... the woman she should be. The happy woman that every one of her protagonists eventually blossomed into.

Living as an independent, unattached spinster, she could fix her own problems. But was it possible that only once she found the right man would she become the perfect woman? Was she too fierce? And was tempering that fierceness with the sweetness of the angel that tiptoed around inside her heart her only hope?

Is Fryderyk... George wondered. She sighed. *Is Fryderyk the man who can help me find what I'm looking for?*

And yet, she shook her head as she remembered what her grandmother had seemed to say. *Maybe he can help me*, she said to herself, *and maybe I can help him, but I'm not going to be his mother. And he's not going to be my child. We've discussed it. And it's settled.*

18   Doubt

Courting… George shook her head. What a word. What a thought. What a concept. What a thing… the goal of so many, and yet not their ultimate goal— it was the foreword, the introduction, the prelude, the overture, toward the saga, the grand concerto, the magnum opus, of marriage. And yet…

She swallowed. Not for her. She'd come within a hairsbreadth of marriage, and in that hairsbreadth, knew she had dodged a bullet. Marriage… much as it made others happy, was not for her. And she knew it wasn't. And if the courting that she and Fryderyk were doing stayed exactly as it was forever, built upon this firm foundation of loving friendship and the unique bond of artistic companionship, she would be happy.

George thought of it. Putting on a wedding dress, standing there beside Fryderyk as an old man said "man and wife," going to sleep and waking up beside her fellow artist, joining herself to him body and soul, united before God and man by vows and paperwork. Permanently joined. Irrevocably bound. Til death should they part. Permanently establishing herself as a second-class citizen, an auxiliary part of her husband, hobbled by the Napoleonic Code that legally obligated her to obey her husband and raise the children whose sole custody belonged to their father.

The Napoleonic Code, the biased laws and webs of hypocrisy from which she had fled from a young age, forging her own path and finding her own future, walking alone in trousers and a top hat in the independence for which she had fought, free from the chains of prejudice against her gender. She could not have both marriage and freedom. But she could have both love and freedom.

She thought of it. And she shook her head. What she and Fryderyk had right now… what they had right now was too perfect to change in any way… too perfect to ruin with the baggage, the particular complexities, of marriage. Too perfect to throw away a lifetime's hard work spent fighting for equality just to claim the status of *Madame Chopin*. With Casimir, she had come close enough to marriage to know that setting a romance in the hard stone of wedlock— combining finances, traveling together, living together day in and day out— and, most problematically, accepting the secondary status of *wife*— was not the next best step, the logical conclusion, of every relationship, however loving. And her marrying Fryderyk… would not truly bring what they had to new heights.

But Fryderyk, now that they were, in so many words, definitely, absolutely, officially courting… would he expect this to lead to marriage, and for her to ask him someday? Was that what he wanted? Was that what would make him truly happy?

And what would he say… if she never asked?

George sighed. And she turned it around in her mind. Because… maybe, rather than waiting for her, he would ask her someday. Though he was rarely the one who took the initiative, if this was genuinely important to him, he would certainly take the lead on it someday, if she never did. At some point, he would grow tired of waiting. And if he did… how could she say *no* without ruining the perfection they were sharing? How could she convince him of the steadfastness of her love without either disappointing him or compromising in a way that would destroy them?

George shook her head. How?

She thought again of the partnership they had formed; the ways in which they endeavored to work together and to help and serve one another. Of the discomfort she still sometimes felt when Fryderyk took it upon himself to help her in or out of a carriage or carry a heavy bag for her. And of the flex inside her heart that urged her to be the one to offer gentlemanly chivalry toward him, rejecting the chivalry he offered her. And she shook her head again as she asked herself the question… did she trust him enough to accept what he wanted to give her and do for her… to let him be a man?

"George," Fryderyk asked quietly one day as they sat on a bench in the park, watching the birds, "how long have you been wanting to court me?"

George felt her face grow hot in a blush. She looked down, adjusting the cuffs of her jacket; smoothing her cravat. She swallowed. And she opened her mouth to release the truth.

"Ever since I first saw you," she admitted haltingly, her voice hoarse with embarrassment.

He looked at her, his keen glance only a pale blur in her peripheral vision. "So why didn't you ask me earlier? I mean, really, really ask me?"

She swallowed again, avoiding his eye by continuing to adjust her cuffs and gloves. "Well, I… I knew about Marja," she stammered as her face grew even hotter, "and if she and you were courting, I didn't want to get in the way of that."

"But then you did start courting me," he followed up with a slight frown which she caught out of the corner of her eye. He paused. "If you were waiting because you thought she and I were courting, then what brought you to the conclusion that that was no longer true? You were correct, but what changed?" He shook his head. "And we... we talked about the idea of courting back during the winter, and I told you how much I cared about you... as my best friend." He looked at her. "What changed?" he asked again.

George fiddled with her sleeve again, keeping her eyes lowered as her heart thudded and her stomach twisted within her. Suddenly the day was becoming very warm. "I know we talked about it... and I don't want to *really* change things... but I just..." She found herself smiling as she remembered how she had felt, taking up her pen to ask Wojciech what was the right thing to do. "Had to take the risk of asking you." George paused, swallowing loudly. "And so, I... I wrote to Wojciech; he's such a good friend of yours, and I thought he'd know... know if it was in any way appropriate for me to ask you..."

Fryderyk gave her another little frown, which she glimpsed in her peripheral vision. "You wrote to him to ask if it was all right to court me— to ask if I was still courting Marja? Why wouldn't you ask me directly? I would have told you."

George felt a sinking in her stomach. She closed her eyes, body wracked with pain, weary heart contracting as it froze, shriveling into an apprehensive fist and retreating miserably behind the high walls that protected it, fleeing wildly from the faintest scent of broken trust... even if she had been the one to break it. This was it... she had failed. Yes, he had accepted her request to court him, but now that he knew the whole story, he was going to reject her.

Told you so, mocked the voice of her mother. *Told you so.*

George felt tears prickling in her eyes. "I... I'm sorry," she faltered through the lump in her throat, still unable to meet his eye as her face burned and her stomach roiled, sweat dampening the palms of her gloves as her shoulders tensed, her jaw tightening and her shallow breath confining itself to her throat. And the painful, striving flex within her troubled heart, the agonizing knot of tangled yarn, drew tighter still. "I just thought… I don't know what I thought."

She felt Fryderyk touch her hand. She flinched, almost withdrawing hers from his gentle grasp. But somehow… she didn't. Slowly, he drew her white-gloved hand to his mouth, pressing it to his lips in a gentle kiss… even as George fleetingly wondered what would have gone through the minds of any passerby, had the park not been so quiet on this particular May afternoon.

"Don't you trust me?" Fryderyk asked softly.

George felt herself blinking back tears. Slowly, she nodded, and slowly she looked up, finally looking into his eyes. His were warm and loving, open to her words and her account of why she had done what she had done. And her heart overflowed as she remembered the pain with which she had wondered if, had she asked him who had cared for him during his illness, he would have told her the truth.

"Yes," she whispered finally, "but I guess I wasn't sure… if I trusted you enough… to hear *no*."

"You wouldn't have," he said, gently shaking his head. "And you won't." He smiled. "If you're going to court me… let me court you as well. I trust you… and I want you to be able to trust me back. So please, don't be afraid… to ask any questions you need to ask. All right?"

George wiped her eyes, allowing the first deep breath she seemed to have taken all day fill her lungs as her anxious body slowly relaxed in relief, letting go of the miserable tension to which it had so desperately clung as she had waited for the verdict he would pass; the verdict that would determine the trajectory of the future of their relationship. Her weary heart stopped pounding. And somehow, she felt it beginning to open, the hard knot of tangled yarn inside slowly, gently loosening just a little. And as she let her heart open, a feeling of peace finally began to descend.

She nodded, slowly unwinding in relief and exhaustion. "All right."

George went home, worn out. She took off her gloves and cravat, laying them aside as she sat down on her bed with a hot cup of tea. *Why hadn't she asked him directly?* she demanded of herself. *What had held her back? Why had she been so afraid?*

She hadn't wanted to ruin what they had. And what with Wojciech already being there, and an acquaintance to both of them, it had just seemed... expedient... to use him as a middleman. She knew why she was afraid. And she knew why she held back. And yet, with Fryderyk, she knew more than ever... that she did not have to.

You're here... The maiden sighed inside her tower, seeing the prince in the distance on his white stallion; the prince who carried the key to her heart, her life, her tower. The prince who could free her to become who she really was.

Fryderyk... George sighed. He may have lacked the physical prowess that her previous beaus had flexed. But his inner strength... his courage, his patience, his determination... that was what took her breath away.

But that wasn't the only way in which he was different from her previous beaus. Fryderyk... he cared. Really cared. When he saw her, his eyes lit up. And together, they shared their art with one another, the author and the composer rejoicing together over their shared passion.

It was… refreshing. And George found herself blinking back tears as he welcomed her into his home for a quiet afternoon of pleasant companionship. Because with him… she had finally found the belonging she had always searched for. Because with him… she could breathe. In the loving embrace of his judgment-free affection, the friendship through which they freed one another, she was safe. And she could just… *be.* Be her authentic self; celebrating every bit of unique weirdness that made her her. Even as she gave Fryderyk space to celebrate every bit of the quirky eccentricity and exquisite sensitivity that made him him. They created a sacred space for one another. And in this sacred space, they held one another.

It was strange, though. And a thousand times, George bit back the words that rose inside her mind; the words her grandmother would say, shaking her silver head in disappointment at how her granddaughter was handling things.

What are you doing, my lad? Why aren't you stepping up? Can't you see that he needs you? He will break if you don't take care of him; if you don't do everything for him. Break like all the others. And he'll leave you because you're not giving him what he needs. Not doing enough. Not being enough. Just like all the others. No matter how faithful you are. But don't be too much… Heaven forbid that you be too much. Because then you'll frighten him off. Don't forget that you are the woman. But don't let him be the man. Because he can't. None of them can. And you know that. They're all breakable little boys; little boys who should have stayed on their mothers' laps.

*So if you stay with him, that's what you're going to have to be.
His mother.*

Why won't you listen? her mother now seemed to ask her
inside her mind, rolling her eyes as she gave a sarcastic *tsk. And
find a man like your father, so you can have what he and I had?
And yet... and yet, you know you'll never keep him like this. You'll
never keep him if you insist on playing the man. But if you insist
on playing the man, you need to find someone who's more man
than you are. Unlike your little Polish corpse.*

George shook her head at Sophie. *Why would you ever think I
would take relationship advice from you?* she countered bitterly.
*You were wrong about everything. Every time. And I refuse to be
like you. Whatever you were, I will be the opposite. Maybe
Grandmother was not always right. But you were always wrong.
Besides which, I am stepping up. I am helping him. Half the time
he needs to cook anything, I'm there to help him, and we walk
arm in arm in the park, especially if it gets lumpy or he's a bit
tired. I'm definitely doing my part, pulling my weight in this
relationship... and then some. And yet... it's all so mutual. He's
not a child, and he does plenty for himself, and for me. And the
ways that he needs me to help him here and there are not the ways
I would help a child. We help one another up hills, we open doors
for one another, we fetch things for one another... we help one
another with everything. And it's beautifully balanced.*

Why do I listen to either of you, anyway? she demanded.
*Mother, Grandmother? You are so confusing— you say to do all
this for him and yet not to be too much... Get out of my head.
You're crazy. You're impossible.* Throwing her hands into the air,
she walked away, ending the conversation. And making herself a
cup of tea, she went on with her day.

George was happy. And yet… and yet, the nights after her agreement with Fryderyk that they would begin courting found her tossing and turning in an agony of doubt. Fryderyk's face danced before her sleepless eyes; his eyes, his hands, his slender frame. And his smile. The smile that lit up his face whenever he saw her; the smile that was always accompanied with a sweet word of gratitude for her presence; for her very existence.

His smiles made her smile. And yet… she sighed. Wondered. And tossed and turned as the thoughts chased one another around her uncertain heart. Because the perfection they shared… could she believe in it? Did she dare hope that she could truly trust in it? His settled separation from Marja notwithstanding, was all this… the friendship that had grown into courting, the ideal artistic partnership into which she and Fryderyk had settled… actually too good to be true? Too perfect to believe? Any day now, would it end? Would Fryderyk tire of her? Realize that she was, in fact, too much or not enough? Meet someone else with whom he got on even better, relegating her once more to the platonic friendship in which she had loved him for so many months before they had begun courting? Go back to Poland to be with his family?

George rolled over in bed as an even worse thought made the pit of her stomach go hollow. Would he, perish the thought, turn out to be the worst liar in history, everything he'd ever said insincere, calculated manipulations intended to draw her close only for him to one day betray her? Or would a sudden illness take him from her? What they had right now, perfect as it seemed… would it last? Or would fate or circumstance whisk it away from them like a gust of wind blowing out a candle? Would every good thing they were currently sharing one day suddenly

206

disappear? His agreement to begin courting notwithstanding, what, deeply, truly, and honestly, did he want out of this relationship? And where would it all go?

Each time the thoughts came, rolling over her mind like waves on the beach, George rolled over, struggling to quiet them; struggling to sleep. And so she went on, weighed down by the exhausting burden of doubt. In yet another, brand-new form of uncertainty mysteriously unlike the bouts of confusing vagueness she had known with her previous beaus, she went on. And she hoped, prayed, that time would bring all the answers to her questions. And that they would be the answers she wanted.

"Congratulations," Wojciech said warmly, shaking Fryderyk's hand and then George's at a salon at Hector Berlioz's home. He raised an eyebrow. "I did wonder about you two. Fryderyk's told me so much about you, Madame Sand, and his eyes light up whenever he speaks of you."

George grinned, feeling her face warming in a blush of delight. "But we haven't said a word. Is it that obvious?"

Wojciech returned her smile. "Love is always obvious."

George just squeezed Fryderyk's hand.

Their love was real. And it was obvious, both to them and to those who watched them from a distance. But how real *was* it? And would it last?

So, George's mother seemed to ask, *now that you're a couple, when are you going to move in together?*

George looked at her. *Excuse me?*

Sophie shrugged. *With all the others, it didn't take long before*

you were sharing a house… and a bed. What about Fryderyk?
When are you going to invite him to live with you? She gave a
saucy wink. *And sleep with you?*

George sighed. And she just shook her head. *I don't know*, she
said simply. *Not yet, that's for sure. Not yet.*

19   The Artists

George's mother and grandmother continued to complain, continued to berate her for everything she was doing and failing to do; her failure to live up to everything they wanted for her at the same time; to perfectly capture the balance she still struggled to strike. And their criticisms ached inside her weary heart; ached until she was almost too tired to enjoy the days she spent walking tall and proud through town, too weary to enjoy the days she spent baking cookies or embroidering beautiful handkerchiefs, too worn-out to enjoy spending time with Fryderyk, which was often the most challenging setting of all in which to live out a true balance between valor and tenderness.

"Is everything all right?" Fryderyk asked softly one afternoon as they sat together on a bench at the park, almost matching in their neat waistcoats and elegant cravats, watching the sunlight sparkling on the lake as another couple shared a ride in a rowboat.

"Hmm?" George looked at him.

Fryderyk gave her a concerned little smile. "With you… is everything all right? Are you all right?"

George shrugged. "What do you mean?"

Fryderyk shook his head. "You just seem… like you're thinking about something important. Like maybe… something's bothering you. And I just… if you want to share, I want to listen."

George nodded. "Thank you," she said softly, sincerely. She swallowed. "I have… I have been thinking." She sighed. "About me… about you. About life. About everything we do together… and everything you mean to me."

He raised his eyebrows. "And?"

She shrugged. "And how strange I am. How I call myself *George* and wear trousers because they're more comfortable. And how I… I try to be the gentleman. Because that's what my grandmother would tell me to do— live up to my father's legend, continue his legacy, fill his shoes. I have to say that it's hard for me…"

She swallowed. "Hard for me to let you, or anyone, help me. Even though I appreciate it. I've just… I've been doing this for so long, earning all my own money and making all my own decisions and always being the one to help myself, and I love it, but I've been doing it for so long… been alone for so long… that I'm not sure I know how to do anything else."

George shook her head. "And yet, I have to be the lady, too. Because that's what my mother would tell me to do. To find joy in the kitchen and in being a loving companion. A lovely lady who is sweet and supportive and feminine and does her hair and makeup every morning and loves it… and who doesn't want more than that."

George looked at Fryderyk. "So, it's not that I don't trust you, and it's not that I'm not grateful, and I certainly don't want to get in your way and not let you do something for yourself or not let you help me… it's just…" She shook her head. "The two dreams in my heart, the two roles that all my loved ones have made me try to play at the same time, their visions of what I should do and what I should be, both the lady and the lad… that's an impossible balance to strike. Or at least it feels that way sometimes. And I feel like I'm being pulled in two directions; like I'm caught in a tug of war between what my mother and my grandmother would want me to be." George shook her head again. "I shouldn't be loading you with my weird sorrows." She gave a wry chuckle.

"The weird sorrows of the weirdo in trousers."

Gently, Fryderyk put his arm around her shoulders, tenderly drawing her close to lay her head on his shoulder. Another pair out for a stroll stole an inquisitive glance at the man who seemed to be comforting his younger brother through an unknown distress, an arm around his shoulder. But George and Fryderyk ignored them.

"Well, I am no stranger to weird sorrows," Fryderyk said softly. He looked at the water, thoughts playing over his quiet face. And he looked at her again. Gently he chuckled. "George... do you think I haven't noticed that you wear trousers? And I'm still here, aren't I?" He sighed. "I love you—"

George's breath caught in her throat. And slowly, she felt a smile creeping over her face as she sat up, gently pulling away. "You do?"

Fryderyk looked at her, eyebrows quirking in confusion. "Of course, I do." He raised his eyebrows. "Haven't you noticed?"

George gave a breathy chuckle. "I mean, of course, I've noticed, but— you've just never... never said the words." She swallowed, looking up at him coyly, feeling her face warming in a blush. "I love you too, by the way."

Fryderyk smiled, gently taking her hand. "I know," he said softly. "And I love you... and I love your weirdness. Your... uniqueness. All the facets of everything you are. Just as you love me in all my exasperating eccentricity." He sighed. "A melody can have more than one theme, after all, can't it? You can wear a dress one day and trousers the next... sometimes be as tender as a mother and sometimes fierce as a knight... but I need both from you." Fryderyk squeezed her hand. "Some days I need your tenderness, and sometimes I need your bold, fearless strength."

He raised his eyebrows. "A true master uses every note on the keyboard; isn't constrained to one octave. You're using the full keyboard. All your themes are beautiful, George. It's all right to embrace them all."

George sighed, blinking back tears of gratitude as she shook her head. And slowly, she smiled. "Thank you. You know, all this talking really helps. I'm always struggling; always afraid I'm too much or too little… What we have is so good that I'm afraid to believe in it… half-afraid that it won't last, that you'll leave, that some secret or surprise we haven't talked about yet will ruin everything, wondering if all of this is too good to be true…"

Fryderyk shook his head. "Not a bit of it," he reassured her. "I need your tenderness, and I need your strength. I need your gentleness, and I need your muchness. You are enough. But you could never be too much." Gently, he squeezed her hand again. "And it will last. This is good, so good, and I thank God every day for what we have together, but it is not too good to be true. It is true. It's real. And it will last. I promise. You can trust me… just as I trust you. I won't leave you. Wherever we go in life, we'll go together. And through it all, every step of the way, we'll communicate with one another, and make every decision together. No secrets. No judgment. And no surprises. I promise. Like I said before, I always want you to feel free to ask me any questions you have. And I will tell you the honest truth… I promise."

George wiped away more tears of gratitude as the exhausting weight of the burden she had been carrying seemed to lift. And silently, she rested her head on his shoulder again, letting him hold her close.

"I'll tell you everything," Fryderyk promised. "Always."

"And I'll tell you everything," George concurred. "I want to hear your questions for me. You've trusted me with your story… and I will trust you with mine."

"And we'll figure everything out together," Fryderyk summed up, gently lacing his fingers with hers.

George squeezed his hand. "Together."

Fryderyk looked out at the water again, releasing a heavy, thoughtful sigh. And lovingly, he looked at her again. Slowly, she sat up straight again, listening for the additional words she could almost see forming themselves into sentences inside his mind as thoughts crossed his face.

"George," he continued after a moment, "you are you. And I love you for who you are… not what your mother or grandmother might have tried to mold you into. And not for what society might have told you you should be. And I truly appreciate what you do for me. And all the thought that goes into it all. I…"

He sighed, giving a soft, wistful chuckle as he returned to the topic with which George had begun several long minutes previously.

"There are moments when I'm not sure who's going to move first. Who's going to help who. And sometimes we do bump into each other. But everything you do for me… everything I do for you… is out of love. And what matters is the love. And we… both of us… will continue to learn and grow and change and figure one another out and figure ourselves out. I will love you in all your uniqueness as you love me in mine. We will discover the future together… discover what exactly we want our love to look like and where exactly we want to take it. And we will work together. All right?"

George looked at him. And slowly, she smiled. "All right."

George smiled as she brushed her hair that night, ready to put her nightgown on and settle in for a night divided between sleeping and writing. He had told her he loved her. And she had told him. And the words hung in the air, a shining, gossamer net gently billowing through the air to envelop their hearts and bind them tenderly together. And weird sorrows notwithstanding... they loved one another. They would work together. And they would be all right.

She felt light. The burden she had carried for so long; the burden of not knowing what she didn't know, was gone, gently washed away by an echoing sense of peace. Everything really was all right. She really could trust him. She really could believe. He really did love her. And he would always tell her the truth. And they really were aiming toward the same future. Even if that future was flexible... they would find it together. Slowly, gently, her worn-out heart opened a bit more, cautiously accepting, receiving, embracing, that peace, gratefully releasing the burden of doubt she had been carrying. Wearily, she chose to trust. Chose to believe. Chose to lower the walls that life had built around the core of her being. And slowly, wearily, the tight, hard knot of yarn inside her well-guarded heart continued to loosen.

Thank You, she prayed as she got into bed at four o'clock that morning after a long, refreshing session of writing, blowing out her candle and pulling the blankets up to her chin. *Thank You for helping us understand one another. Thank You for... using his words to remind me of what is true. Thank You for finally allowing us to say the words,* I love you. *And thank You for helping us work together.*

214

He loves me, she said into the silence before her mother or grandmother could say anything. *I already knew, but he actually told me. And I told him that I love him. Which I do. And that's that.*

George sat on Fryderyk's couch, halfway through the next chapter of her story. Steadily, her pen moved across the pages of her notebook, tracing out the story that was rising inside her mind. And as she wrote, she listened. Listened to the twining notes of the stately polonaise Fryderyk was playing, filling the quiet afternoon with breathtaking beauty.

She sat absorbed in her work as he sat absorbed in his. But some part of the back of her mind took a moment to notice. And silently, she was grateful, so grateful, for the quiet companionship in which she and her beloved could create side-by-side.

"He's so different," George said for what felt like the thousandth time. Inside her mind and coming from her lips, the words were never far from her heart. "From the others, I mean."

Claudette nodded as she played a card in the game she and George were playing at Claudette's apartment one evening. "How so?"

"In every way," she said. She sighed, heart glowing as she considered the many advantages Fryderyk, and her relationship with him, had over the many beaus of her past and the bonds she had shared with them. "He's gentle, he's kind, he's considerate, he's a good listener, he doesn't find me to be too much or not enough, he has a great sense of humor, he's a fellow artist..."

Claudette smiled. And she played a card of her own. "What

can I say?" she asked softly. "I'm happy for you."

She loved him. He loved her. They had said the words. And as of now… they were officially courting. So… George sighed, drumming her fingers on her knees as she sat by her bedroom window one moonlit night, looking out on the courtyard outside her apartment. What was next? Kisses? Hugs? More than that?

George closed her eyes. She thought of him; of his bright eyes, his soft, brown hair, his noble nose, his fine chin, his slender torso, his delicate, long-fingered hands. He was beautiful, inside and out. And she… she desired him. She knew she did. Desired his companionship. Desired his art. Desired his love, his heart. Desired his touch. She blushed as she thought of it— kissing him, holding him in her arms, asking him what he wanted to do next. And she shook her head. Maybe someday. Maybe someday, they would be ready to have that conversation. Maybe someday, she would be ready to ask him. And maybe, someday, he would choose to give himself to her.

George went on with her days. And she wondered.

"Is something bothering you?" George asked softly as Fryderyk stood across from her beside his carriage. They were about to ride to the park together, but at the moment they stood in silence, neither taking the initiative to assist the other into the coach.

Finally, Fryderyk extended his hand. Taking it lightly, George hopped into the carriage, then offered her own hand to help him in in turn.

Fryderyk closed the door behind them. He settled into his seat. And he sighed.

216

"I'm just… thinking," he muttered as they began to drive, the carriage trundling down the bumpy road. Biting his lip, he looked down, picking thoughtfully at a loose thread on the cuff of one of his pristine white gloves.

She looked at him, feeling a slight frown of concern creasing her forehead. "About what?"

He shook his head. "About me… about you. About life. About everything we do together… and everything you mean to me. And about…" He swallowed. "Independence."

George raised an eyebrow. "Independence?"

Fryderyk shook his head. "About me… and independence. Adulthood. I mean, I know I get up every morning and decide what to eat, and teach lessons and go shopping and visit with you and all those things— I know those are all true— but… it just feels… like something's missing. In me. Something that… maybe someone else can help me fix. Someone…" He looked at her. "Like you."

George blinked, cocking her head slightly as she looked at him. "Like me?"

Fryderyk sighed again, looking down again and shaking his head with a flush of embarrassment. "I'm being stupid," he muttered, biting his lip.

George took his hand with another frown of concern. She shook her head. "No, of course you're not being stupid. Just— tell me more. I'm listening."

He swallowed, looking out the carriage window at the trees and buildings slowly sliding by as the wheels rumbled slowly over the road and the horses' hooves clip-clopped on the street. "I'm just…" He bit his lip again. "Not what I should be. Not strong; not hale and hearty like all the other men I see around me.

217

Not… not a soldier marching to the front lines, fighting to free my country. And I'm not… not really independent. I always need so much help— from my parents, roommates I've had, my other friends, you. Estelle cleans my apartment, Céline takes my laundry away and brings it back every other week, I eat most of my meals at restaurants… and I don't drive— I'm not driving this carriage at this very moment. And the horse and the carriage are hired; I don't own them. There's so much, so many things, I don't do for myself. I manage… but at the same time, I don't manage. And I'm… I'm ashamed. Because I should be doing all these things for myself, and helping my loved ones at the same time. Shouldn't depend on others like a pathetic little child. But my disappointing body…"

He looked down at his thin hands. "It has other ideas. And I'm left with no other option but to hold these hands out—" He held them out— "and ask. Receive. Let others do things for me that I should be doing myself. Because I… I never made the decisions at home. I always listened to my parents, my teachers, my doctors. Always got their permission for everything. And I'm not sure if I know… how to make the decisions now. And I don't feel… like a real adult.

"I'm sorry," he choked, brushing the back of his gloved hand against his nose. "This is embarrassing. Now I'm loading *you* with *my* weird sorrows."

George shook her head. "Fryderyk, I am no stranger to weird sorrows. I still have a lot of stories of my own to tell you. But this…" She took his hand again. "This is good. Thank you for telling me. Thank you… for trusting me with this." George looked at him. And she sighed. "All those things you just said… that's all fair. All fair." She shook her head. "Fryderyk… it's all right to be

218

disappointed. I'm disappointed a lot, too."

He looked at her. "You are?"

She nodded. "I am. More than you might think. And life… life is hard." George squeezed his hand with another sigh. "But you are… you are independent. That's what independence is… doing everything you possibly can, maximizing your abilities, identifying what you need and taking action to get it, staying on the forefront of what you're capable of." She smiled. "And you're doing that, right?"

Fryderyk looked down, then slowly met George's eyes with a small smile of his own. "I suppose I am."

She kissed his hand. "Then that is perfectly enough. You, my friend, have a lot to be proud of." She looked at him. "And you are an adult. After all, you're making your own decisions. That's all that it means to be an adult. And I see you doing that every day. And you know what else I see you doing every day?"

Fryderyk looked at her. "What?"

"Honoring your country with your music," she said softly. "With every note you write, you tell the world about her. And with every note you write, you fight for her."

Fryderyk just looked at her. And slowly, he smiled.

20 Companionship

George sighed. She had spoken the truth— Fryderyk had a lot to be proud of. And yet, the voices of her mother and grandmother still chided her. *How can you tell him he's being an independent adult,* her mother asked with a derisive scoff. *He's a child, and that's all he'll ever be,* her grandmother insisted, shaking her silver head.

But George shook her head. *No,* she said calmly. *He's not a child. He's doing everything that adults do, and he's established his own independence. And he is doing enough.*

George thought of him, climbing slowly and deliberately in and out of a carriage, making a distinct effort to hold a door open for her or fetch something for her, acknowledging her with a little nod of gratitude as he walked up or down a hill without her help, or sometimes with it. Thought of him writing day and night, pouring out his soul, his artistic vision, weaving melodies that others would someday love and purchase the sheet music for; thought of him teaching a steady stream of students of different ages and skill levels, earning his bread as he faithfully guided them through the intricacies of each beautiful piece; thought of him glorifying his beloved country with every piece he wrote in her honor. And she knew she had spoken the truth. Faithfully, Fryderyk was doing everything he could. And that was enough.

He loves me, George said to her mother and grandmother before they could speak. *And I love him. We help one another. He is good to me... and I am good to him. And that is enough.*

But again, she shook her head wearily as she wondered... what was real? Which of these? The angelic little lady who danced at the edge of her imagination? The perfect ideal that taunted her with her clumsiness, her brashness, told her over and over that surely there must be a man out there who could unlock her heart and set her free?

Maybe the delicate, feminine, domestic maiden who languished in the tower that life had put her in, waiting for a knight on horseback to transform her into the happily homebound, corset-confined angel who would finally live happily ever after in the life women, real women, were supposed to live... the tame happily-ever-after that George's own parents had never really gotten to share and that she had recreated countless times in her novels, unable as she remained to grasp it for herself? Or the independent, fierce, forthright literary spinster who paid her own rent, bought her own trousers and waistcoats, took herself out to dinner, lit her own cigars, tied her own cravat, and made all her own decisions?

Too many ideals crowded together within George's heart, incompatible dreams fighting for prominence, each demanding that she choose it. Because she could not have them all. Because how could she be forthright and independent and find a domestic happily ever after all at the same time?

Back and forth she went, jumping back and forth over the chasm that separated her two dreams. *You'll never be happy until you're a traditional woman; a trim, dainty homemaker*, part of her mind said, holding out a glowing image of a cheerfully domesticated housewife standing happily at her stove, at peace with every element of life, the same angel of domesticity who bullied and tormented her. *You'll never be happy until you stop being fierce.*

But you don't want that, countered another part, unveiling a picture of herself striding through town in a waistcoat and a top hat, a manuscript in a folder, ready to be submitted to her publisher, tucked under her arm and a purse full of money she'd earned herself and would spend exactly as she chose jingling in her pocket. *It's so limiting.*

She thought of Claudette, and the joy her feminine friend took in perfecting her makeup, styling her hair, arraying herself in the latest fashions. Thought of just how girly Claudette was. And of how happy it made her. And of how happy Pauline's adherence to the societal norms of clothing, hair, and makeup made her.

George shook her head with a perplexed sigh. All those happy, feminine women, finding so much joy in beautifying themselves, keeping up with their households, some of them surrounding themselves with children. Even as Claudette took an earnest interest in politics; analyzing the world around her and concerning herself deeply with the future and her place in it. Claudette, in particular, truly seemed to have it all; have found a way to bridge her own chasm between societal norms and independence. How did she do it?

Be a lady… be a lad… be Papa's little girl… The voices of George's mother, her grandmother, and her four-year-old self chased one another around her heart and mind as they always did, whirling around and around in endless confusion, doing nothing but sparking questions that had no answers. Where could she find the freedom she was looking for, the strange balance between fighting her own battles and knowing that she was deeply loved by someone who would come through for her as she came through for him and who loved her for her? And how could she find a way to truly unleash her womanly heart… without forcing herself into

222

the horrible, limiting notion of what it meant to be a "lady" in France?

She looked from one side of the chasm to the other; from her dream of independence to her dream of domesticity. And she shook her head. Where… where could she find both? Where could she find true balance?

Help me figure this out, she prayed simply. *And help me, in all the right ways, to help him. Help me… help us… find what I am… what we are… looking for.*

Maybe she was still searching for elements of what she hoped to one day find. But George smiled as she accepted the peace that now filled her heart. She was not too much for Fryderyk. And she was not not-enough. What they shared was not literally too good to be true. And it would last. He was not going anywhere. Except… except into the future at her side. Maybe they had not yet discussed every possible facet of the future they hoped to share. But George felt peace fill her heart as she trusted… that they would build that future together.

Softly, she smiled. Finally, after so long, she could let down her guard. Because finally, she had found someone she could trust.

"What did you think of the upcoming vote for President of the Chamber of Deputies?"

"I see that Hippolyte Passy is challenging André Dupin. He's been in office for what, coming up on seven years, isn't it?"

"Too long, if you ask me. Longest term since the years of the Bourbons— Auguste Ravez served for nearly nine years. We need someone more like Passy. He took part in Napoleon's invasion of Russia back in the teens, and he's served our people as Minister of Finance and Minster of Commerce."

George cleared her throat, approaching the two men who were conversing at Delacroix's party. "But which will serve his people, both male and female, better, improving the lot of women and championing the causes of all of those who are less fortunate?"

They looked at her. And she looked back. "They'll... they'll figure it out. Don't you worry," one of the men said haltingly. "I don't... don't know if politics is something a... a lady needs to worry about, *mademoiselle*."

"Oh, don't you?" she said calmly. "How unfortunate. Shame how with your head buried in the sand, you'll miss out on the glorious future that awaits once women finally have an equal say in government."

"For an equal say, women would have to bear equal responsibility," the other man countered, raising a dismissive eyebrow. "And how is that ever going to happen?"

"I don't know," she said airily. "We already do far more than half the housework. Maybe if men bore equal responsibility for childcare and household management, women would have the time and energy to inform themselves and take part in civic engagement. And equal rights would certainly go a long way in creating equal opportunities. Just food for thought. Good day."

And leaving them chewing on a veritable meal of food for thought, George went to find someone else to speak with.

George took Pauline out for coffee. And they continued to talk. Even... even as Pauline continued to sob into her handkerchief as she showed George the response, now much tearstained by its

224

recipient, that she had received to her refusal of Musset's proposal. The calm, accepting response that in no way suggested that Alfred was as broken up about Pauline's decision as she was.

"I told you, dearest, I know how much it hurts," George reassured Pauline, wincing herself as Pauline's fingernails dug into the back of the hand George had offered to the crying teenager from across the table where they sat in the busy restaurant one Tuesday.

A number of other restaurant patrons glanced over, curious as to the exact nature of the young woman's emotional crisis, but George just waved them off with polite, reassuring little smiles with which she hoped to convey that everything was under control.

She offered Pauline a sympathetic frown. "And unfortunately, it will go on hurting for a good while, but you'll survive. I promise."

"But how?" Pauline howled, her heartbroken wails now catching the eyes and ears of more and more of her fellow diners as she dropped salty tears into the coffee cup she was clutching.

George offered another reassuring smile to the world at large. And moving her chair so she could sit beside Pauline, she put her arm around her friend's shoulders.

"By moving on," she said. "By focusing on your art, your career, the things you love."

"But I love *him*," Pauline wailed.

"Other than him," George conceded with a little nod. "You, my lady, are one of the greatest opera singers I have ever had the honor of listening to, and you are an amazing pianist. You have so much to offer the world... so much to delve into within yourself. Men are... you know, to a certain degree, they're all beside the point."

"But you've had plenty of them!" Pauline contradicted. She began counting on her fingers. "Casimir, Jules, Didier, A-A-Alf-fred..." And wilting forward to faceplant into her handkerchief, she dissolved into fresh wails. Carefully, George moved the coffee cup a little further from her friend's flailing, lest it bite the dust.

With a heavy sigh and yet another winning smile for their rather concerned audience, George rested a consoling hand on Pauline's shaking back, rubbing gentle, reassuring circles. "I have," she acknowledged, nodding at her own hypocrisy. "And they're not all that bad. When you find the one you click with... it is one of the best things in the world. And if settling down with someone is the thing you want most in your life, I'm sure there's a man out there with whom you will be very happy."

Pauline looked up with a sniffle. "There is?"

George gave a soft smile, sensing her mind beginning to tiptoe toward a plan, a hopeful possibility of a kindhearted, dependable, financially-secure member of their academic circle to whom she might one day introduce Pauline. Even if Louis Viardot was quite a lot older than Pauline. Once Pauline's heart had healed a little more, it might be worth George at least mentioning him to her. At least to see where it would go.

"I'm sure there is."

...and so you're not good enough. And you will never be good enough until you get over this ridiculous phase, put the trousers away, and show yourself worthy of finding a partner in a man.

George rolled her eyes as the image of her mother tormented her in her imagination. *I know you mean well*, she groaned, *but*

226

sometimes I wish you would just shut up!

"Excuse me?"

George looked up at Claudette, who was gazing at her in some amount of confusion over the cup of tea she had been raising to her lips as she joined George for lunch one rainy Saturday. Across the room, Marquis was snoring in his basket as the raindrops pattered on the roof of George's apartment building.

George hung her head with a heavy sigh, suddenly realizing that her angry retort had been out loud. "Sorry, just arguing with my mother. My dead, ah, mother."

Claudette sighed. "I'm sorry. But what did I tell you about your dead mother?"

"That she can't boss me around," George repeated.

Claudette nodded. "That's right. So don't let her."

George just shook her head.

A thousand times, George thought of her mother. As she tied her cravats, put on her boots, buttoned herself up into waistcoats and tailcoats, she pondered. And she remembered. Remembered her mother and the sorts of things she would say if she were watching.

That's not beautiful, Sophie seemed to chide, rolling her dark eyes and tossing her proud head. *That's not lovely. That's not like me.*

But I don't want *to be like you*, George responded bitterly, rolling her own eyes at the unnecessarily-revealing red dress Sophie was wearing. *You hurt me. More than you'll ever understand. And I... I want to be as unlike you as possible. You were wild, loose, untrustworthy, insane. And everything you were... I hate. And I promise you... I will never be like you.*

George thought of the kisses the others had given her; the passionate embraces she and her beaus had exchanged in the twilight of the love-nests they had shared throughout Europe. And she wondered. Wondered about Fryderyk. And if she would ever share those embraces with him.

She thought about the first time she had mentioned a kiss, long before they had begun courting, and the way he had politely refused. Of how that had made her feel. And… of how far they had come since then. Without any kisses at all. Without ever waking in one another's arms with hearts full of sweet dreams of the night they had shared; without the final embrace of the Divine Mystery. And yet… with joy. With satisfaction. And with the shared experiences that only a pair of artists could ever know.

She thought of the way he had never even spoken of sharing a kiss on the lips; never offered her one. Thought of the way they would each occasionally kiss one another on the hand and she had once kissed him on the forehead… and how those kisses seemed to be enough for him.

She thought of the way they connected. The joy they brought one another. And the peace of the space, the freedom, that they created for one another… as an artist and an artist who loved one another very much.

She shook her head. And she… was no longer sure that she ever needed to share a kiss with Fryderyk to know that he loved her.

Thank You, she prayed. *Thank You for the ways that Fryderyk is different. And thank You… for the ways in which I am becoming different, too.*

She shared her heart, her art, with Fryderyk. And she shared them with Claudette. George smiled as Claudette also embraced her work, welcoming it into her soul as George read her every word of her works-in-progress. Claudette offered feedback of her own, the counterpoint of her perspective helping George to deepen sections on which Fryderyk had not commented, further honing her work with the observations of another mind, heart, and soul. Gratefully, George considered the feedback of her readers. And lovingly, she shared her works with them.

"I got a letter from home," Fryderyk said one day as he and George sat together in his sitting room in Paris, enjoying the late-spring sunshine pouring through the window.

George looked up from the needlework she had brought on her visit with a smile. "Oh, that's lovely. How is everyone?" she asked. "Are they well?"

"Overall," Fryderyk said cheerfully. "My papa wrote me a few lines… He always gives me such good advice. He asked me how my savings are coming— not as well as I might have hoped, but I'm trying— asked me about my work, and gave me some excellent suggestions in regards to a conversation I need to have with my publisher…"

Fryderyk shook his head. "He's taught me so much. Taught me to be a man; to always look out for others, even when it's hard. Especially when it's hard. Taught me… that even though my body is a disappointment to me, I do have what it takes. And never to be afraid to do what's right." Fryderyk sighed. "I may not have been able to see him in person in far too long, but he's always there for me. Always has been. And I know he always will be."

George squeezed his hand, even as she choked back tears. "I'm glad."

Fryderyk saw her tears. And a gentle, concerned frown touched his face. "What kind of man is your father, George?" he asked.

She shook her head. "I don't know," she said, blinking back her tears. "His name was Maurice... He died when I was four. My mother Sophie never remarried— she and my grandmother spent the rest of my childhood playing tug of war with me until I ended up in a convent for a few years. And then I went back with my grandmother; lived with her for the rest of her life. But my father..."

George sighed, folding her hands in front of her. "I never knew him; not like I wish I could have. He was a soldier; a brave soldier... My mother always used to point to the sunset and tell me that a great battle was going on in the distance, and my papa was surely right in the middle of it. I always used to play 'war,' even when I was three years old— I would make little fortresses with the furniture and kill off the enemies of France.

"He was my hero; the hero I worshiped, waiting for the day when he would come home. And he did come home, our war hero... but all too soon, he was gone."

George swallowed, pausing as she considered how to go on. Because the next part of her story, the next person she needed to talk about... was someone she did not always mention to those who did not already know her full story. Someone she barely even knew... but who would be part of her heart forever. Someone it was not even always appropriate to mention, instead finding creative ways of describing herself as the child of a complex family spread over multiple households. And yet, when she chose not to mention him... she felt as though she were being dishonest.

George sighed, weighing her options… silence or candor. She looked at Fryderyk; at the love for her that shone in his eyes; at the trustworthy friendship and compassion he offered her, at the good care he would take of all her secrets, as she took good care of the things he told her in confidence. At the bond of courtship they had established with whispered words of love. The trust he'd placed in her… that she could offer back to him. And she… decided that the time was right to open her heart. And slowly, carefully, with a catch in her voice, she went on.

"My baby brother Louis… my mother's baby boy… he died when he was only four months old, and a week later, my father was dead, too— his horse threw him on the road. He… he was gone. I didn't understand; I kept asking when Papa was coming back from 'death.' But he never did." George looked down at her folded hands. "And he never has." She swallowed. "They told me he broke his neck in the fall. And I know that that's the way it happened, but even now… I don't know how an accident with a horse could kill a person."

Fryderyk looked at her, his own eyes shining with unshed tears. "I'm sorry," he whispered. "About your father… and about your brother."

"Thank you," she murmured, taking the supportive hand he offered. She sighed again. "So… I've spent my life wondering what kind of man my father was. And what he would think of me… what I've become."

Fryderyk looked at her, giving her a little half-smile. "I think he'd be proud," he said softly. "I know he would."

21   Gratitude

George went home. And she thought. Her father's voice never popped into her head; not like her mother's voice, her grandmother's voice. Because she didn't know what he would say. But she thought of him, welcoming every shred and scrap of filmy, poorly-lit memory her mind could conjure up. She could never see his face, but he was there… he was there in Casimir, in Jules, in Musset, in Mallefille; in all the others. In some strange way, he was there. And in some strange way, she was searching. Searching for what he would say.

She shook her head. Another voice that never rose inside her mind was Louis'. Because, as a very small infant, the only ways he had expressed himself verbally had been in the form of loud crying and soft cooing. Loud cries and soft coos that she could remember if she tried hard enough; that she hung onto with every ounce of her strength as she longed to hear them again. But even more, she longed to see him as he was now, an adult only four years younger than she was. And she longed to hear what he would say.

She shook her head. She longed for her father; the Papa she'd barely known. She longed for the brother whose presence in her life for so many years had been only in the form of his absence. And she longed… for home. The strange, intangible concept from a thousand storybooks; the heartwarming cocoon of safety and security she had rarely known. And the question she had always carried inside her heart. What was "home," really? What did it mean? And where, outside of the simple, literal place in which she existed, would she find it?

She had told Fryderyk about Louis. Opened her heart; trustingly revealed to him that she was the sister of a dearly departed little brother. He had listened. He had offered his sympathies. And he… she knew… would honor the trust she had placed in him. Just as she honored the trust he placed in her. With him, her secrets were safe. And with him, she could accept peace.

George closed her eyes, letting the tears fall as a new thought gently rose; rising into the dimness of the shadows into which she had pushed her thoughts of her brother for so long, in front of the insistence of some part of her mind that she leave him in the past and simply carry on without him. And she went to her room and opened her journal to explore it. Slowly, she opened the door of her heart just a crack, tentatively letting the feelings in. And hesitantly, she raised a candle into the shadowiest corners of her soul to take a good look at the grief that was all that she had left of her brother.

I have thought for a long time that since Louis was my mother and father's child, not mine, and their grief was intrinsically much greater than mine, that I have no right to speak of him— only they can decide who to talk to about him and when. And yet… they're gone. And I can't ask their permission.

But… maybe that's not the right way of looking at it. After all… he was my brother. And the loss of him… that doesn't just belong to my parents. It belongs to me as well. My loss is real. My grief is real. And I will never understand exactly how they felt; I can't grasp their exact loss… but maybe my loss and grief aren't automatically less than theirs. Maybe… they're just different. And maybe it's time to own my loss. Claim it… as mine. And decide for myself whom to tell that I have a brother in Heaven.

George closed her journal with a sigh. And she wiped away the tears that had run down her cheeks. Her loss was real. And it was up to her... and only to her... to decide with whom she would share it.

She went to bed early that night, worn out by emotion. Raw heart wrung dry of tears; tears she had not expected to shed. Soul aching with pain she had not realized was still there; grief she had thought long gone, belonging in the past, that, upon reexamination, still hurt far more than she had expected. Silently, George closed her eyes, pulling her blankets closer. Maybe she had more work to do than she had realized.

Late afternoon passed into evening. And as they sat together on George's couch after sharing the dinner they had cooked together, Fryderyk began to yawn.

Wistfully, George smiled. And slowly, she opened her arms. "May I?" she asked.

Trying simultaneously to stretch and to cover his mouth as he gave another yawn, Fryderyk looked at her. "May you what?"

George tried not to chuckle in loving confusion at the way that the implied part of her question had not hit its mark. "Put my arm around you," she clarified.

Fryderyk continued looking at her. And slowly, a smile touched his face. "Yes," he said slowly, scooting a little closer to her and bending to rest his head on her shoulder. "Thank you."

Gently, George put her arm around his shoulder. And she smiled.

They were happy. And yet... things were not perfect. And

from time to time, George still found herself gritting her teeth as Fryderyk canceled or rescheduled activities, wilting as he went home from an activity early, exhausted by coughing, losing sleep on the occasions when he remained, for one reason or another, uncertain as to whether he would be able to join her for dinner on a particular evening until the very morning of, tossing and turning the night before as she prayed that by morning, he would be feeling well enough to spend the day together.

When she finally met with him, unrested but blissful, her jaw unclenching in relief even as her shoulders continued to ache with the knots they had tied themselves into, half of her always wondered what she had been so worried about while the other half of her asked her why all of this was making her feel, and behave, like an idiotic teenager. And then those thoughts would put themselves away as she threw herself, heart and soul, into the activities they had planned for their day, returning to her apartment that evening weary but glowing. And many, many nights brought her beautiful dreams of the music he played for her.

It was thrilling. But it was challenging. At times, they struggled to balance their entwined social lives into "his," "hers," and "theirs," sometimes double-booking themselves and having to choose between two social obligations; other times finding themselves unexpectedly sitting alone on a day they had expected to spend together, disappointedly wondering what the other was up to. Peeking constantly out the front window as they impatiently waited in breathless anticipation for the other to arrive for their next activity; waiting anxiously for the postman to come, hopefully bearing another loving note from the other, either an invitation to another visit or outing or a thank-you in honor of the most recent day they had spent together. And trying not to let disappointment simmer into jealousy or resentment when things didn't work out quite right. Trying to inflate her compassion for him into infinity, using it to push away the annoyance she occasionally tried not to feel when a "bad lung day" forced him to cancel or cut short one of their precious days together.

Sometimes, it was awkward. Sometimes, it was uncertain. And sometimes she had to talk to herself as to a selfish teenager, berating herself for egotistically regretting having missed out on the joy she had hoped for when Fryderyk had sent only his regrets for having to stay home sick on a day they had planned to spend shopping together. And her throat ached with tears as her annoyance melted into compassionate regret for the miserable day he was clearly spending in bed, alternating between coughing and drinking tea, comforted only by his cat. Always her empathy won out. But the lovestruck teenager who demanded to spend every waking moment with Fryderyk would not back down without a fight.

Both were growing. But slowly and steadily, they found their way forward. And with everything they did together, whether the results were perfect, awkward, or somewhere in between, they grew closer.

"George, may I—"

"Yes," George said without looking up from her needlework. She smiled. "Yes. Whatever you have in mind… yes." She looked up. "Because you do not need to ask me."

Fryderyk looked at her from where he sat on the couch in his sitting room, a soft smile slowly spreading over his thin face.

"I was just thinking about going shopping," he said.

236

George nodded. "Have fun," she encouraged him. "Don't let me stop you." She picked up her needlework, folding it up and placing it in her bag. "I was just about to be on my way, anyway."

"You don't have to go," Fryderyk cut in, holding out a thin hand.

George shook her head with a chuckle, looking up at the clock on the mantlepiece. "No, no; I'd really better be going. Oh, dear, look at the time— I need to go feed Marquis." She got up, stretching, then took Fryderyk's hand and kissed it. "So, where are you shopping today?" she asked, going over to the door and putting her shoes on.

Fryderyk got up from the couch, stretching his own slender arms. "To the rue du Faubourg Saint-Honoré," he said. "I need some new gloves, and I wanted to pick up some flower arrangements."

George smiled. "Well, you have a good time. I'll see you on Thursday, all right?"

Fryderyk paused. Slowly, the fact that she truly meant it settled into his heart. And slowly, he smiled.

"I'll see you Thursday."

She went home. But she was smiling. Because she had meant what she said. And he… he knew that she meant it. She imagined him getting ready to go; calling for his carriage and riding into town for an exhilarating shopping spree. And she hoped… truly hoped… that he would have a good time.

She hoped and moped like a lovesick girl of sixteen. But still, she wrote. Every night, George cast aside the hopes and fears of the day and entered her own private universe; the mirror-world where she could find herself; could process the very hopes and fears that troubled her days. In a state beyond waking she considered her waking world, dialoguing with it and contemplating it, studying the events and reflecting upon every possibility. In the shadow-realm inside her own heart, she found healing for the events of her life. And in her the interior landscape of the depths of her own mind, she found relief.

"Oh, lessons this week were a nightmare, so to speak…" Fryderyk groaned one day as he met George for lunch one weekend in Paris. As the restaurant was terribly crowded on this early Saturday afternoon, they had chosen to sit at one of the outdoor tables in front of the restaurant, watching other diners streaming in and out of the restaurant's swinging doors, gazing at the blossom-laden pear trees that lined the Paris street, feeling the breeze on their faces. Fryderyk fairly sparkled in a brand-new waistcoat of pale gray, a snappy black jacket, and a dazzlingly-white cravat, but George had gone the simple route, wearing one of her most comfortable dresses, one whose puffed sleeves didn't get in her way.

George looked up from her onion soup with a concerned frown. "Aw, really?"

Fryderyk chuckled, cutting a bite of lightly-seasoned chicken and watching the steam rise. "Yes. All these duchesses and countesses and baronesses… they pay well; they pay beautifully, but they don't all… *play* beautifully."

George grinned. "No?"

Fryderyk chuckled again. "No. They do their best… and I do my best, helping them coax the right notes out of the instrument. But it's not just about playing the right notes… it's about bringing the right *feeling* out of the piano. I've had students who have played with great precision but no emotion… Students with less precision who put their hearts and souls into the piece are the ones with the right idea. 'Put all your soul into it,' I always tell them. 'Play the way you feel!' And some of them 'get' that, and others don't."

George smiled. "They'll get there. I'm sure of it."

Fryderyk shook his head. "We'll see."

George shook her head, sitting at her dressing-table one night. Slowly, she had opened the door of her heart, illuminating its dark corners with a candle as she carefully prodded the areas that hurt the most. As regarded her brother… she had a lot of healing to do.

But he was not the only person from her past who made her soul ache. The grandmother who chided her and the mother whose madness had so shaped her life stood always at the edges of her mind, spying on her, tormenting her.

Mother… George bit her lip as she thought of her *maman*; the woman who had given birth to her but whose main presence in her daughter's life had been her absence. Numbly, she had pushed away her thoughts of her mother for so long, hiding them away like her memories of her brother. The past was the past, and if she forced it away, doggedly moving forward with her life, it would eventually stop following her, wouldn't it? Would eventually stop applying; stop being true?

But it hadn't. These recent thoughts… only showed her how much her past, the thoughts of her brother, the memories of her mother, had not stopped following her. She shook her head, taking a deep breath. They wouldn't stop, would they, until she took them out and finally looked at them?

Slowly she opened the cupboard in the back of her heart, cautiously untying the bandage that was still wrapped around the stinging wound that had stabbed her very soul; the wound that lay beside the echoing emptiness that was the void left by her brother's absence. And she looked at the wound wrought by her mother.

Inside it, she found memories. Memories of every harsh word, every unearned slap, every broken promise. Every bad day she had spent attempting to coexist with her crazy mother; every stressful visit she had spent with her at her grandmother's quiet estate in Nohant. Every night she had lain awake listening to pacing, crinkling, and all manner of little tapping noises, wondering which hat or dress her mother was going to stay up all night making over, only to reject it in the morning and rush out to buy a new one.

Every time she had run away in tears from the towering rage that had come upon Sophie for no reason at all, widening her wild eyes, loudening her strident voice, harshening her words and her hands until she would seize Aurore by the shoulders and shake her, demanding things Aurore did not understand; accusing her of disobediences that had never occurred. All the anger. All the fear that had grown. And the careful wall of distrust that little Aurore had slowly built to protect herself from the slings and arrows of her mother's irrationality; the apparent insanity that had no explanation.

She thought of how she had grown up; grown up to find herself disgusted by her mother and everything she stood for, everything that represented her. Grown up to array herself in shirts and trousers and top hats, striking out on her own at right angles to the life Sophie had lived, the choices she had made. Sophie had

240

ruined her own life, and wrecked George's heart. And her daughter wanted none of it.

She had been crazy. Just crazy. And that was not George's fault.

In George's grown-up heart, anger rose. And bitterness. She clenched her fists, closing her eyes against the anger; against the seething oceans of pain and heavy basketfuls of broken promises; against the impossibility of defining her mother's mental unwellness. *Why, Mother?* she demanded inside her mind. *What was wrong with you? And why did you ruin my life?*

George listened. But there were no answers.

Am I lovable? George asked herself in her diary. *Really? Am I worthy of love? This broken, crazy author who writes to keep herself from going stark raving mad and can never... never... seem to be happy for long? How can someone like Fryderyk love someone like me? He's just as fragile as the others. So won't... won't I kill him if I give him everything that I am? Won't I be too much for him? And can the faithfulness that never seemed to be able to resuscitate any of my romances with any of the others really be enough this time? Can we make this romance healthy from the start?*

We're so different. Too different? But then, he's exactly what I like; exactly the kind of man I always seem to find my way to... someone I can look after. And yet... maybe not quite in the same way as the others. Not as a surrogate mother this time. But... can we do this? Can I give him room to be himself... and can he give me room to be myself? Can we thrive together? Can we be a team?

She shook her head. And she smiled. Worthy of love… How could she ever even think of asking, ever consider doubting, if she was worthy of love?

She remembered the convent where she had spent two years as a teenager, smiling at the memories of what she had learned there. And the peace she had gained. Peace that gently enveloped her heart now, reminding her that no matter what happened, regardless of which beaus might one day abandon her and which relationships might fail, the One Who had created her would never leave her nor forsake her.

There was Someone… Who loved her enough to die for her. And abandoned though she may have been by many, carrying on in the absence of her father and mother, she was not alone. The One Who had died and risen again to redeem her would never abandon her.

Being that I'm worthy of love… a voice said into the stillness.

George looked up. And she realized, to her surprise, that the maiden in the tower was speaking. She looked at the maiden. And she listened.

Because of the worth God has given me, I deserve to be loved by my parents, by my friends, by my significant others. But what… The maiden paused, seeming to look away into her thoughts. *What about… what about being loved by myself?*

Was I wrong? the maiden asked, eyes suddenly brightening as she looked out the window of her tower, gazing at the world that lay far below. *Wrong to wait for a prince? What am I waiting for? I am waiting*, she concluded, stepping back into the shadows of her tower. *But I'm not sure what for.*

22   Independence and Interdependence

George went into town, buying herself a new pair of shoes, a couple of cravats, some gloves. "Pardon me, Monsieur," or "Excuse me, *jeunne-homme*," was all she heard as she strode through the crowded streets of Paris, chuckling to herself as she heard it. Blending into the crowd as she silently rebelled, appearing as a small, unassuming young university student or the son of some prominent newspaper editor, she bought what she needed, receiving no questions as she bought the accessories that completed her look so well. Walking tall in sturdy boots, garbed in a jacket and trousers, her top hat raised her stature to a solid 1.6 meters— not tall, by any means, but not short enough for concerned passerby to stop the *petit garçon* and ask him where his mother was.

She exercised her authority to buy her own things with the money she had earned for herself, authority that was underlined by the attire she wore; the attire of the dominant gender. As the decision-maker, breadwinner, and bill-payer at her house, George took herself shopping. She bought what she needed. And she went home.

She remembered the first time she'd been addressed as *Monsieur*— once, on a teenage horseback-riding expedition, she had found herself passing through a town far away enough from home that it was full of strangers. Seeing her riding outfit of frockcoat and trousers, they had all addressed her as *Monsieur*, convincing themselves rather quickly that the stranger was an important nobleman sent by the government to inspect the province. Within moments, *Monsieur* was being fawningly offered home-brewed wine and guided around the town to "inspect" the local stables, the local wool industry, and all manner of other things. Men tipped their hats to *Monsieur*, and the ladies blushed and curtsied as the young dandy walked by.

She had gone home that night with her heart pounding. As a woman, she could taste the freedom and authority denied her by the society in which she lived. By dressing in trousers, she could exercise her right to live on her own terms... make her own rules. By dressing in trousers, she could be free.

"So... what have you been working on recently?" Claudette asked as she and George took a walk in the park.

George adjusted her top hat as the sun came out from behind a cloud, making her squint. "A rather exciting story about the corsairs of Croatia. The hero is from Turkey, and he's been telling his companions all about the dangers of these terrifying pirates."

"Sounds intriguing," Claudette said. "Not that you'd know anything about piracy or anything, though. Except for stealing hearts..."

"Oh, you," George groaned, rolling her eyes and playfully jostling her shoulder against Claudette's. "I'm more like Anne Bonny or Mary Read. Yes, I love, and yes, I've had plenty of adventures, but I love my freedom most of all."

Claudette smiled. "As you should. As you should."

June came. And George spent a weekend, only a weekend, in Nohant, finding her beautiful estate in surprisingly good shape after a period of disuse. Quietly, she prepared her heart for something new; an observation she had never made before. And as the twelfth of June arrived, she walked to her brother's tree, sitting down in its shade to think and remember as she marked another year, reflecting beneath the tree that marked the site of Louis' grave.

She sat beneath the tree. She looked down at the gravestone beside the trunk, which bore the dates of his birth and death; the dates that marked the span of his little life, the meagre days he had spent on this Earth. And she looked up at the tree, into the kaleidoscopic canopy of green leaves. A gentle breeze ruffled the leaves, gently blowing her hair back from her face. And she closed her eyes, her heart suddenly aching ten times more. Because beside her, she seemed to feel… another presence gently touching her. A gentle presence, silent and peaceful, quietly reminding her that he was all right… that he still *was*.

George wiped away the tears she had just realized were streaming down her cheeks as a sob broke out of her. And kneeling beneath her brother's tree, she wept. He was in Heaven, she knew. At peace in the presence of the Lord. But as she wept beneath his tree, she shuddered with gratitude at the feeling that floated serenely beside her. Here, in the shade of his tree, she had found her brother.

One day in Paris, George arrived for her biweekly visit to find Fryderyk with his sleeves rolled up, laboriously dusting his sitting room bookshelves. Another day, he set the table while she cooked dinner, and brought her a ladle, a pitcher, and a dishtowel before she could even ask for them. One day she arrived to find him cooking up some chicken for lunch; on another she found him at the sink, doing dishes. And whenever she took action to help him that was in any way noteworthy, he always thanked her sincerely.

He could do things when he felt up to it; when his body cooperated, she observed with a smile. He really could. And he cared. As grateful as he was for her help, he wanted to help her. And he did as often as he could.

He did things for himself. She did things for herself. And they did things for one another. Fryderyk played his music for George; she read her stories to him; he made lovingly homemade pierogis for her that stuck hopelessly to the bottom of the pot; she made epically burned cookies for him— although Funeral March Stew remained a comical, carefully-unrepeated anecdote in the annals of their growing relationship. In sickness and in health, in art and in life, in companionship and love, in laughter and in friendship, they worked together, a hero and a heroine whose lives were becoming more and more lovingly intertwined with each day that passed.

Together, they talked. They played cards. They cooked dinner and made cookies together. They went on carriage rides and walks in the park. They smiled. And they laughed. As the dog or the cat did something unexpected, as a pun came out of nowhere, as a humorous memory tapped one or the other of them on the shoulder and inspired a funny story, as Fryderyk made George slap her knee with the hilarious impressions that had her a centimeter from swearing that the proprietor of Fryderyk's favorite restaurant, the shoemaker, Franz Liszt, or Eugene Delacroix was in the room with them. Together, they laughed. And together, they found joy unlike any they'd ever known.

"Are you all right?" Claudette asked one afternoon as she and George went shopping. "You seem… different."

George picked up two pairs of boots to compare, carefully considering their relative merits. And she smiled.

"I feel different," she admitted. "But it's a good different."

"Where should we go first? The museum? The library? Lunch? And where did you want to go to lunch?"

George and Fryderyk struggled to keep up with Pauline, who, her face alight and her eyes sparkling, was striding along much more quickly than her tiny frame might have suggested possible, the tour guide who had promised to give them a different look at the great city of Paris than they had ever experienced. And so, their collective years of life in Paris notwithstanding, they had joined her.

Pauline glowed. Having finally, over time, thrown off the dark mantle of her heartbreak over Alfred, she was ready to embrace joy again. And, after attracting the attention of every dog and bat in Paris with the high-pitched squeals with which she enthusiastically congratulated them on having become a couple, she was ready to take on Paris.

It was thrilling. It was exhausting. And George and Fryderyk were both flagging by the end of it. But over the course of that busy Saturday, they found their breath stolen at the museum by a series of sculptures they had never noticed, discovered a new favorite coffee shop, took a walk in a park they had each passed many times but never visited, and each came home with a new hat.

Each new discovery might have been small on its own, but Pauline had been right. Coming home from their adventure, they saw their city with new eyes.

He was exhausted. Happy, but exhausted. Wearily, Fryderyk sat down at his piano at the end of the long, exciting day, visibly relaxing as he played a delicate mazurka. Slowly, he sank into it, the weariness in his tense shoulders dissipating as his hands moved gently over the keyboard, tracing out familiar melodies and beloved chords. Silently, George watched him decompress. And she smiled. That truly had been quite the day.

George sat in her armchair by the piano, listening to Fryderyk play as she worked on her embroidery. The sweet, gentle nocturne twined through the still afternoon air, a soft, perfect accompaniment to a sleepy afternoon of needlework.

She heard a breath. And she realized that it was her own. Fryderyk's music had gone still.

She looked at him. "Everything all right?" she asked softly.

He sat up straight with the hint of a startle, wiping a slightly sappy smile off his face. Then he shook his head, giving a gentle chuckle.

"I was just thinking..." he whispered, "about how beautiful you are. Just... admiring you."

George laughed out loud for pure joy. And there was nothing she could say but, "Thank you."

George smiled to herself. A few months ago, if Fryderyk had told her how beautiful she was, she would have laughed it off as silly, meaningless, irrelevant. Mallefille, Musset, and all the others... With each of her previous beaus, the day had quickly come when this one or that one had forgotten to remind her of how beautiful she was. And for them... for them, her previous beaus had needed her to be strong... not beautiful. Warrior, healer, and matronly mother; not maiden and lover. Protector and comforter, yes, but as a mother hen would shelter her chicks under her wings, not as a shieldmaiden ready to fight alongside her man as his powerful counterpoint.

With Fryderyk, however… with Fryderyk, it was the opposite. In all those previous relationships, each of her lovers had begun by praising her beauty, but before too long, their infatuation had faded into needy, whiny reliance, references to her physical beauty rendered as awkward-sounding as compliments offered to one's own mother, aunt, teacher, nanny, or nurse. But Fryderyk… yes, he needed her, but he had needed her from the beginning. And in caring friendship, the two of them had settled into a bond of giving and receiving, in which comments on one another's appearances, no matter how sincere, would have seemed both irrelevant and borderline inappropriate.

A bond of giving and receiving that was graced with a sincere, continually-expressed gratitude that all of George's other romantic partnerships had either lacked completely or quickly lost. A bond of friendship that had deepened into love and romance, growing into a place where Fryderyk could, and would, in a genuine expression of attraction to her, offer sincere, loving compliments on her beauty. And maybe just a little sentimentally, he gazed at her now, not in preparation to ask her to do something for him, and not in the hunger of lust, but in sincere, slightly awestruck appreciation. Loving appreciation… that warmed her heart. Loving appreciation… that she might, she thought to herself, just be ready to accept… ready to receive.

George smiled as the present in which the two of them now stood and the future into which they hopefully gazed together seemed to embrace her with love. Now… now, Fryderyk's words seemed to touch something deep within her; something real, something true. And something seemed to be loosening inside her; something that had been tightly knotted up for a very long time like a snarled-up ball of tangled yarn. Part of her was not sure how she would feel if the knot ever came undone. But part of her... wanted to know.

He doesn't mea—

Stop, George said firmly as her mother's voice rose reproachfully inside her mind, the cruel whisper of an angry harpy. *Just stop. Please. He does mean it. I know he does. I... I trust that he does.*

Am I beautiful? George asked herself with some indifference. Silently, she shrugged. *Does it matter? Fryderyk seems to think so... and I'll appreciate that.*

George and Fryderyk's companionship... it was quiet. Yes, sometimes they went to the theater, but more often, they simply came over to one another's houses to pass a gentle afternoon together. In that quiet, loving companionship of tender friendship, they held sacred space for one another, freeing one another to be who they truly were. And in that freedom... they found belonging.

Always, they worked together. George helped Fryderyk with cooking, organizing, planning... and he opened doors for her, helped her on with her coat, held her hand as she stepped in or out of a carriage, offered his arm as they walked up or down a hill together, pulled her chair out for her, took her out for tea or to lunch. And slowly, gradually, almost sneakily, George felt something shifting... the hard, stressed knot inside her heart almost beginning to loosen. Because, almost in spite of herself, she could not help but think… that it felt good to receive. Sometimes she didn't know whether to laugh or cry. And sometimes, she could not silence the nagging voices of her mother and grandmother, who continued to insist that she be even more supportive and submissive to Fryderyk and do everything for him while simultaneously politely dismissing his offers to help, support, and serve her.

Around and around in impossible circles she went, tormented by the incompatible demands of the memories of who her mother and grandmother had been. And she found herself stumbling, exhausted by the constant strain. But when she gave in to the temptation of acceptance, allowing Fryderyk to go to the effort of helping and caring for her, accepting the tender, intentional love he offered… she sighed. She relaxed. And she wondered… just because she was strong enough for both of them, did that mean that she could never accept anything from him?

George looked up at the tower and the maiden within. The maiden… whose face now shone with a curious smile. Because she had the same questions as George did. She was strong… but would receiving help from Fryderyk negate her strength? George's heart ached with the question. Because she… wanted to know.

George sat down on the couch beside Fryderyk, releasing a heavy sigh as she gave him a wistful smile. "You know what?"

Fryderyk looked at her, returning the smile as he waited for what she would say. "What?"

She took his hand. "You… are such an incredible, incredible blessing."

He chuckled. "Really?"

"Really. What you have done for me… is so powerful. With you… I'm finally in a relationship where I feel valued; where I'm treated like an equal and a peer. Other men I've known… have tended to treat me like a mother. I've been the comforter, the consoler, the muse, the chef, the maid, the nurse. Not the true companion I've always longed to be, standing side-by-side with a man as a counterpart… as a true counterpoint.

"You… you are the only man I've ever known who doesn't want to change me. You say… that I'm not too much. But that I'm not not-enough. And you don't try to put me in a box like others I've known. You don't insist that I step into my father's boots as my grandmother's laddie, or my mother's, ah, dancing shoes. You don't tell me to put on an apron and stay in the kitchen for you or to put on my editor hat for you. You don't… you don't tell me what to do or who to be."

Fryderyk looked at her. And slowly, a small smile touched his face. "Why would I?" he asked softly. "I know what it's like. I've been put into metaphorical boxes and tucked literally into bed by my parents, my doctors, my prospective in-laws. And I have no intention of doing that to you."

George swallowed. "I can't even express what a relief that is. For you, when I come over, to not boss me around— to just be… happy. That I'm there. Exactly as I am."

"In all your complexity," he agreed, lifting her hand to his lips and kissing it. "In all your many facets." He smiled. "Just like you do for me."

George squeezed his hand. And she just smiled back.

Fryderyk nodded, giving a wistful sigh. "I've felt like a child in the past," he said. "Because of my health. People worry about me— *Fryderyk, how are you feeling? Are you tired? We should probably go home now; it's seven o'clock. And don't forget to take your medicine before bed and wear your socks with your slippers.*" He rolled his eyes. "Marja actually wrote about that to me; she accused me of not wearing my slippers over my socks just because I hadn't specifically told her in a letter that I was wearing them." He shook his head. "Honestly, I wonder what kind of marriage we would have had… if it would have been a matter of her faithfully standing by my side 'in spite of' all my issues rather than loving me for me… appreciating the rest of me— my personality, my art— *despite* my body and trying to politely ignore it, rather than appreciating my body as part of me. And I wonder how happy we would have been for how long. Maybe it was better to have these things impede her relationship with me in the first place, rather than giving them the chance to erode our relationship after we had gotten married."

With a nod and a sigh, George reached out to squeeze his hand. "Maybe it was." She winked, feeling her face warming in a blush. "I *do* appreciate your body, you know," she said cheekily. "If I may say so, you are an extremely handsome gentleman."

"If not for my nose," Fryderyk countered, raising his free hand to tap it. "As you can see, it's rather… outsized."

George rolled her eyes. "You mean outstanding," she said. "You have a lovely nose," she said sincerely. "It's not disproportionate at all. It's very distinguished."

Fryderyk just gave a sarcastic chuckle. "If you say so."

23   Understanding

Quietly, their chuckles faded into a companionable silence. Fryderyk gave a sigh, and silently, they each found themselves looking reflectively down into their own laps. Looking up again, she gave him a wistful little smile. "You know how it feels, then. For certain parts of yourself to be a... distraction... to certain other people. As for me, in a bizarre way, I've found myself treated both like a mother and like a child by my other sweethearts. And not just because of my height; *they* made me feel like a child, in how they treated me; how they talked about me. *This is Aurore; isn't she tiny?* That was how it always began— they wanted me as an ornament to hang on their arm."

She shook her head, remembering how admiring kisses and occasionally-backhanded compliments had devolved into unmade beds, uneaten sandwiches, and sleepless nights of angry tears as the first blush of infatuation with her delicate, tiny beauty had faded into whiny dependence, whining, pouting, childish artists clinging petulantly to her skirts. How passionate embraces had decayed into long nights of sitting at feverish bedsides of those whose health could no longer tolerate even the most joyful excitement, though some of them had not wanted to take *no* for an answer. How the lover had become the mother. And how, each time, that painful progression had signified the end of yet another relationship.

"And then, as time went on," she sighed, "I became *Maman*. And I looked after them and cleaned up after them as gratitude turned into entitlement and they started impatiently demanding the things they'd come to expect. Started... ignoring me. Stopped caring. And just saw me as a resource, as a means to an end, someone who could facilitate *their* art, *their* careers. A financially independent person who cared enough about them to let them live with me and eat my food and be nurtured… whether or not they ever gave anything back."

"I won't do that," Fryderyk said, shaking his head and taking her hand again. "Never. I'm too grateful for all you do for me… I see how hard you're working."

George gave him half a smile. "I just got so sick of it— becoming *Maman*. If we're courting… I really don't want to be stepping in for my beau's mother."

Fryderyk sighed with a small smile of his own. "And you won't be. Likewise, I'm glad to be treated as a whole person, not a half-dead invalid. Yes, I'm so sensitive it actually hurts at times, and maybe I've never quite known the reason, but Marja and the others were always fussing over me like I couldn't do anything for myself; reminding me to do things like eat dinner and wear a coat; whispering about how they thought I 'wasn't long for this world' when they thought I wasn't listening. I saw the letters they wrote home— *Fryderyk's not well.* And I got sick of being treated like a colicky baby."

Fryderyk sighed, looking down at his and George's hands, their fingers intertwined. "They never really gave me the freedom to truly do everything I can for myself; genuinely step forward as an adult. Didn't… didn't respect my adulthood and the decisions I was fully prepared to make for myself. And I… sometimes I hardly felt like a real adult. Felt like maybe I wasn't fully prepared to make my own decisions. Felt… like I was still waiting for some milestone I couldn't define, where I'd finally be free." Fryderyk paused. "But you…" He smiled at her. "You're… you don't boss me around; treat me like I'm six."

George shrugged. "Why would I? Look at you; you're twenty-eight years old. You don't ever need to ask anyone's permission for anything. Least of all me. All right? If it's important to you, you go for it." She swallowed. "I'm here to help... but I'm not here to tell you what to do; be your adult. Stop waiting to be grown up, Fryderyk. You already are."

Fryderyk just blinked back a sudden brightness in his eyes.

Stop waiting to be grown up— you already are. George held those words up as the memories came to tell her that they were not true; that of course, Fryderyk was just a child; just a child in need of a mother who would tie herself to her kitchen stove with her own apron-strings. Fragile though his body was, he *was* an adult. And she could let him be one.

Facets, she thought. *Or were they fragments?* The disparate bits of herself that she was trying to force together into some sort of cohesive whole, cutting her fingers on the sharp edges in the process as though she were cleaning up the pieces of a broken mirror. The shattered bits of her heart, soul, mind, and psyche that she was still struggling to integrate, reconcile, into unity.

She sighed, seeming to catch a distorted glimpse of her warped reflection in the cracked surface of a broken mirror. And she turned away from the image. She was still broken. Very much a work-in-progress.

George looked into her wardrobe, at the racks of shirts, waistcoats, and trousers that hung among her dresses. She looked down at the dress she was wearing right now. And the angel of

256

domesticity, of sweet, demure femininity, seemed to look reproachfully at her, intentionally obscuring George's view of the independent side of the chasm.

You should get rid of them, the golden-haired angel seemed to say, pointing contemptuously at the shirts, the waistcoats, the trousers, her tiny nose wrinkling. *These men's clothes. You don't need them. Stop wearing them,* the angel continued, shaking her head dismissively. *Being a real, feminine woman, a good girl, is the only thing that will make you happy. And women… real women… good girls… don't run wild. And they don't wear trousers.*

But trousers are what I feel most at home in, George countered. *They make me feel free.*

And wondering why she had chosen a dress this morning, George changed her clothes.

George listened. But although she might have expected to hear the familiar voices of her mother and grandmother chiding her for her choice of companion, clothing selections, and life choices in general, they said nothing. She listened into the silence. She lived her life, in all its joys and challenges. And she wondered.

She continued attending to Fryderyk; continued helping him. And yet, as she stepped forward, offering her strength on his behalf, lifting his burdens, capably assisting him with the requirements of day-to-day life, he reminded her… that she was beautiful. Told her she was precious. Told her that he would always be there for her just as she was there for him. That she was worthy of all the gentlemanly care that he could ever offer. And slowly… she began to believe him.

In her turn, she continued to offer him all her loving support; reminding him that he was strong, that he was capable, that he was handsome. Bashfully he deflected her compliments, fixating on the prominence of his nose or the small dimensions of his biceps, but she was always there with a kind word, praising the graceful curve of the nose he was embarrassed by, lauding the strength both external and internal with which he was maintaining mastery of his own life, earning and managing his own money, cleaning his own kitchen. Silently, he listened to her sincere words. And slowly… he began to believe her.

George shook her head. And she smiled, whispering a prayer of gratitude as her own words came back to her; the words she had spoken to Fryderyk during the very first carriage ride they had gone on together. That here below… the people placed on Earth by God to live their lives here had been given to one another to show love to one another, love that reflected the love of God for His people. And to come to know Him more through their relationships with one another. To look out for one another, and to lift one another up.

George nodded, smiling as she received all of those reminders… as she considered all the things that she and Fryderyk were doing for one another. God was with them. And He had given them to one another.

"How do I look? Do I look all right? I have no idea if this is going to go anywhere but I want to look my best—"

"You look fine, dearest," George reassured Pauline as they stood in Marie d'Agoult's powder room one summer night, minutes before Louis Viardot was expected to arrive at the party.

Gently, she brushed a lock of hair out of her friend's eyes. "Absolutely lovely."

"But what will he think of me?" Pauline squeaked. "What if he doesn't like me? What if he *does* like me?"

"Well, seeing as you haven't met more than the once, you won't know until you find out!" George said cheerfully. She offered her arm, which Pauline clung to. "Off we go," she said. "Let's not leave it a mystery any longer."

Steadily, George made her way out into the drawing room, feeling Pauline's knock-kneed shaking beside her. A number of other guests had arrived; George noticed Delacroix and Liszt speaking with Didier and tried just to be glad that Mallefille was out of the country and exceedingly unlikely to turn up. Alfred de Vigny was speaking with Pierre Leroux, and Victor Hugo and Honoré de Balzac were deep in discussion.

"Ah, Monsieur Viardot…"

"There he is," George murmured to Pauline. Pulling the staggering teenager along with her, George offered a nod to Louis, who was being greeted by Wojciech Grzymała. They exchanged a few words; then Wojciech stepped away to speak with Balzac.

"Monsieur Viardot, may I present Michelle Ferdinande Pauline García," George announced. Offering a manly bow to match the shirt, trousers, cravat, and top hat she had worn today, she stepped aside as Louis offered a bow of his own.

"Señorita," he said, offering a gloved hand. Pauline offered her own, and he raised it gently to his lips and kissed it. Pauline went bright red. "Señorita," he said again, "Monsieur Balzac and I find ourselves unsure on a particular point in the history of flamenco music…"

Pauline's eyes brightened. She glanced at George, who nodded with an encouraging little smile. And allowing Louis to take her hand, she joined him and Balzac in another part of the room.

George watched them go. And she smiled.

She read. He listened. He played. And she listened. George and Fryderyk continued to share their art with one another, rejoicing in the shared experience, growing closer with every day that passed. One quiet afternoon, and then the next, George found herself so spellbound by Fryderyk's music that she crept closer and closer, finding herself underneath the piano almost without knowing how she had gotten there, just as she had the first time she had visited Fryderyk's apartment. She opened her heart, letting the music pour into her. And as it ended, she climbed back out from under the instrument, offering Fryderyk a half-shaky smile, which he returned, his eyes shining like the stars.

"What did you think?" he asked in a breathless whisper; a whisper that already knew the answer, but at the same time, really wanted to know.

She just sighed, soul too full for words. "Beautiful."

A singular instance was repeated at occasional intervals, then slowly became a habit. And George chose not to hold herself back. Too many times to count, she folded herself up under Fryderyk's piano as he played, letting herself drown in his music. He just smiled and kept playing, rejoicing with her in the intimacy in which their very souls were sharing. He didn't mind. And before she knew it, she was listening from under the piano more often than not.

George went to the marketplace, filling her basket with fresh fruits and vegetables. Except— she needed one more eggplant, and there was an absolutely perfect one just out of reach. She stood on tiptoe, straining to reach it, fighting to keep her balance and keep from collapsing onto the vegetable stand, sending produce cascading everywhere.

"Can I help you, my dear lady?"

George looked up, seeing a tall older man standing behind her, a benevolent smile on his face. Dressed as she was today in a long skirt, she had been instantly recognized as a woman.

"Thank you," she said, lowering her arm and taking a step back. The man reached the eggplant she wanted easily, presenting it with a flourish.

"What a nice meal that'll make for your dear husband," he said fondly. "Feed him up, eh?" Tipping his hat, he went on his way.

"What a nice meal indeed," George said softly, placing the eggplant in her basket. And she continued with her shopping.

"You know how much I need you?" George asked at the close of a long, quiet afternoon visit at Fryderyk's that had somehow lasted until almost nine o'clock in the evening. They sat side-by-side on the couch in his living room, sharing a blanket, watching through the window as one by one, the stars lit up the sky.

Fryderyk smiled as he reached out to squeeze her hand. "I need you, too."

George smiled, joy rising inside her heart with a sudden idea. "Why don't I make myself useful, then?"

He raised a quizzical eyebrow. "Hmm?"

She nodded. And her breath caught as her excitement rose. "I mean it. I'll come over a couple of times a week, and I'll do whatever you need. You want me to cook, clean—"

"Maybe not cook," he said with a raspy, wheezing little laugh.

She smiled and shook her head, giving him a playful wink. "Maybe not. But I can clean pretty well. Not that your place is a mess, but every house needs tidying every now and then."

"I do have a maid," Fryderyk said. "But she was off this week. And she doesn't clean my bedroom."

"Well, I don't mind. And not just helping with the cleaning— I can read to you, sit up with you... Let's see, what else am I good at— oh, I can write quickly, quite obviously, so if you ever need to dictate anything, I can do that. Anything you need. Anything at all. I don't know when I've spent my time better than tonight. Or any time that I'm with you, Fryderyk."

George paused with a breathless smile of pure delight. Fryderyk returned her smile, then seemed to shrink as he shivered. "Do you want another blanket?" she asked, giving him a concerned little frown.

"Yes, please," he said. He nodded at the chair across from the couch. "There should be one over there."

Standing up, George crossed to the chair, gathering the blanket into her arms. And a rustling caught her ear. George chuckled, glancing down at the wide, flouncy skirt that she had chosen today; the heavy skirt that was slowing her down just slightly.

"Fryderyk?" she asked, turning back around.

"Hmm?" He raised his eyebrows, inviting her to continue. Approaching the couch, she carefully arranged the blanket over the afghan that was already draped over him, tucking him in warmly.

She chuckled, smiling as she felt the words forming behind her lips. "Well, we've been talking recently about setting one another free… and how when I'm around you, I'm free to be the woman who wears trousers…"

He continued looking at her. "Mm-hmm…"

George let her smile turn into a grin. Playfully, she raised her own eyebrows. "Would you mind if I wore trousers tomorrow?"

Fryderyk chuckled as he shook his head. "Not at all. I know when we first met that the fact that you wore trousers rather… overwhelmed me, but since I've gotten to know you, and trust you, I wouldn't mind." He looked up at her a bit cheekily as she sat down again beside him. "In fact, I think I'd rather like to see you in trousers again."

George just laughed.

Maybe, she thought. *Maybe I can let you love me. Maybe I can believe that you really do love me, even in a best friend sort of way. Maybe I can let myself be myself around you. Maybe we are enough for one another. Maybe you are able to handle me. And maybe I really am all right exactly the way I am.*

24   The Dream Meets Reality

George got up shortly after six the next morning. For a woman who was known to go to bed at six in the morning and get up at noon, that was saying something. She fed the dog and put him out, then put on a simple white shirt, a cravat, and a comfortable pair of gray trousers. Good for cleaning in.

She made some coffee and ate a quick breakfast, then gathered up a mop and two dusters, tied up her hair, and marched over to Fryderyk's apartment before it was even light. After knocking heartily at his front door, she paused, biting her lip as she suddenly hoped he was actually up. Double-checking her pocketwatch, she saw that it was only seven-fifteen.

Fryderyk was slightly out-of-breath when he got to the door, wrapped warmly in his dressing-gown and still tying his cravat. "Oh, George, you're here early," he said, eyebrows raised in surprise. Looking her up and down, he blushed. "And you're—"

George chuckled. "How do I look?"

He just shook his head. "Beautiful."

She just smiled.

"Thought I'd get an early start," she said, then walking past him into the apartment, which was as dim, warm, and dusty as ever. "All right. What should we start with? You did eat breakfast, didn't you?"

"Not yet, actually," he said, following her back inside. "I was just finishing getting dressed when you arrived."

She stopped, setting down the dusters and propping her mop carefully in a corner. "Oh. Well, then, what would you like?"

He paused, putting his hands in his pockets. "Well, George, I

264

don't know if…" He trailed off.

She snorted with laughter. "Oh, I know what you're thinking. I know how bad my Funeral March Stew or whatever we were going to call it was, but that was months ago. Don't give me that," she said playfully as he raised his eyebrows incredulously. "Come on. You like eggs? I can make really good scrambled eggs, I promise. That sound all right?"

He just chuckled. "If you're sure."

George smiled. "All right, then. I'll get some started for you."

She strode confidently into the kitchen, stoked the fire in the stove, heated up a frying pan on the range, and cooked up three eggs. Sweat ran down her face as she stood over the hot stove. It was still very warm inside the apartment, even for winter— at least she wasn't using the oven.

"You get yourself some milk and sit down; these'll be ready in a minute," she said. Obediently, he poured himself a glass and sat down to wait. Soon she was emptying sunny, fluffy eggs onto his plate, watching him eat them with more gusto than she had anticipated. She would have to make scrambled eggs more often.

"I'll get started while you finish eating," George said, and Fryderyk nodded. Taking up one of the dusters, she marched into the dimness of the still, muffled sitting room and took a look around— or tried to. It was so shadowy in here that she could barely see.

As her eyes adjusted, George found the nearest footstool with her knee and almost tumbled over forward. From somewhere in the dark room, Valdeck gave a yowl of panic, and Fryderyk gave a startled,

"Huh?"

"I'm all right," she yelped as she threw her arms out, catching herself on the arm of a chair.

"Good!" she heard his concerned voice reply.

George regained her balance and her composure and began formulating her plan of action. She started by heading to the large picture window and hauling back the heavy curtains. Early-morning sunlight flooded the crowded room, illuminating the sparkling frost of dust that lay over every surface. At least now she could see enough to work. George choked up on her duster and began her anti-dust crusade on a rickety, fragile-looking bookshelf filled with delicate knickknacks. Three enthusiastic seconds later, a vase crashed to the floor.

With a gasp, George dove, but it was too late. The vase was done for. "Ohhh, Fryderyk, I'm sorry," she moaned, kneeling down and carefully beginning to pick up the larger pieces. The cat arched his back and hissed, then launched himself into the air to observe from the top of a chair. From the kitchen, Fryderyk craned his neck to see what she'd broken.

"The green and white vase?" he asked.

"Yes," she mumbled, her face growing hot with shame. "I didn't mean to; I just wasn't being careful…"

He just shook his head with a little smile. "Well, at least that was a gift from someone I never want to see again. Maybe it's for the best."

George just winced.

"Who… who gave it to you?" she asked a few minutes later.

Fryderyk chuckled. "A pompous, self-important snob… Sent it to me just to make sure I knew he was wealthier than I was."

George shook her head with a little smile, even as she set aside the broken pieces of glass for disposal. "Sounds like you know some pretty interesting people."

He smiled. "I certainly do. Present company included."

George just chuckled.

As George cleaned, Fryderyk joined her in the sitting room, regaling her with the origin stories of all the little knickknacks that filled his shelves. Paris, Poland, Germany… each had a story behind it, happy, sad, or funny. And with each story that Fryderyk told, George's fascination grew.

"I had a friend pick up six of these for me in Vienna," he said, pointing to a series of china figurines, "and this one over here—" He pointed out a miniature teacup— "I got in Berlin. And this…" he said, his voice filling with pride, "is the most special of all." Carefully, he picked up a small silver urn, holding it cautiously in both hands. "Soil from home," he said softly. "Good Polish earth. So I'll never… never forget."

George nodded. Gently, she patted him on the shoulder. "How could you forget?"

The knickknack shelves clean, George turned her attention to a dusty bookshelf. "Well, that's better already, isn't it?"

Fryderyk said nothing. Wondering if he'd heard her, George turned to look at him— and paused in confusion. Fryderyk's face had gone white, a picture of horror. Shaking from head to foot, he began backing up, pointing a quavering hand at something that seemed to have reduced him to abject terror.

"What's wrong? What is it?" George's heart began to pound, and she whirled around, duster held aloft like a weapon, searching the half of the room at which he was pointing for the threat.

"SPIDER!" he howled, his eyes wild.

"Oh." Her sense of calm returning, George tossed aside the

duster and began peering around for the spider as Fryderyk bounded onto the dark-red couch and perched there on his knees, practically gibbering as he shook. "Where is it?"

"Right there! Right there! Oh, kill it, kill it!" Fryderyk flailed a shaking hand in the general direction of the window.

"I'll get it, I'll get it, it's all right." As George watched, trying to tune out the distracting howls, an ugly, hairy little piece of work with visible fangs came scuttling out into the open.

She didn't have time to think; just ran over, shot out a bare hand, and walloped it with a satisfying crunch.

"There, it's dead, see?" She held out the remains for him to see. Shuddering, Fryderyk turned away with his eyes squeezed shut and his hand over his mouth, nearly gagging. "See? All gone. All dead." She wiped the spider legs and guts off onto her trousers.

But the war wasn't over. Just as George was about to reclaim her duster and get back to work, Fryderyk turned pale again and wailed,

"There's another one! Oh! Oh! Kill it! Kill it! Kill it!"

He'd said "kill it" three time for this one. Deftly, George spun around and brought her hand down on another hairy little monstrosity with a distinct squelch. This was kind of fun, if not for all the shrieking with which Fryderyk was regaling her. Who knew *what* he'd do if a mouse got in the house. Based on this performance, probably break a blood vessel. Thank goodness for Valdeck.

Two very exciting minutes later, George finally killed a third spider with another crunch.

"I think that's the last one."

"Good." Fryderyk was visibly shaking, so drained from the

burst of panic that he looked like he was about to collapse. "Thank you… George. I'm sorry I'm—"

She rested a hand on his trembling shoulder and shook her head. "No, don't be; it's no big deal; phobias aren't anything to be ashamed of…"

He raised his eyebrows sarcastically. "It's not a *phobia*, George."

She looked at him. "Fryderyk, respectfully, if it sends you jumping up onto the couch screaming, it probably is a phobia. But we took care of it, all of them, and they're all thoroughly squashed and I certainly hope we found all of them. I'm going to dust some more, all right?"

He gave a shuddering sigh and nodded. "All right, George."

Then he looked at the wall, and his nose wrinkled. That was kind of a cute expression, the same one he'd worn so many months ago when she'd made that awful soup.

"Oh… there's a bit of one still on the wall." Fryderyk's look of revulsion intensified— he looked absolutely sickened.

George hurried over and examined the spot that was nauseating him. "Really? Oh, where?"

"There," he groaned, pointing a bit weakly.

George pulled her sleeve over her hand and wiped the spider's squashed little corpse off the wall. It only left a small spot. "There, how's that? You can barely see the spot."

Fryderyk looked at it and nodded, still looking a little queasy.

"That's lovely, George."

For the rest of the day, Fryderyk's eyes seemed extra-large, and George found him checking chairs before he sat down, looking under and behind things, examining things before he picked them up. Checking for spiders, she was sure. Oh, thank God, thank God that it hadn't been a mouse. Silently she shook her head as she wondered— if there had been a mouse, what would he have done if she had not been there? She didn't mind being the spider-killer— she found it rather fun— but again it occurred to her… she had never met anyone so afraid of spiders. And again she wondered… what was it that made Fryderyk so unique— so different from anyone she'd ever met?

After a short break, George did the dishes while Fryderyk sat at the kitchen table and wrote. Within five minutes, she broke a plate. Fryderyk continued writing, but eventually shook his head and asked,

"How do you keep your own house?"

She groaned and scrubbed harder at the next dish. "I kind of do and I kind of don't!" Shaking her head, George rolled up her sleeves and set to scouring a pot. "Whoever said that women are the weaker sex never scrubbed burned soup off the bottom of a pot!"

The dishes done and put away, George swept the kitchen, gathering up a dustpan full of fluffy dust bunnies. The dust removed, she moved on to mopping, filling the mop bucket with hot water, then dropping the mop in with a splash. The cat sped across the kitchen floor, hopped lightly onto the counter, and looked down, watching her.

Once the mop was thoroughly soaked, George hauled it out, slapped it onto the floor with a wet splat, and went to work scrubbing at the floor. Fryderyk set down his work and peered over at her from the easy chair in the sitting room, where he'd settled himself with a blanket to continue writing. She smiled and

270

hoisted the mop in salute, then stepped forward onto a spot she'd already mopped and skated nearly a meter before grabbing the counter, gasping and laughing.

"I'm all right," she guffawed, backing away from the counter and picking the mop up off the floor. Fryderyk's concerned expression changed to a laughing smile as he shared the joke, realizing that it was all right for him to laugh.

"Where's Valdeck?" Fryderyk asked suddenly, craning his neck to look for his cat.

"On the counter," George said, pointing. "He's watching me. How'm I doing, Kitty? No, don't get down—"

But it was too late. Valdeck had jumped off the counter onto the wet floor. He screeched as all four paws shot out from under him in all four directions, scrabbled helplessly with his claws on the slippery floor, skated a meter, and catapulted himself through the air to land in his master's lap, shaking all over, his fur standing on end. Fryderyk petted him and fussed over him while George stood by and chuckled.

"He's probably never even seen the mop," Fryderyk said as he continued soothing the confused cat. "He's always upstairs with me while my maid Estelle cleans every week."

"Upstairs?"

Fryderyk swallowed, looking down shyly. "Yes, well, Valdeck and I, we don't really like standing around staring at Estelle, watching her clean. Might as well stay upstairs in the sitting room, play the piano a little…"

Silently, George smiled. He hadn't told her everything, had he?

"Well, the mopping is finished and I haven't hurt myself, so that's a small victory," George finally announced after a dangerous adventure, staggering in weary satisfaction into the sitting room. "Guess that about does it for the downstairs, then."

"Thank you so much, George," Fryderyk said sincerely as she flopped down on the ottoman at his feet with a sigh. He poked a chilly hand out of the blanket and stroked her sweaty hair. She smiled at his gentle touch— Mallefille could nearly have knocked her over merely by stroking her hair, even if he honestly meant to be gentle. And she bit her lip, blinking back tears as she thought of her father and how he had stroked her hair all those long years ago. "I wish... I wish I could help more," Fryderyk said regretfully. "Cook, clean, tidy." He shook his head with a wry chuckle. "But I can't even carry a laundry basket— weighs as much as me!"

George turned toward him with a little smile of her own. "Aw, now you don't have to worry about it because now you have me," she said, patting his pointed knee under the knitted afghan and the sleeping cat. She sighed, biting her lip in poignant pain. He needed her. He really didn't have anyone to take care of him. A maid kept his apartment clean, but that wasn't a relationship. And his parents lived so far away.

And yet, here she was, doing the things he needed her to do, filling that role, taking care of a person who needed to be cared for. Here she was... being a woman.

She sighed. "But it's all done now, anyway. All done."

"I actually do have a maid, like I said," he said awkwardly. "Her name's Estelle. She was off this week; that's why it's so dusty."

"That reminds me," George said carefully. "Fryderyk, on the nights that I've seen you to bed, I can't help but notice that your bedroom is really dusty. May... may I clean it sometime?"

272

Fryderyk gave a slightly embarrassed smile. "I know it's a wreck. Estelle doesn't... actually clean the bedroom. She cleans every other part of the house, but my bedroom's off limits."

George nodded. "Well, that makes sense."

Fryderyk tried to laugh, then stifled a cough. "Actually, I hardly see her at all. She knocks on the door, I let her in, and I tell her that the list of what needs done is on the table along with her pay, and go upstairs. I don't think she's ever seen my room."

George nodded again. "Well, since I have permission to go in your room, I wondered if I might clean it today."

Fryderyk shrugged. "If you like. I suppose the dust isn't very good for my cough."

George smiled. "I think not."

25   A Fussy Friend

Fryderyk settled into his easy chair, Valdeck curled up on his lap. After a short rest, George got up again and headed for the stairs.

"Now, you just rest there awhile, and I'll go up to clean, all right?"

He coughed again and nodded. "Thank you, George."

She shook her head. "How can you breathe in there every single night? You're right— that really can't be very good for you."

Fryderyk nodded and shivered, putting his arms around himself. George detected an extremely small draft and started looking around the room for another blanket for him.

"I know. I don't like it. But I can't do it myself and I'm not letting Estelle in." And that was final, George gathered. She just nodded.

George found a soft, gray, hand-knitted blanket on another chair and draped it around Fryderyk's thin shoulders. He cuddled up in it and lay back, resting his head on the back of the chair.

"Thank you."

"Well, I'd better go up and get started," she said. "Try to rest."

He gave her a tired smile as she mounted the stairs. "I will. Be careful," he added in a half-teasing tone. "You've already slipped and broken a vase and a plate."

George just rolled her eyes with a chuckle of her own. And she made her way upstairs to the dark, warm, shelf-crowded, fabric-swathed, dust-muffled bedroom.

"Let's see, then," she said to herself, putting her hands on her hips and examining Fryderyk's room. Two chairs, comfortable

274

and overstuffed. A large armoire, similarly stuffed, revealing glimpses of velvet coats, silk shirts. A large bureau, certainly full of even more clothing, stood next to that. Several bookshelves filled with folders stuffed with handwritten musical compositions and printed sheet music. Vases of violets everywhere. A very nice room, except that every step she took on the sound-muffling rug raised thick clouds of dust like that which lay softly over every surface. Everything was gray, colors and patterns obscured by the film of dust.

First things first. Crossing to the window, she opened the heavy curtains, blinking as bright morning light streamed into the room, illuminating every speck of sparkling dust that lay like hoarfrost over every surface. Additional motes of dust floated into the air from the curtains themselves. George tied a hanky around her face so she could breathe, rolled up her sleeves, and set to work. Years of education in household management taught to her by her grandmother rose to help her, reminding her that the first thing to go after would be the rug, and then the furniture, working from the top of the room to the bottom.

She looked down at the oriental rug, where the dust lay so thick that she couldn't see the pattern. Fetching a clean bedsheet, George rolled up the rug inside it, dragging the whole package outside to the backyard and hanging it on the clothesline to beat it free of dust, gray clouds of fluffy dust cascading through the air as she lambasted it with the rug-beater she'd found in the same closet from which she'd procured the mop. Hauling the clean rug back inside, she propped it, rolled up as it was, against the wall in the hallway just outside Fryderyk's room, waiting to be rolled out again once the rest of the room was clean. Returning to the kitchen for a moment, she put the mop, the bucket, and the rug-beater away in the closet.

Now that the dust was gone, George could see how beautiful the colorful Turkish rug was, its vibrant patterns almost seeming to glow. The heavy curtains, likewise full of dust, received the same treatment as the rug had, revealing brighter tones of olive-green. Then she swept the bedroom floor itself, gathering up a whole dustpan full of wispy dust-bunnies.

With a creak, she forced the bedroom window open, letting cool, fresh air pour into the room. And she emptied the dust out of the window. Being that there was so much of it, maybe the birds could use it for their nests come next spring.

The next thing George approached was a fragile-looking bookshelf that wobbled gently as she approached. As she began brushing at it with the duster, as gently as she reasonably could, its spindly frame trembled alarmingly. Then, out of nowhere, a voice from downstairs broke the silence; a sudden voice that made her jump, jabbing the duster into the set of shelves with sudden force as she endeavored to register that Fryderyk was calling for her and listen to what he was saying.

"I should have mentioned, the bookshelf is—" *Crash.* "Kind of unstable."

"Oh, no!"

George groaned as the dust settled— to some extent, anyway— and she was left staring at the carnage of what had once been a bookshelf. Books lay scattered on the floor, open and crumpled; three tiny vases lay in puddles of water, rumpled violets strewn over the wet floor. One china figurine was broken, and a marble bust lay at an angle, the side of the subject's face pressed into the floor. She bent over and carefully picked up the three framed pictures that had fallen, wiping the water from the flower vases off of the mercifully-undamaged glass.

In one portrait, that of a family, she recognized Fryderyk's facial features. That must be the Chopin family. Another picture portrayed a lovely young woman— probably Marja Wodzińska. A third, of an older man with curly hair and impressive sideburns, was definitely the Professor Elsner George had met. She also found a small bust, which had to be of Fryderyk himself, and which had only gained… one small chip in the tumble.

The bookshelf itself wasn't actually broken, which was a blessing. George picked up everything that had once been on it, then put her shoulder to it and got it upright again. Then she began the slow, delicate process of putting the books, picture-frames, vases, marble bust, and small, delicate knickknacks back onto the set of shelves, even though she knew that wasn't the way they'd been organized when she'd come into the room. Well, this did give her a chance to take each item individually and dust it, she reflected, and to clean the empty bookshelf, wiping up the film of dust with a damp cloth. She just wished that she could have emptied the shelf her own way, and on purpose.

Before too much longer, the entire set of shelves and all its contents were thoroughly cleaned and everything was back where it was supposed to be— or at least back on the shelf. Cautiously, George wiped down the other bookshelves as well, marveling as the silver frost of dust disappeared to reveal the warm, gleaming tones of shining chestnut, oak, and mahogany. That was better. Much better.

Slowly and methodically, George cleaned that room from top to bottom. She refilled her bucket of water again and again, pouring it out black with the dust that she was cleaning from the many surfaces in Fryderyk's room. And she discarded many dustpans full of fluffy dust bunnies. Slowly but surely, the room became cleaner. And the air became more breathable.

That just left the bureau, and then the floor itself. George rolled up her sleeves, got another damp cloth, and began wiping down the bureau. She didn't remove the two vases of flowers before beginning, but found the left one with her elbow.

She let out a yelp of panic and dove for the falling vase. She caught it before it hit the floor, setting it carefully back on the bureau with a shuddering sigh. She had a little water to clean up, but that wasn't… it didn't quite qualify as a disaster.

Fryderyk had heard the noise of panic. "Now what are you doing?" he asked from downstairs.

"Spilling your flowers, but I caught them!" she called. "All good! Nothing to see here!"

Fryderyk just chuckled.

Finally, it was time to return to the floor, where the dust of the rest of the room now lay thicker than ever. She swept the floor again, gathering up another dustpan of dust-bunnies. Then she got down on her hands and knees, wiping down the hardwood floor with a damp rag, which came away as black with dust as her washing-water had been earlier. With every bit of dust she wiped away, the colors and textures seemed to grow brighter, the once dull, gray surfaces now gleaming vibrantly, every inch of the room shining. And finally, she stood proudly regarding a sparkling, dust-free bedroom, breathless with satisfaction at the accomplishment that had followed all her hard work.

Closing the bedroom window and leaving the fresh, clean, worn-out bedroom to take a metaphorical nap after the ordeal she'd put it through, George stumbled downstairs, sweaty, exhausted from so much excitement, and covered in dust.

"Room's clean," she panted, collapsing once more onto the ottoman with her duster in her lap. Again, Fryderyk located his hand, unearthing it from among his blankets and gently reaching out to stroke her hair.

"Thank you so much, George," he said fervently. "I wish I could have helped; I wish it hadn't been in such bad shape for you, so much work…"

"That's all right; that's all right," she said, waving it off. "It's done now and everything is back pretty much where it was, except for the dust and a few spiderwebs. And the spiders," she had to say, raising her eyebrows as she teased him.

He smiled, winking good-naturedly at her joke. "Well done."

George bit her lip. "And I am sorry about the vase and the plate and the figurine I broke."

Fryderyk raised an eyebrow. "Oh, you broke a figurine?"

George looked down. "Yes… I'm sure you heard the bookshelf fall," she said sheepishly.

He hesitated. "Yes. I did."

She gave a nervous little laugh. "Well, I only broke one figurine, and I put a chip in the marble bust. It's you, right?"

He nodded. "Yes, me. My friend Jeanne-Pierre Dantan made it." He paused, giving a slight frown. "Where's the chip?"

"Just in the base."

He relaxed, his forgiving smile returning. "Oh. Well, that's not too bad." He chuckled. "Couldn't you have broken the nose? You see I could stand it. Always used to joke about flies landing on it when I was a teenager."

George shook her head with a chuckle of her own., rolling her eyes good-naturedly at his constant criticism of his own nose. "Oh, stop it. Your nose is just right."

George sighed and settled into the contented satisfaction of a freshly tidied house she'd cleaned herself. "Well, what's next?" she asked.

Fryderyk smiled. "We could eat soon, if you want." Pushing the blanket away, he slowly stood up from the easy chair. "Let's get this folded up on the back of the chair." Slowly he bent to pick up the heavy afghan, laboriously beginning to fold it.

"Here, let me," she said, and took it from him. George rolled it up into an ungainly ball and threw it over the back of the chair in a lumpy heap.

Fryderyk looked at it, then raised an eyebrow at her. "Let me show you how to do it. Go on, let me have it."

George took the blanket again and handed it to him. "There, now you take that end, and we'll fold it together," he said. George and Fryderyk each took two corners, and Fryderyk began folding his end.

George started folding her end without referring to Fryderyk's technique. She was just getting her end neatly folded in half when he made a disparaging noise.

"No, not in half— in thirds, like this. Watch me." Inquisitively, George disarranged her end and watched Fryderyk carefully fold his end in perfectly equal, tidy thirds. "Now try." In an instant his manner had changed; suddenly, he sounded like a piano teacher.

George's stomach plummeted as she seemed to shrink, feeling like a pupil. She took a deep breath and did her best, trying to fold her end of the blanket into what might have been equal thirds.

"How's that?" she asked almost nervously. She shook her

head. She'd never met anyone this particular about the way their blankets were folded. And she'd never felt a twinge of anxiety as to whether she had folded a blanket correctly. Or not since her grandmother had been the one scolding her.

"Just fine, for a first time," he said. George tried not to snort. First time? "Now we fold the whole thing in half, and then it goes over the back of the chair. Here we go."

Matching up their respective ends of the blanket, they carefully arranged it over the back of the chair. Task finally accomplished, George straightened the last little bit, stood back, and smiled.

"How's that?"

Fryderyk examined everything and smiled at her. "Very good, George. You're learning."

She patted him on the shoulder as she rolled her eyes. "But I'm not there yet?"

He just chuckled, the tall, imperious teacher fading away as the friend and sweetheart she knew reappeared. "George, I don't know if you'll ever get there, but I sure do like you anyway."

Her stomach grumbled. "What time is it? I've been cleaning all morning."

"Lunchtime," he said. "Or after lunchtime. It has to be one o'clock by now."

She checked the clock. He was right. Apparently his stomach could tell exact time.

George strode into the kitchen and began to make toasted cheese sandwiches for lunch, first opening the door of the stove to stoke the fire that was still gently smoldering inside. Fryderyk headed over to the cupboards for a glass. He put one hand firmly on the counter for balance, hauled one cupboard open, and frowned.

"George, where did you put the glasses? The plates are in here instead."

George looked up from the frying pan where the sandwiches were sizzling. "The glasses? Oh, they're over there." She pointed. "In the far-left cupboard."

He sighed with a shadow of a scowl. "Oh. Well, they go in this cupboard, just so you know for next time."

George nodded. "Oh, thanks for telling me. I'll do that next time."

He nodded and poured each of them a glass of milk.

"Why don't you get yourself a plate," she said a few minutes later. "These are almost done. Maybe you could get me one, too."

Fryderyk paused. "Why don't I?" he asked, tilting his head quizzically. "But I will if you're asking me to."

George paused, pondering Fryderyk's literal interpretation of the turn of phrase she'd used. "Ah... please get a plate for each of us, is what I should have said. Uh, thanks."

Fryderyk just nodded. He reopened the cupboard where the glasses should have been and got out two plates, which he set at each of their places at the dining room table. Returning to the kitchen, he opened yet another cupboard, seemingly just for the sake of suspicion.

"And I see you put the cooking knives in here, which go in the drawer over there—" He pointed— "where I'm guessing you put the dishcloths and towels."

"Yep," she said. "How did you guess?"

He shook his head. "Well, maybe later I can help you reorganize. I appreciate you washing all the dishes and putting things away; I just wish you'd asked me where things went so you

282

would have saved yourself the work of putting them away again *right*."

"You could always leave them where they are now," she muttered to herself, but not with any real resentment. "If you want a butter knife or a fork, I put them in the drawer over there," she said, pointing with the spatula. He got two of each.

After a silent pause, Fryderyk checked another low cupboard, then looked up, foiled again.

"But where are the napkins?"

"Up there," she said, pointing to a higher cupboard. "That one was completely empty."

"Well, that's because I can't reach it," he said just a little tartly. "Would you get me a napkin, please? And one for yourself, I suppose."

"Sure." George left the sandwiches, which by now were on the browner side of golden-brown, and fetched two napkins. "There you go— oh, no, they're burning!"

George thrust the two napkins at Fryderyk and raced to the stove, where the frying pan of toasted-cheese sandwiches was beginning to smoke. Grabbing a towel to use as a potholder, she snatched the frying pan off the stove.

"Well, they're still edible," she said cheerfully, bringing the frying pan of very hot sandwiches to the table just as Fryderyk slowly, carefully, and deliberately pulled her chair out for her. Silently, she brushed aside her grandmother's insistence, the demand of the angry, flexing ache inside her heart, that she should have been the one to pull his chair out for him. "Here you go." She put two sandwiches on each plate, then sat down.

"Thank you, George," Fryderyk said hesitantly from where he

had sat down across from her, poking at one of the sandwiches with his slender white finger and wincing at how hot it was. A bit of a sour expression was playing about his mouth, and she thought she saw his nose wrinkle just a tiny bit. "Crispy... just the way I like them."

Interpreting his expression, George identified the white lie he was telling her. "Here, we'll switch. Mine aren't as dark." She swapped the plates.

George took a bite. "Well, these *are* crispy," she commented, crunching noisily on the blackened sandwich. She wiped the charred crumbs from her mouth and took a big gulp of milk. "Milk helps it go down," she choked as she crunched into it again, the sharp, crunchy crumbs scratching at her throat on the way down.

Fryderyk smiled and took a sip of milk. Well, George thought, at least these weren't as bad as the Brussels sprout soup she'd made, and at least she hadn't burned down the apartment. She had two good things going for her about this meal. Things were going great.

Over her own loud crunching, George heard a loud scraping and looked up. Nostrils still flared and his jaw set into a polite smile, Fryderyk was endeavoring to scrape the black sooty stuff off the toast with his knife.

"I'll make you another one," she said, and got up.

She barely heard him mutter, "Thank you."

26 Friendship

They finished up, and George put the dishes in the sink. "There's still a bit to do upstairs," she said. "Want to come too, now that the air's at least breathable?"

"Yes, I'd like to."

Carefully they climbed the stairs together, Fryderyk panting as they reached the top. Gently George laid her hand on his back as he recovered.

"Let's see, now— would it be helpful for me to change your bedsheets while I'm here?"

"Today actually would be a good day to change them, since the laundress is coming to pick up my laundry later today." He gave a half-embarrassed chuckle. "Ah, thank you."

She smiled. "Not a problem. Not a problem."

He showed her the full hamper and she took the bedsheets, added them to the hamper, and set it aside for the laundress. Finally, she returned with an armful of clean sheets.

Fryderyk was waiting at the bookshelf she'd knocked over earlier, busily rearranging the objects with both hands.

"I'm sorry; I don't know where anything goes," she said. "I just picked them up and put them on the bookshelf."

He shook his head with a dismissive, forgiving smile and a little shrug. "That's all right. I'll just put them where they go." He looked around the room, offering an appreciative smile. "It looks beautiful in here," he said sincerely. "So much better than before. I can actually see the patterns on my lovely rug, and the shelves look amazing. And..." He took a deep breath, releasing it as a heavy sigh. He smiled. "I can actually breathe for once. Thank you so much for all your hard work. I'm sorry it was so bad."

George smiled. "My pleasure— and no problem. All right, let me put the clean sheets on." Wearily, Fryderyk settled into the armchair to watch, the sleepy cat curled up in his lap.

George proceeded to arrange the white linen bedsheets and heavy red comforter in the way she would on her own bed, with the foot of the top sheet stuffed under the mattress, lumpy and wrinkled.

She stepped back, satisfied with her work. "There we go. How's that?"

He looked at it, one eyebrow slowly creeping upward. And only minutes after accepting Fryderyk's fervent gratitude, George again felt herself feeling like a pupil in the presence of a tall, imperious teacher.

"George, look at it. How does that compare to how it looks when you make your bed?"

George felt herself chuckling. And this time, her spark put up its fists with a playful comeback. "Well, I don't really make my own bed, so I can't really say," she said unashamedly. "I'm not that fussy. I just kind of throw the blankets back toward the head of the bed and get on with my day."

Fryderyk sighed. "Well, let me explain how to make a bed with square corners."

She raised an eyebrow. "Explain?" she asked. She put her hands on her hips. "I didn't say I didn't know *how* to make a bed with square corners; I said I don't *care* to make my own." She chuckled. "But let me see what I can do."

George crouched down and set about making square corners, raising the foot of the mattress with her shoulder so she could cram the sheet under it and somehow contrive to smooth it out.

"All right, how's that look?"

286

"Almost done," he announced.

It looked done to her. "What's the last step?" she asked.

"Well, I like to have the top edge of the sheet and the blanket folded down about twenty-five centimeters."

"All right." George took the edges of the sheet and comforter and folded them over, arranging them as smoothly and evenly as possible. They were folded between twenty and thirty centimeters down, that much was certain. "How's that look?"

He examined it and smiled. "Good job, George. For a first try."

She returned the smile, even as she rolled her eyes. "For a first try, just like with the afghan? That's all the credit I get? I went into battle there, you might say. Seems a shame you're just going to lie down in it," she said, admiring her work, the beautiful results of the ten minutes of pure warfare she'd just spent; her sweaty struggle with sheets, blankets, pillows, and mattresses. "I can honestly say that I've never made a bed that nicely before."

Fryderyk smiled. "Well, you've learned something important today."

George just rolled her eyes.

George unrolled the rug that had been waiting in the hallway, settling it again into its place on the bedroom floor. The vibrant colors and patterns of the radiant Turkish rug seemed almost to glow as she rolled it out again, shining a thousand times brighter than they had when they had been obscured by all that dust. Carefully, she also put the curtains back up, marveling at the deep, jewel-like green that was now properly apparent. Slowly making their way back downstairs to the sitting room, she and Fryderyk collapsed on the couch, both out of breath.

"All this cleaning has worn me out," George panted, pulling

off her cravat and wiping her sweaty face. Being a happy, domestic goddess was exhausting, even if it was satisfying.

"How about you rest and I'll play the piano for you?" Fryderyk asked, pulling the afghan he'd settled down under closer around his shoulders and slowly getting up.

She yawned. "That would be lovely." She turned and watched him sit down at the piano, wrapping the blanket around his shoulders again. He grunted in frustration as he struggled to get it comfortably adjusted, and she got up and fixed it for him. He smiled at her thoughtful gesture, reaching out and gently touching her hand. She smiled too, eternally amazed at how exactly alike their hands were. They were artists' hands.

Fryderyk straightened his sheet music and got ready to play. George sat down again on the couch as the cat hurried over and curled up at Fryderyk's feet.

Fryderyk pointed at the handwritten title at the top of the manuscript. "This is a fairly new one, one of the etudes. When he prints it, my publisher Monsieur Pleyel will probably call it *Winter Wind*."

Fryderyk began a piece in a minor key, soft and slow. But the gentle mood did not last— abruptly, it transformed into a powerful tempest, Fryderyk's delicate hands flying over the keys as the essence of the perfect winter storm whirled and whistled through the room with all the power and menace of a blizzard throwing itself against the outside of the houses.

It moved into major key for a moment, its spirit a little friendlier, but not for long. The piece stormed along wildly, Fryderyk looking almost frightened as his hands disappeared into a blur of violent music. The same descending theme reappeared, and George could just see the trees beaten by the winter wind.

288

Soon the piece crashed down and moved into a ferocious crescendo, the last glissando ringing out into silence.

Fryderyk sat there panting from the effort, wiping his pale brow. George released the breath she suddenly realized she'd been holding, shivering in the blizzard she could almost feel chilling her bones. She glanced out the window at the winter afternoon. It was still mostly sunny outside, but there, on the western horizon, she could see large, dark clouds piling, approaching them in a stiffening breeze. Had he… summoned a storm?

"You brought a storm in with your music," she said, pointing out the window. "Although in the middle of summer, I assume we'll get thunder instead of snow."

Fryderyk looked, raising his eyebrows as he saw. "Well, now I know never to write a piece about the ten plagues of Egypt," he said with a small chuckle that turned into a cough. He stifled it in his elbow.

George smiled. "Yes, with a touch like yours, that might not be a very good idea. That piece was amazing," she said, nodding at the sheet music of this new etude. Amazing he could play it without collapsing, she thought privately.

Fryderyk smiled, then paused. "But it's not quite right…" He repeated a phrase in isolation, and then stopped abruptly, grabbing up his sheet music and making a small change. George shook her head. She knew that nothing, not even the most beautiful piece, was ever quite perfect.

Dinnertime came and went, the blue twilight deepening into a gentle night. George was putting away a stack of clean dishtowels, just delivered by the laundress, who had also taken away the dirty bedsheets, when she noticed a slip of paper in the bottom of the kitchen drawer. Setting the stack of towels aside, she retrieved the paper before putting the towels where they belonged.

It looked like a short letter. And the first words were *Dear George.*

She read on, kneeling there on the kitchen floor, blinking back another happy tear with every word she read. *Dear George*, it said, *I want to thank you for everything. Your love, friendship, and companionship are a gift for which I thank God. And so is your incredible faithfulness; your generous kindness— helping me cook, helping me with the housework, keeping me company.*

I wish I could do more for you. But I can never, never thank you enough for everything you have done for me. Thank you, my beloved, for joining me in life's duet.

Yours,

Fryderyk

George held the letter to her heart, blinking back tears. *Love. Companionship. Gratitude.* Infinite care… the reciprocation of the love for him that filled her heart; the love that made her want to spend the rest of her life in the easy familiarity they had formed… and to share more and more with every year that went by.

Wiping her nose, she stood up, making her way back into the sitting room. She could finish putting the clean laundry away later.

"I got your note," she said, holding it out. Nestled in his easy chair, Fryderyk looked up from petting the cat and smiled.

"Good," he said with a little nod. "But even that note… it can't really say everything I want to say. Can't really say how grateful I am."

She bent to give him a gentle hug. "I hear you loud and clear."

Soon it was nine o'clock. And as Fryderyk began to yawn, George took her leave, giving him a gentle pat on the shoulder before wishing him a pleasant evening, putting her coat on, and heading out into the cool June night. And with a smile in her heart as she remembered the wonderful day they had spent together, she went home.

Take care of him, her grandmother seemed to say, the steel in her blue eyes commanding her granddaughter to obey. *Take care of him as he needs to be taken care of.*

George nodded. She would.

It was raining. George raised the collar of her frockcoat, bending her head as she splashed through the running streets of Paris one late spring day in 1838. And she barely glanced at the stores and shops she was passing.

Until she saw the hat shop. George turned her face away from it as her stomach swooped, memories clawing at her in bitter fury. The hat shop. Just like a dozen others in Paris, a hundred others in France, not particularly distinctive in and of itself. And yet, to her… infinitely distinctive, standing out to her like the proverbial sore thumb.

She shook her head, blinking back tears. Because the little four-year-old inside her mind was frowning up at her with big, sad, brown eyes, tugging insistently at her hand.

Stop, she whined, pointing at the hat shop. *Go in.* Maman *is in there. You know she is. This is her shop. The shop she promised she'd open. She promised. So all you have to do is go in, and she'll be there. And everything will be all right again.*

George paused, looking up at the hat shop through tears, even as her mind demanded she walk up to the door and go in. She swallowed, seeing it in her mind— the love, calm, and clarity on her mother's face, the embrace they would share, the way Sophie would lead her through the business she had opened, welcoming her daughter to take her place beside her as co-owner of the shop she'd founded. Everything would be all right again. Everything would be perfect.

She shook her head again. Because that wasn't true. And the part of her that was still waiting for her mother, dead and buried as she was, to open a hat shop, was misinformed. Those beautiful hopes… were simply not possible.

George wiped her eyes. And she turned back to the street, hurrying away. *I can't,* she said to the child. *I wish you were right… oh, how I wish you were right. But things don't work that way. They just don't.*

Why not? the little girl asked.

George bit her lip. *Because she's dead,* she said softly. And with a shuddering sigh, she closed her eyes, steeling herself for the question she knew was coming next.

When is Maman coming back from death?

George felt a painful shiver course through her, blinking back tears as the pain wracked her.

She's not, George whispered. *I'm sorry… but she's not. She can't.*

The little girl looked up at her, tears of her own running from her big, brown eyes. *I'm still waiting.*

George nodded, releasing a heavy sigh.

I know.

"Thank you for listening," George said to Claudette as she set aside the chapter she'd just read of her latest manuscript. She looked up at her friend, biting her lip in sheer gratitude for the rapt interest on Claudette's face. "Thank you... for caring."

Claudette looked at her. "Of course," she said. "I'm your friend, aren't I? And besides that—" She winked— "you are actually a pretty good writer, if I do say so myself."

George just smiled.

George joined Pauline for tea again. And carefully, tenderly, she continued to encourage the lovesick young woman.

George sipped her tea. "You know, Alfred de Musset is not the only man on God's green earth."

Pauline gave a sad sigh, biting her lip as she looked away. "I suppose he's not," she murmured dejectedly.

George allowed herself a small smile. "You know, Louis Viardot is a wonderful man. He's a little older than you... all right, he's a lot older than you, he's almost forty, but— well, you know him, don't you? Or you've met him? He was your sister's attorney; he helped her get her divorce from Eugene."

"But my sister's dead," Pauline whimpered, eyes sparkling with tears. "Remember? She had that horse accident in '36 and died two months later..."

"I'm sorry," George murmured, squeezing Pauline's hand even as she shuddered, a strange twinge shivering through her at the thought of Maria's deadly equestrian accident. She'd died just the same way that George's papa had... Shaking her head, George brushed away the thought, returning to the moment. "But all that to say," she continued, "Louis is very academically-minded— he has a literary background, he's a part of the artistic circle here in Paris— Leroux introduced us way back when, and it seems like he's good friends with everyone, he's financially secure, he's the director of the *Théâtre Italien*, he's as solid as a brick…"

Pauline gave another sniff, wiping her nose. And slowly, she looked up. "Are you trying to set me up with him?"

George smiled, giving a little shrug. "I don't know. Maybe I am."

George sorted through the day's post. And she sighed. There was yet another letter from Mallefille; another missive from the lovesick globetrotter who could not help but tell her exactly where he was at all times, and remind her of how much he missed her. And, he promised, of the fact that one day, he would be back.

She scanned his letter. Finding nothing in it that merited rereading, she threw it in the fire. And she went on with her day.

"I wish I'd never met Mallefille," George said one summer day as she and Fryderyk sat on her couch, sipping their tea.

He looked at her, forehead crinkling in confusion. "What do you mean? What's that got to do with anything?"

"I got another letter from him," she explained. "From my end, we broke up ages ago, but he won't stop writing to me to tell me where he is and what he's doing. As though I care." She shook her head. "He was a pig," she said bitterly. "He didn't mean to be, but he was. A boor. Yes, a fellow artist; a playwright— he wasn't dim, by any means— but he was… selfish. And jealous. Did nothing but show me off on his arm like a little china doll and comment about how small I was, and when we were alone, he would accuse me of cheating on him. Bossed me around, was suspicious of everything I did, picked horrible fights with me where I didn't even know what was going to happen next. And it got to the point where I was uncomfortable just being around him... where I didn't even feel safe with him. Breaking up with him was the smartest thing I ever did... but I still don't know what would happen if he came back from roaming the Continent. Don't know what he would do. To me, once he saw how much I've moved on... or to you, for being the one I've moved on with."

She sighed, looking at Fryderyk with a small smile. "I can't tell you how different you are from him; how different courting with you is from courting him. You... you care about me for who I am; you really understand me as an artist; you aren't just letting me court you— you're courting me back. Because I... matter to you. In a way that I never did to Mallefille."

Fryderyk took her hand with a concerned little frown. "Of course, I care about you— of course, you matter to me. And of course, I'm going to court you back. I need you— a thousand times, I need you— but in all the ways that you need me... I'll be there. I promise."

George felt herself swallowing back tears as she nodded. "Thank you, Fryderyk. I... I promise, too."

26   Danger

George continued taking life one day at a time. But the voices of the past did not remain silent for long.

He doesn't mean that, her grandmother's voice seemed to say, shaking her head sadly. *Or even if he does, he can't. Can't come through for you. Can't help you. Can't be the man. Can't protect you. He'll blow away in the next breeze. You will always have to protect him.*

He's not the warrior type, her mother seemed to say, flouncing by as she always did. *Not like your father was. And he won't be able to follow through. You've seen how he doesn't follow through. He's an inconstant little wisp of cloud, not a man you can rely on.*

Papa got hurt, and he went away, the little girl said, her big, brown eyes welling up with tears. *And I wasn't a good enough girl for him for him to come back. And if you're not a good girl, Fryderyk might leave and never come back. Because that's what happens with daddies.*

George shook her head. *You're wrong,* she responded. *He's strong. And I know he'll be there for me just as I will always be there for him.*

Time passed. And George continued to think. Continued to let the blur of houses and apartments in which she had lived fill her heart and mind; continued to let the memories of love and pain overflow the ocean of her aching soul.

Home, she thought over and over. *Such a word. Such a thought. So many things… all at once. But what… what does it mean to me? And will I ever find my way to it?*

296

George and Fryderyk made the rounds of George's social circle over the beginning of the Parisian summer of 1838, visiting with acquaintances and friends. Now and then, an ex would come out of the woodwork. George cringed her way through the visits, fending off embarrassing conversations with Didier, Michel, Bocage, but although she was annoyed and uncomfortable having to speak with them, she never felt unsafe. Until…

"George," a soft voice said. George looked up, and up again, into the face of the tall Hungarian at whose home a glittering collection of artists and philosophers had gathered for an evening of music and poetry.

"Yes, Franz?"

Liszt looked down. He swallowed. And he adjusted his cravat.

"George," he said again, "I have bad news."

George looked at him steadily, even as her heart began to pound, stomach twisting as her brain seemed to seethe and churn, bubbling and boiling inside her skull with a sudden, overwhelming sense of convulsive dread. Silently, she swallowed. And through the lump that choked her throat, she pushed out a response.

"What news?"

Liszt swallowed again. And quietly, he said, "Mallefille is back in France. Back… in Paris."

George closed her eyes as her heart pounded, her stomach swooping as though she'd missed a stair in the dark. The world around her had gone silent, the dazzling party bustling around her existing a universe away from where she floated in the silent eye of a sudden cyclone. Mallefille, whom she had thought long gone; Mallefille, who had gone to roam the Continent in search of a balm for his aching heart; Mallefille, whom George had never particularly wanted to see again. Back in France. Back in town.

She shook her head. Slowly, she returned to the world around her, letting in the sounds of the merry partygoers who surrounded her. And she opened her eyes, letting in the bright candlelight that sparkled on the brooches and tie-pins of the assembled artists.

"Thank you for letting me know, Franz," she said softly. "It was good of you to tell me. Thank you," she whispered again, the words barely crossing her lips. "Thank you."

George went home. She thought. And she worried. Mallefille. Back in France; back in Paris. She had thought— hoped— wished— that he was gone forever; that he would spend the rest of his life chasing rabbits and barmaids and would find some form of happiness that did not involve George. And yet... that dream had not come true. He was back. What... would that mean?

She kept an eye out for him. Every party, every shopping trip, every time she left her apartment became fearfully fraught with the heart-pounding question of whether she would see him; what she would do if she did. And her long, restless nights were filled with anxious, violent dreams of what might happen, every long hour weighed down by a growing sense of dread.

Keep us safe, she prayed as she kept her eyes peeled. *Keep him away from us. Please send him back to Germany, to Austria, to Russia, to Africa, to America, anywhere but here. Please... give him somewhere else to be.*

"You remember how I said not too long ago that I wished I'd never met Mallefille?" George said out of the silence of a quiet afternoon she was sharing with Fryderyk at his apartment.

Fryderyk looked up from the polonaise he was perfecting at the piano. "Yes," he said. He looked at her; at the way she was twisting her hands, biting her lip. And a frown of concern touched his face. "Did something happen?"

George looked up. "He's back," she said simply. "Franz told me, at that party the other night. Back in France. Back… in Paris."

Fryderyk nodded, his solemn face unreadable. He offered a hand, which George took. Biting his own lip, he looked away, heaving a heavy sigh. And he met her eyes with his.

"I'll keep you safe," he promised.

George swallowed back painful tears. And she just closed her eyes.

This is bad, George's mother and grandmother, the four-year-old, and the angel all seemed to agree. But they had very different thoughts on what she should do about the situation.

Show Mallefille that you've moved on, George's mother suggested, flouncing by with her hair long and loose, her shoulders bare, and the long train of a bright red dress flowing behind her. *Introduce him to Fryderyk and show him your new love.*

Remind him that you're his equal, her grandmother said, blue eyes snapping as fiercely as her apron. *And if he comes anywhere near you, punch him in the nose.*

Fryderyk wants to keep you safe, the four-year-old said, *but I'm not sure if he can. And if he can't beat Mallefille, he'll go away forever… just like Papa.*

Give Mallefille another chance, the angel insisted, pouting at

George with her annoying pink cheeks and perfect, rosy lips. *After all, if he loves you enough to keep writing to you, maybe he has changed.*

George shook her head. And she turned away from the voices. Until another one made her turn back.

This is bad, this voice agreed with the others. George looked around for the source of the voice. And finally, she saw the tower and the maiden within... the wise, patient maiden who, rarely though she spoke to George, seemed much more aware and perceptive than George ever would have realized.

This is bad, the maiden said again. *But... all is certainly not lost. Keep your wits about you. Don't trust Mallefille. But trust Fryderyk. And most of all... trust yourself.*

The days went on. And finally, the evening came when George saw Mallefille at a party; this time a salon held by Eugene Delacroix. George managed not to say a word to him; to avoid so much as making eye contact with him. And with the other guests, Mallefille listened as Fryderyk performed his Ballade in G minor. But on a night like this, with the noose of danger tightening more closely around her and Fryderyk's throats with every moment that passed, George could not lose herself even in the beauty of the ballade with which she had fallen in love all those months ago. She took it in; appreciated it. But she could not close her eyes. And she could not let it sweep her away. Not this time. Not tonight. Not with the very sword of Damocles hanging over their heads, the horsehair by which it dangled about ready to snap.

A rustle of fabric made George turn her head, heart thudding at the approach of an unknown individual. "That's bold of you, George," a familiar voice hissed. Marie d'Agoult stood there, looking down at her with a strange combination of pity and disgust. "Bringing your new beau to show him off to your old ones. Bold... and possibly dangerous. You may have moved on, but I can think of someone who hasn't forgotten you... and isn't likely to."

"Hello to you too, Marie," George said, shaking hands tersely. The duchess was not an easy person to like, an easy person to be friends with, but George had always done her best... and she always would. She looked at Mallefille from across the crowd; Mallefille, who was greeting this one, then that one. And yet, who, as of this moment, hadn't seemed to have noticed her. Until—

"I'm ready to go." George bumped right into Fryderyk, who, having finished his ballade to a hearty round of appreciative applause, had stepped unexpectedly into her bubble of space. Losing her footing in the tiny high-heels she was wearing, she found her stumble being righted by the strength of two slender arms garbed in jacket-sleeves of fine velvet; by two fine-boned hands that grasped hers as she got her footing again. George looked up at him, half-chuckling in embarrassment and gratitude. Breathlessly, she smiled. And he smiled back.

They stood there for an instant holding hands, alone in the crowd. The crowd that was populated by so many people; a sea of faces over whom George's eyes swept, taking them in in a merry blur.

Until one face stood out in sharp relief.

Mallefille was standing there, leaning against a doorframe. As tall and broad as ever, he had his burly arms folded in front of his chest, and his heavy moustache fluttered with every heavy breath he took. He was looking right at them. They had been seen.

"Good night, Fryderyk."

"Good night, George."

George got out of Fryderyk's carriage, heading up the walk to her front door as the carriage continued on, making its steady way down the street. But as she turned the key in the lock… a sound from behind her made her blood run cold.

"Fryderyk?" she asked, whirling around. She peered into the shadowy forms of bushes and trees; into the dark corners that made up the front yard; the spaces on each side of the building. Her heart hammered in her chest, her mouth growing dry as her palms grew slick with sweat, a wordless prayer for protection echoing inside her mind. She swallowed, gulping back as much of the fear as she could. "Who's there?"

No one spoke. George pushed the door open, then backed into the apartment, trying to keep her eyes on every dark corner of the outdoors at once.

She slipped inside safely, then slammed the door behind her, bolting it against the outdoors. George stumbled inside, shaking from head to foot, wondering what she had heard; why it had frightened her so badly. Cautiously, she crept to the front window, peering through the curtains.

A shadowy figure was striding purposefully away from her apartment, away from the exact place from which the noise had seemed to come. A build, a walk, she recognized as belonging to Mallefille. A knife glittered in his hand.

The next day, George arrived at Fryderyk's apartment to find him somberly pondering a letter at his kitchen table.

There was nothing for it but to launch straight into it. "You know how much I like this free coming and going," she said, "but something happened last night… and I'm thinking we should give each other our keys and lock up at night." She shook her head. "I always want my life to be open to you, but now I'm worried… about other people."

"Other people like Mallefille?" he asked in a whisper, his lips dry, his face pale. He slid the letter over to her. "He knows. This letter was on my doorstep this morning."

Stomach twisting, heart beginning to pound, George read the letter. *You have stolen that which is most dear to me. I intend to get it back. Meet me at dawn on Thursday, in the field by the mill. And choose your weapon from the pair of matched pistols I will provide.*

Fryderyk looked up at her from where he sat. "How early will I have to leave on Thursday?"

George's breath caught in her throat as her heart froze. Gasping, she sank to her knees beside Fryderyk's chair, grabbing his hands in hers.

"You can't mean to go through with it? Are you crazy? Fryderyk, he'll kill you!"

Fryderyk shook his head, his jaw set. "Maybe. Or maybe I'll kill him."

Rising to her feet, George threw her hands up. "Or maybe he'll kill both of us! He turned up at my house last night just as you were dropping me off— and he had a knife!"

Fryderyk gasped, eyes going wide. And his hands flew into the air in a dramatic gesture of his own. "You see? That's what I mean! I have to protect you! He's a maniac!"

"But it's not *safe*, dueling!"

Fryderyk gave half a chuckle. "George, that's the point."

"Come on!" George cried, shaking her head. "You'll be killed and end your career just as it's beginning, just like Évariste Galois the mathematician back in '32. What a bright star the world lost that day— all over a stupid affair of honor that he could have walked away from. He was only twenty, and you're only twenty-eight. I won't let you risk your life, your art, your career, for me."

"But I can't walk away." Fryderyk shook his head, eyes blazing with an unhesitating certainty, a firmness of purpose, that she had never seen before. The courage of a warrior who, had his body been stronger, would have dedicated his life to fighting for his country on the battlefield. "George... I have to. I have to keep you safe. Stand up for you."

"Stand up for what?" George cried. "My honor? I don't care about that. You know I don't." She gave an angry scoff. "Come on, all our time together and you think I care about a thing like that? Let Mallefille and all the others think what they want. You've done nothing worth dueling over, and he had no right to suggest something so ridiculous."

Fryderyk shook his head. "What if Mallefille doesn't stop until I do?" He took her hand, softly cradling it in his and gently raising it to his lips to kiss it. "You've taken care of me so many times and in so many ways. You make my life in France worth living. Now... now it's my turn to take care of you."

Tears blurred George's vision, the brave beloved in front of her wavering before her sight. And her heart flexed, telling *her* to stand and fight for *him*, guard him, protect him. Because no matter how great his dedication was, how could he stand up for her?

George shook her head. "Don't do this," she whispered through her tears. "I'll talk to him. I and all my friends will talk to him. Talk sense into him. Just give me time— time to stop him."

Fryderyk glanced at the letter. "Thursday, he said. That makes three days."

George nodded, turning away and beginning to pace the kitchen. "Three days. We don't have much time, but we'll figure this out. All right— I'll write to Wojciech, I'll write to Pierre Leroux, and they'll stop him. I'm the object of this duel, and I'm calling it off— women do not belong to men by right of brute force. Mallefille's or yours. You are absolutely forbidden to shoot one another over me, no matter how much you love me."

Fryderyk nodded. "Three days," he repeated. "Do what you can. But if you can't…" He sighed, then swallowed loudly. "I'm going to do it. Go through with it. Because I love you… love you too much to see him stalking you, threatening you, just because of me. But if Mallefille thinks I'll walk away and leave you with him, brute that he is, he's crazy."

George blinked back tears. And grabbing the nearest piece of blank paper, she began writing a distress signal.

George wrote to Wojciech and Pierre; to every other friend she could think of, begging them to speak to Mallefille; to make him see the madness of his ways. She sent the letters off. And she waited.

Letters sent, George ran all the way to Claudette's house. And over the endless cups of coffee that poured from Claudette's silver coffeepot, she poured out her problem. And how Fryderyk's solution only demonstrated that he seemed to have gone insane.

"He's crazy, all right," she agreed with George. She sipped her coffee. "Crazy about you."

George just shook her head.

I love you, she heard Fryderyk's voice repeating in her imagination. And blinking back tears, she shook her head.

So this is how you show me— come now, is this the only possible way you could have shown me? By marching off to be killed?

She bit her lip as more of Fryderyk's words rang inside her mind. *If Mallefille thinks I'll walk away and leave you with him, brute that he is, he's crazy…* Heaving a heavy sigh, George shook her head again. Who was crazy?

George sought silence in which to wait for her fate, and that of Fryderyk and Mallefille. And yet, the little girl still asked… *Do you love, me, Papa? Do you care? Am I worth fighting for?*

She thought. And she prayed. *Stop both of them*, she begged. *Help me fix this. Get us out of this nightmare. And don't… don't let anyone die.*

27   Courage

George tossed and turned all night, plagued by a pounding headache and endless, racing thoughts. Sounds and images flooded her imagination, visions of what she desperately prayed was not about to come. Visions of beloveds past and present lying still and silent in the bloodstained grass in the quiet of the dawn. The visceral, gut-wrenching crack of a gunshot and the sudden whiff of gunpowder. A flash of fire as a body fell heavily to the ground with a broken gasp. Images of bloody shirts, cravats, and handkerchiefs, of solemn funerals marking the sudden departure of an artist who had gone before his time, felled by his own reckless pride. The taste of the tears that would run down her face as she sobbed at Fryderyk's grave... the taste of the fear to which she would be condemned if he was the one that fell, forever looking over her shoulder for Mallefille. And the emptiness that would fill her heart as she faced life without Fryderyk. But even with Fryderyk victorious, she could taste the bitterness they would share in the soul-destroying wake of the murder he had had to commit to protect her. What would the blood on his hands do to him? To his art? And to them as a couple?

But one of the duelists was going to have to die. Because that... was how duels worked.

Fryderyk had gone crazy. What ever could have possessed him to say *yes*? How could he have gotten himself into such a life-threatening mess? Why couldn't he see that her honor and reputation didn't matter to her? Why had he insisted upon charging straight into a confrontation that would risk his very life?

What were they supposed to do now? And could… could she save him?

She thought of Mallefille. The big brute, the half-crazy playwright, whom she had once loved. And for one fleeting moment, she wondered… could she talk sense into him herself? If she went to him—

But no. She rolled over in bed, punching her pillow into shape. No. To do that would be just as brave, possibly, but even stupider, than what Fryderyk was preparing to do. Because if Mallefille had a knife— and, clearly, two guns, as well— then there was no way, no way at all, that she could trust him not to try to kill her— in the same way that Mallefille trying to kill Fryderyk, and Fryderyk trying to kill him, was the entire point of what was to come. There was no way that any kind of meeting her and Mallefille could be safe. She sighed. The help of Grzymała and Leroux was going to have to be enough.

Mallefille was clearly prepared to take revenge on her for choosing Fryderyk over him by murdering her, or murdering Fryderyk in the duel that was to come. But… George rolled over again, squeezing her eyes shut against the terrible possibilities. What if instead of murdering her, he kidnapped her? What if he took her hostage and shot anyone who tried to help her? What then?

George tried to close her eyes; tried to force herself to go to sleep as images of coffins, funerals, and bloodstained clothing filled her mind. How could all three of them get out of this alive?

Now she had a secret. George thought of Pauline. And of what her sweet, young, innocent, bright-eyed friend would say in this moment. Only… in this moment, Pauline's eyes would not be bright. They would be overflowing with tears as she sobbed in terror. Terror that, in being shared by George with Pauline, would not be truly dispersed or diluted. Terror that would simply plunge Pauline, who was little more than a child, into helpless misery. George shook her head, heaving a heavy sigh as she pondered a different example of the challenging balance between silence and candor. And in her heart, she chose silence. A cautious, compassionate silence. She would not say anything to her young friend until it was all over. She would not say anything to Pauline… until she had news.

The problem that would soon decide the trajectory of the rest of their lives had more layers than an onion. George was in danger. Fryderyk was in danger. George had to protect Pauline and her tender heart. Valuable moral support notwithstanding, there was little that Claudette could do directly. Leaving the country in the dead of night would only drastically complicate things for Fryderyk and George, and would still not fully rule out Mallefille finding them someday. And Pierre and Wojciech had to receive George's letters immediately and take action of their own. George thought of the letters moving slowly across town, moving from hand to hand until they finally arrived on Pierre and Wojciech's doorsteps. Every moment was precious. Every second counted. Because the thing they had too little of was time.

He can't do it, the memories of George's mother and grandmother whispered to her as the long, restless night wore on. *If he even follows through, Fryderyk will faint before it's time to fire his gun. He'll die, and so will you. The only thing for it is to stop Mallefille.*

You can't rely on Fryderyk, they insisted. *You can never rely on men. He can't protect you; can't take care of you. He can't even take care of himself. You are the one who has to take care of him; save him. And you must.*

Then the little girl looked up at George, all big, sad brown eyes. *Papas do crazy, brave, courageous things*, she said, *and then they die, and then they can never come back. Papas, and other men who love you... really, really love you. Like Fryderyk.*

George just looked down at her with a sigh. What was there to say?

Don't try to do anything, the angel of domesticity insisted, grabbing George's hand and dragging her bodily toward the sweet, homey side of the chasm. *This is man stuff. Let them figure it out. You just sit still, stay in the kitchen, and they'll get back to you once it's all over. And you will find the happily ever after you've always wanted with the courageous winner.*

George gritted her teeth. And she chose not to so much as deign to tell the angel to be quiet.

George's strength seemed to harden within her as her heart and body flexed, jumping to the tough side of the chasm. And the knot of yarn inside her that had seemed to be beginning to loosen drew tighter than ever. And the lonely maiden inside the tower went inside and shut the door. George waited for her to speak. But this time, she said nothing. Although her words still seemed to float in the air— *This is bad, but... all is certainly not lost. Keep your wits about you. And most of all... trust yourself.*

George got up. And in her diary, she considered everything that the angel, the maiden, the four-year-old, and the memories of her mother and grandmother had said. But in their words, she found no answers.

Finally, George fell asleep. And she dreamed.

"Aurore? Aurore!"

George walked down the corridor, following the little voice that was calling out to her. A vague tapping approached her, and she held out her candle to see who was coming. But no arriving candle approached her.

The tapping grew louder. And around a corner came the end of a stick, then the length of a cane. Upon the cane, there was a hand. The hand of a tiny little child. The child who walked behind it stared into the blackness; the blackness that was all he could see. The little boy was blind.

"Aurore?" little Louis called. "Aurore, where are they? Where's Maman? *And where's Papa?"*

George's throat closed on the words she was struggling to formulate, cutting off her answer. Accusingly, her little brother looked up into her face; looked at her with the eyes that could not see.

"I can't find them. Did... did something happen? Why didn't you protect them, Aurore? Why didn't you protect them?"

Protect them... protect them... *Louis' words echoed through the darkness of the corridor, filling it up until there was nothing but his words, bouncing off the ceiling and against the floor, ricocheting from one wall to another, the sounds shattering into a million pieces that began their own mad dance of pinging off every available surface. Far from the joyful discovery of her early childhood, this echo brought nothing but pain. And George stood there and held her head as the sounds grew louder and louder, accusing her like a pointing finger, like the admonishment of a*

priest, like a sentence passed by a judge. Louder and louder they
grew until the corridor itself seemed to shiver and quake, the
ceilings cracking as the walls began to splinter and give way—

George sat up, staring into the candlelit bedroom and gasping, clutching her chest as she took in where she was. Only a dream. Only a dream. Her departed baby brother had only been a dream.

George shook her head. She got out of bed and went to the pitcher of water on her dressing-table to wash the cold sweat from her face. She checked that the doors were locked. And she got back into bed.

She closed her eyes, willing herself go back to sleep. But Louis had been right, she could not help but think. She was the protector. And right now, Fryderyk was the one who needed her protection.

Tuesday morning, poorly rested, she went to Fryderyk's again, waiting anxiously on his doorstep until he answered the carefully-locked door. They chatted about nothing, trying to distract themselves and one another from the fear, from the question of whether the others would write back; whether they would be able to get involved before it was too late. Although Fryderyk did inform her that he had chosen a friend to nominate as his second— his friend Daniel. And before the mail was due to arrive, George went home.

She waited silently at the front door, heart pounding, staring out into the empty street. The clock ticked behind her, counting the hours; the hours until Thursday. The postman had not yet arrived. She scanned the street over and over, eyes stopping at

312

every house, praying that he would come soon, soon, and that he would bring her the replies she longed for. Mercilessly, time ticked by. The time that they had so little of; that they desperately needed to save their very lives.

He was late. George tapped her fingers on her legs, wiped her sweaty palms on her trousers, shifted her weight from foot to foot. What time was it? A good half-hour after he usually got here. She thought about making a cup of tea, but the doorway and its view of the street held her like a magnet. She must not move until the post arrived.

Marquis barked. George jumped, staring up and down the street for whatever her little fluffball had heard. And she gave a shuddering sigh of relief. There he was, three buildings down. Step by step, the postman made his steady way up the street, passing the buildings one by one, finally making his way up to her very door.

George tore the door open, standing there in a tizzy of anticipation as the postman drew today's stack of letters from his bag and handed them over. Thanking him shortly, George turned around and dashed back inside, throwing them all onto the nearest table and sorting through them madly. A bill, a letter from her publisher, something from Claudette… there. *A. Grzymała* and *P. Leroux*. George ripped open the two envelopes, scanning their messages.

I'll do what I can, Wojciech promised. *I'll take him to the tavern and make him understand*, Pierre swore. George held the letters to her heart, sinking down into the nearest chair and closing her eyes, soul overflowing with gratitude. Her friends had come through.

"They wrote back," George announced, hurrying through Fryderyk's front door half an hour later, half a heartbeat after he had hurriedly unlocked the door for her. She handed him the letters. "They'll do what they can."

The same show repeated itself as George waited for the post on Wednesday. And yet... there was no more news. George threw down the day's mail in disgust, letting it scatter out upon the kitchen table. No updates on their promises of help; no words of comfort, no declaration that they had talked sense into the mad playwright. No report that her friends had gotten hold of Mallefille and forced him to understand.

And no peace. George agonized her way through the rest of the day, forcing down a simple sandwich for dinner that she barely tasted, tossing and turning and praying through another fitful night of restless agitation, agonizing over every hour that slipped by, helpless urgency pressing down upon her heart and lungs like a millstone. And she got up to face another day of waiting.

This time, she didn't visit Fryderyk. She couldn't bear to. Couldn't bear to see his face what might be for the last time, to hear his voice, to hold his hand and discover whether it was warm or cold, firm or shaking, to sense his fear, to feel his agonizing, stupid courage; his thoroughly ridiculous impetuousness. And so she sat inside her apartment and drank coffee until her hands shook.

Then there was a knock on the door. Stomach clenching, she got up to check who was at her door. And she released the breath that had been holding itself just below her collarbones. It was Fryderyk.

With fumbling fingers, she unlocked the front door.

"Come in," she said breathlessly, ushering him inside and quickly locking the door behind him. "Are you— are you all right?"

He swallowed. And he gave a silent shrug; half an uncertain smile. She looked at him— he, too, seemed to have suffered a sleepless night; his eyes were shadowed, his hair messy, and his fair face was paler than ever.

"I heard from Daniel," he said rather hoarsely, "and he agreed to come with me as my second. He's going to inspect the pistols that Mallefille brings for us, and… well… do all the things that seconds do."

George nodded. And she tried not to think about what he meant.

Fryderyk swallowed again. "Although there's no calling it off through my issuing a formal apology… as I've done nothing to apologize for. And I won't leave you to his mercy." He shook his head. "There's only one way to settle this… through blood."

"Do you want me to come?" she asked very softly. She raised an eyebrow. "If the duel is over me, I suppose it would be only fair."

Fryderyk shook his head, raising his hands as if to hold her back. "Don't come," he said roughly, his voice breaking hoarsely. "I don't want you there. I don't want you to see me get shot; don't want you to witness that violence… don't want you to see me fail. I can't defend you against Mallefille if you're there and I have to protect you in person. It's too much. I can't deal with all of this at once. If I saw you, I would crumble. And I couldn't do it. And then where would we be? I'll have to be focused… and I couldn't focus if I knew you were there. And I wouldn't be able to help you… and there's nothing more you can do to help me. We've already done all we can. Your presence wouldn't make a difference in the outcome… and it honestly wouldn't help me."

Gently, he squeezed her hand, offering what was clearly supposed to be a reassuring smile. "No," he said softly, shaking his head. "You stay where you are, and Daniel will tell you as soon as there's news."

George looked at him, choosing to ignore the thousand angry thoughts that wanted to ask Fryderyk who he thought he was, telling her what to do, whether he really even knew, understood, and loved her as a person, and why he wanted to sideline her in the deciding moment. And the courageous maiden inside her heart seemed to shake her head.

"I understand," she said softly. And that was true. She even appreciated his intention of protecting her emotionally. But just because she understood… didn't mean she had to listen.

Author's Note

As I set about retelling the journey shared by George Sand and Fryderyk Chopin, I had many questions to answer and narrative decisions to make. Who, and what, historically came between them, wrecking their chances of remaining together in the long term? And what would have needed to have been different for their relationship to have survived?

I identified many factors that a careful examination of the facts allowed me to rearrange or omit, some more subtle, like George and Fryderyk's ability and willingness to admit and work on their own flaws and truly listen to one another, some far more dramatic, such as Aurore's previous marriage and the existence of her two children. Other things were adjusted, too— on a lighter note, I have also chosen to make the home in which Fryderyk is living when he and George begin their relationship a dark, dusty two-story house that reflects his health and personality rather than a tiny apartment like the one he historically lived in at that time.

From 1836-38, Fryderyk historically lived as roommates with Julian Fontana, a fact that I omit. George's friend Claudette is fictional, as is Fryderyk's cleaning lady Estelle. The cat Valdeck, real though he was, also seems to have belonged to George, rather than Fryderyk.

Although, in my references to George's childhood and adolescence, I imply that she has not seen her mother in many years, historically, George was reunited with her mother late in Sophie's life, visiting her in a nursing home in the days before her death. References to George revising her works in progress are fictional; historically, George did not seem to have revised her works, instead birthing them straight from her heart onto the page in their finished form, spending days and nights in meditative journeys through her own subconscious, as I have described. From what we can tell, also, Fryderyk, bashful and conservative as he was, did not address his beloved as *George*, but rather, *Aurore*.

Marja Wodzińska, Fryderyk's intended, is historical, as are many of the events I describe surrounding her— from her slow separation from Fryderyk at the behest of her concerned family, to George's epic 32-page letter to Wojciech Grzymała begging him to reveal whether Fryderyk and Marja were still a couple. Although the specific content of Grzymała's response to George has been lost to history (and the letter I describe George as receiving from him is therefore technically fictional), we can read between the historical lines to see that he must have answered George's question with the exciting news that in courting Fryderyk, George would not be stomping all over an active betrothal. The quotations I provide from the (dramatically abridged) letter George writes to Grzymała are historical except for the line in which she states that Fryderyk needs to know that she is not currently in a relationship.

Some details of George's early life have been portrayed very much as they happened, while others have been adjusted. Little Aurore was born to an aristocrat and a dancer, was intrigued by her own echo, and enjoyed playing "war." She first discovered the freedom conferred by male attire on a horseback ride a few towns away from home, as I have described. However, although her paternal grandmother seems to have viewed her as a sort of stand-in for her father, the person who would fill the Maurice-shaped hole in all their lives, she may not have actually liked seeing her granddaughter in trousers, and did not live to see Aurore step forward as *George*.

In some of these alterations and omissions, my story is inspired by the film *Impromptu*, an enjoyable but heavily fictionalized account of Fryderyk's life. I also gleaned useful insights from a video essay presented by Cinema Therapy, a YouTube channel created by duo licensed therapist Jonathan Decker and filmmaker Alan Seawright. In a video essay on the film *Runaway Bride*, they analyze the trust issues and fear of intimacy experienced by the title character, vulnerabilities I believe George also experienced.

My own experiences have also provided me with various concepts to explore. Spending one morning a week doing laundry and playing cards with an elderly woman with an eye for detail gave me many stories which I was able to adapt for the persnickety Fryderyk. Blankets and dishtowels have to be "just so," after all!

As he approached adulthood, Fryderyk apparently did not experience some important milestone of preparing to go out on one's own, specifically as a son separating from his mother, and it seems that he always struggled with making his own decisions as an adult. As a fragile child, he may have been almost literally "praised for breathing" and sheltered longer and more intensely than most children. Through childhood he was guarded from physical strain, kept from playing sports, and was homeschooled, probably for safety's sake.

At the age of twenty-six, he reassured the woman who might have become his mother-in-law that he was wearing slippers, since she had asked him if he wore slippers and warm woolen socks and went to bed early, mother-henning that could not have helped facilitate his growing up into an independent adult.

Various comparisons of Fryderyk to a corpse were inspired by historical comments by both George Sand and Franz Liszt, referring rather affectionately to Fryderyk as such.

On George's side, it seems as though she desperately wanted to mother everyone (or at least all the local artists) but her own children, with whom she had very difficult relationships. She would take in one ill or unstable artist after another, and then, just as things got really hairy, she would find another "injured bird" and separate from the previous one.

Chopin is often described as having had tuberculosis, which is a possible explanation for his lifelong symptoms, but not the only possibility, a mild form of cystic fibrosis being another candidate. An additional possibility is rheumatic heart disease, which could have led to a heart condition called bacterial endocarditis, which in turn could have caused pericarditis, which a recent visual examination of a preserved heart believed to be Fryderyk's suggested may have been his immediate cause of death.

Although we don't have any specific record of him having endured either illness as a child, we cannot prove that Fryderyk never had scarlet fever or strep throat, either of which can develop into rheumatic heart disease. The autopsy performed after Fryderyk's death also indicated more damage to his enlarged heart than to his lungs, and was described by the doctor who performed it as not only revealing a condition distinct from tuberculosis, but a disease the doctor had never encountered, an unknown condition Fryderyk had endured for years and could not have ultimately survived.

The "mental conversations" I portray George imagining having with her mother and grandmother are my own invention, but are inspired by her self-awareness and the ways in which she used her writing as a way to delve into her own heart, mind, and past. Odd though those conversations, seemingly shared with her memories, might seem, I'm not wishing to portray George as mentally ill—she's living with trauma.

Elizabeth Harlan's biography simply titled *George Sand* was an indispensable resource, providing a fascinating glimpse into the complex life that made its way, in many ways, onto the pages of her books, as was a psychoanalytic paper written by psychologist Helene Deutsch, a paper that helps modern readers follow the thread of trauma that spun its way from George's painful life and into the plotlines of her many novels, as well as illuminating the dark corners of the almost-hypnotic process by which George saved her own sanity by writing. Additionally, I have had the privilege of being inspired by some of Fryderyk's own letters, as compiled in the book *Chopin's Letters*, collected by Henryk Opieński and translated by E. L. Voynich. I also gleaned a great deal of information from *Chopin in Paris*, a biography by Tad Szulc, and extensive online research.

In this story, I present to you a recipe of fact, wishful fiction, and tributes to a number of memorable films. I hope you will find it as delicious as Fryderyk's favorite Polish gingerbread!

Featured Pieces

Below I provide a list of specific pieces played by Fryderyk in the book, including popular nicknames as applicable. Nonspecific references are not included. Works are arranged in order of their date of publication, not necessarily their date of composition.

Ballade in G minor, Opus 23
Etude in A minor, Opus 25 "Winter Wind"

Pronunciation Guide

Casimir: Kas-i-meer

Fryderyk Chopin: Free-*dare*-ik Show-*pan* (also *Fred*-er-ick)

Delacroix: *De*-la-kwah

Didier: *Di*-dee-ay

Dudevant: Due-de-*vawn*

Dupin: Due-*pawn*

Emilja: E-meel-ya

Wojciech Grzymała: *Voy*-check G'zhee-*ma*-wa

Jasia: Yasha

Justyna: *You*-stin-ah

Liszt: List

Ludwika: *Luhd*-vi-kah

Mallefille: Mal-*fee*

Mikołaj: *Mee*-ko-why

Musset: Mu-*say*

Pierniki toruńskie: *Peer*-ni-kee toh-roon-skee

George Sand: George Sahnd

Viardot: Vee-are-*doh*

Marja Wodzińska: Marya Voh-*jeen*-skah

Zelazowa Wola: *Zhe*-la-*zho*-vay *Voh*-lee

Selected Sources

The Lioness and the Little One by William G. Atwood

Chopin's Letters by Fryderyk Chopin. Comp. Henryk Opieński. Trans. E. L. Voynich.

The Sacred Romance: Drawing Closer to the Heart of God by Brent Curtis and John Eldredge

The Therapeutic Process, the Self, and Female Psychology by Helene Deutsch, Fellow of the American Academy of Arts and Sciences

Chopin's Funeral by Benita Eisler

Wild at Heart by John Eldredge

Captivating: Unveiling the Mysteries of a Woman's Soul (revised and expanded) by John and Stasi Eldredge

George Sand by Elizabeth Harlan

Lives of the Musicians: Good Times, Bad Times (and What the Neighbors Thought) by Kathleen Krull and Kathryn Hewitt

Story of My Life by George Sand

Winter in Mallorca by George Sand

Chopin in Paris: The Life and Times of the Romantic Composer by Tad Szulc

Frederic Chopin Son of Poland Later Years by Opal Wheeler
Cinema Therapy. "Therapist Reacts to RUNAWAY BRIDE."
https://www.youtube.com/watch?v=C2lTqETtppo
https://heroinejourneys.com/heroines-journey/

www.ingramcontent.com/pod-product-compliance
Lightning Source LLC
Chambersburg PA
CBHW051331020726
47501CB00007B/2025